Time slowed as Rayanne's mind scrambled to make sense of what she was seeing.

She made a grab for the wall as her knees gave way. Surely this was some kind of joke.

"Who are you?"

Her question was little more than a whisper, but the man heard it all right. There was no mistaking the temper in those ice-blue eyes. His outfit matched the one he'd worn in the picture he held clutched in his fist: scuffed boots, a faded shirt, dark trousers and a worn duster. It couldn't really be him, but every cell in her body screamed that it was.

"Wyatt McCain?"

His name was the last thing she said as the floor rushed up to meet her.

IMMORTAL COWBOY

ALEXIS MORGAN

Published in Great Britain 2014
by Mills & Boon, an imprint of Harlequin (UK) Limited,
Eton House, 18-24 Paradise Road, Richmond, Surrey, TW9 1SR

© 2014 Patricia L. Pritchard

ISBN: 978 0 263 91391 0

89-0414

Harlequin (UK) Limited's policy is to use papers that are natural, renewable and recyclable products and made from wood grown in sustainable forests. The logging and manufacturing processes conform to the legal environmental regulations of the country of origin.

Printed and bound in Spain
by Blackprint CPI, Barcelona

Alexis Morgan grew up in St Louis, Missouri, graduating from the University of Missouri, St Louis, with a BA in English, cum laude. She met her future husband sitting outside one of her classes in her freshman year. Eventually her husband's job took them to the Pacific Northwest, where they've now lived for close to thirty years.

Author of more than nineteen full-length books, short stories and novellas, Alexis began her career writing contemporary romances and then moved on to Western historicals. However, beginning in 2006, she crossed over to the dark side. She really loves writing paranormal romances, finding world-building and developing her own mythology for characters especially satisfying.

She loves to hear from fans and can be reached at www.alexismorgan.com.

I want to dedicate this story to the memory of one of my favorite uncles, who shared his love of Zane Grey with me. I blame him for my lifelong love of stories about gamblers, cowboys, lawmen, and gunslingers with hearts of gold.

Prologue

No one was ever alone on the mountain. Sometimes voices whispered in the mists, uttering words too faint to be understood. Eyes watched from the shadows, the weight of their gaze sitting heavily on those few brave enough to venture far up the slopes. The most sensitive of the visitors might feel the fleeting touch of hands without substance, leaving a chill on their soul. Smart folks didn't linger for long.

Chapter 1

Rayanne charged into the dappled shadows under the trees, following the narrow path that led toward town, the dense growth making it impossible to see more than a few feet ahead.

Where was he?

Her breath came in fits and jerks as she broke into a run down the game trail. A few feet in, her shoe caught on a root, sending her sprawling forward to land on her hands and knees. Ignoring the warm trickle of blood down her shin, Rayanne lurched back to her feet, wishing she'd taken the time to exchange her flip-flops for running shoes. But there hadn't been time for practical matters, not when Uncle Ray needed her.

The trees thinned out ahead, affording her a better

view of the town. There wasn't much left of Blessing, but that was no surprise. The last residents had abandoned the place over a hundred years ago, leaving behind only the few buildings too stubborn to fall down.

No sign of her uncle in any direction. What would she do if he didn't come back soon? At thirteen, she could take care of herself for a while, but the mountain was a scary place to be all alone. She yelled Ray's name several times with no answer except the soft rustle of leaves.

Should she go back to the cabin and call the authorities for help in finding him? No, he'd never forgive her. Uncle Ray wanted nothing at all to do with the government that had taught him how to kill and then did nothing to repair the damage it had done to his soul.

So that left it up to her. As his namesake, she took her uncle's well-being very seriously.

Ignoring the pain in her side, she sprinted toward the old church, the one place that would give her the best vantage point. It sat right smack in the middle of Blessing, directly across from the saloon. Inside the sanctuary, she waited a few seconds for her eyes to adjust to the dim interior before making her way to the staircase that led up to the belfry. Out of habit, she avoided the missing second step, using the banister to pull herself up directly to the third. The rest of the stairs were sound enough, allowing her to reach the roof quickly.

The hinges on the door creaked in protest when she pushed it open and stepped out onto the narrow confines of the belfry. She carefully skirted the hole where a bell used to hang. It had probably been sold off for scrap metal by one of the former residents, but that was old history. Right now, all Rayanne cared about was finding her uncle.

She hated heights, and each step across the rough wood floor took all the courage she could muster. Dread made her feet heavy as she crossed the short distance to the front edge of the roof. She latched on to the worn wooden railing in relief. But the second she touched it, the air around her rippled and blurred. Her stomach heaved as she clutched the railing and waited for the world to quit rocking.

When the floor beneath her feet finally steadied, she risked a quick peek at the street below. She blinked twice and looked again.

"What the heck?" she asked, not expecting an answer.

The town below was no longer a skeleton of what it used to be. Instead, the street was lined with buildings that hadn't been there only minutes before, all constructed out of fresh-hewn lumber.

And there were people—men, women and children—going about their business as if they strolled through Blessing every day, all wearing clothes straight out of a history museum. Were they reenactors? She couldn't imagine Uncle Ray tolerating such an intrusion on his privacy.

Besides, how could she have missed seeing them on her way through town? As she scanned the faces to see if Uncle Ray was among the throng of people, a shout went up, drawing everyone's attention to the far end of town. A group of men on horseback appeared in the distance, riding hard for the center of town, sending everyone on the street scurrying for cover. Something was dreadfully wrong. Rayanne ducked down even though the railing wouldn't provide much cover.

Just as the last child was dragged inside the old store and the door slammed shut, a solitary man appeared in the doorway of the saloon, carrying a rifle in his right hand. He paused long enough to inhale deeply on his cigarette before tossing it on the wooden sidewalk and grinding it out with the heel of his boot.

He stepped out into the street and the bright sunshine, moving with a lethal grace. Just like the others, he wore an authentic-looking costume: a cowboy hat, boots and a duster that had seen a lot of hard miles. His hat sat tipped back slightly, giving her a glimpse of coal-black hair. From the faded blue of his shirt to the scuffs on his boots, whoever had designed his costume had an amazing eye for detail.

Her pulse tripped and stumbled as the stranger turned to face the oncoming riders. He pushed his duster open, revealing a lethal-looking pair of revolvers. The holsters rode low on his hips, looking all too comfortable there as if he'd been born wearing them. There was a deadly stillness about him that she could feel even from her perch two stories above the street.

A few daring people in town peeked out of windows and through cracks of open doors. Playacting was one thing, but the scene unfolding in front of her felt too real, dangerous. If Rayanne could've run away, she would have. But her feet ignored her orders and remained right where they were.

The riders slowed their horses to a walk and fanned out across the narrow confines of the street. If the man was nervous about being badly outnumbered, he gave no sign of it. Instead, he planted his feet in a wide stance, as if hurricane winds couldn't have budged him.

Was she witnessing an actual gunfight straight out of the Old West? The tension radiating from everyone in sight certainly seemed real enough. She should go back to hunting for Uncle Ray, but at that moment nothing could've dragged her away from the drama unfolding before her. When the riders started forward again, time stopped and the seconds stretched to the breaking point.

The hinges creaked behind her, warning her that she was no longer alone. Thinking it had to be her uncle, Rayanne smiled in relief and turned to scold him for worrying her so. Instead, a man she'd never seen before stepped through the narrow doorway, ducking to avoid the church bell.

Before she could wonder much about its sudden reappearance, she saw that he, too, was heavily armed. She shrank back into the corner, hoping that he wouldn't notice her even though she huddled in plain sight.

He ignored Rayanne completely as he crouched down to peer over the railing. When he brought his rifle up to his shoulder, there was no doubt in her mind that he had his sights centered on the lone man below and meant to do him serious harm. When he pulled back on the hammer, preparing to shoot, her voice finally broke loose. Her terrified warning echoed down the street.

The man on the street spun to face the church. For a long heartbeat, his pale blue eyes met Rayanne's just before he fired his own rifle. The man beside her jerked and stumbled. He had a puzzled look on his face as he slowly sank to the wooden floor, his fingers trying to hold back the red stain spreading over the front of his shirt.

For a few seconds, silence reigned. Then blood, hot and bright, rained down on Rayanne's face and hands. At first she only whimpered as she frantically tried to scrub her hands clean on her clothes. But when Rayanne saw the man's eyes staring up at her, dull and lifeless, she screamed and kept on screaming until her throat was raw and her face burned with the hot acid of tears and fresh blood.

Her uncle finally appeared and pulled her into the solid warmth of his arms. He stroked her back, murmuring words of comfort in that awkward way of his. After a few moments, he stepped back.

How odd. Ray no longer towered over her. Either he'd grown shorter or she was taller. He'd also aged, the gray streaks in his red-gold hair more pronounced. All of that was strange enough, but it was the sadness in his smile that caused her heart to stutter.

"I've always loved you, Rayanne. I always will. I'm so proud of the woman you've become."

Woman? She was barely a teenager.

Ray brushed her hair back from her face. His eyes, so like her own, looked at her with such serious intent. "You have the gift, same as me. The mountain and Blessing need your special touch. Don't let anyone tell you different. Promise me that much."

She had no idea what he was talking about, but she nodded, anyway. "I promise."

"That's real good, sweetheart." Then he looked around. "It's time for me to go."

He smiled one last time as he slowly faded into shadow with no substance, leaving her alone on the rooftop bereft and still splattered with blood.

Rayanne bolted from her bed and went stumbling across to the bathroom, barely making it to the toilet in time. Kneeling on the floor, she heaved and retched until there was nothing left to come up. After a bit, she pushed herself back to her feet, waiting for another wave of nausea to pass before stepping closer to the sink.

It had been years since the nightmare had been so vivid, and she needed her mirror's reassurance that she was twenty-eight, not thirteen. Even with her face pale and her hair a tangled mess, it helped to calm her nerves a little.

She grabbed the robe hanging on the back of the bathroom door, an old flannel one Uncle Ray had loaned her one summer. Having that little piece of him close by always comforted her. Her next stop was the kitchen to brew a cup of chamomile tea. Along the way, she turned on every light she passed.

Anything to keep the shadows at bay.

After putting the kettle on the stove, she sank down on the nearest chair and waited for her heart to stop pounding. Dawn was still an hour away, but she wouldn't risk going back to bed for fear the dream would play itself out again. She'd had as much terror as she could handle in a night, thank you very much.

Things might be different if she had someone there to help ward off the fear, but she didn't. Bright lights, hot tea and a warm robe would have to suffice.

Just as the kettle started to whistle, the phone rang. Rayanne stared at it for several seconds before reaching for the receiver, her hand trembling hard enough she almost dropped it.

"Hello?"

"Rayanne? I'm sorry if I woke you up, but I thought you'd want to know. Uncle Ray passed away during the night. It was his heart."

Her mother's stark words stole the oxygen in the room, leaving Rayanne struggling to breathe around the lump of grief in her chest. Had Ray really come into her dream to say goodbye? She wouldn't put it past him.

"Rayanne? Did you hear what I said? Ray's gone."

She forced herself to answer. "Yes, I did, and I'm really sorry, Mom. I'll call you later about the arrangements."

Then she hung up and let the tears come.

One week later

Rayanne taped up the box and set it down on the floor by her office door. She had more packing to do, but right now a break was definitely in order. Dropping into her chair, she popped the top on a bottle of water and then picked up the book that had come in the morning mail. Flipping through it distracted her from the quagmire of her own thoughts.

The past seven days had been hell, plain and simple. They'd honored her uncle's request that they not make a fuss over his passing. In truth, he'd had few friends, and they weren't the kind to stand on ceremony.

Two days later, a lawyer had contacted her about Ray's estate. Her mother had been with her when the call came in and insisted on accompanying Rayanne to the appointment. What a disaster that had been. She'd spent the ensuing days either berating her late brother for forcing Rayanne to move up to his mountain cabin to claim her inheritance or demanding that Rayanne contest the will. The attorney had repeatedly emphasized the terms of the will were rock solid, but her mother had a habit of hearing only what she wanted.

Rayanne had finally quit answering her mother's calls. Eventually, she'd have to deal with her, but right now she had other priorities.

Lost in her thoughts, a knock on her office door startled her. Who could it be? Surely her mother wouldn't have tracked her down here. Setting her book aside, she unlocked the door. When she saw who it was, relief had her smiling.

"Hi, Shawn, I'm glad it's you. I was afraid my mom had decided to drop in for a visit." She looked around at the surrounding chaos in her office. "Sorry about the mess. I was just taking a short breather before I finish packing."

She pointed toward the stack of boxes she'd yet to fill in hopes he'd take the hint. He didn't. Instead, he shoved a pile of papers aside to make room for himself on the corner of her desk. He picked up the book she'd been reading.

"Still studying up on dead towns, I see."

"The correct term is ghost towns, not dead ones."

She let a little of her irritation show. Even though he was teasing, she wasn't in the mood. She took her research seriously. Normally, Shawn respected that, but he'd been in a strange mood lately.

She took the book from him and set it aside. "What's up?"

"When were you going to tell me that you'd asked for a leave of absence from the university?" His voice was a shade too cool for the question to be completely casual.

Oh, that. Whoops. "I only got the approval late yesterday afternoon, and I asked the dean to make an announcement this morning at the staff meeting."

Shawn's eyebrows snapped down tight over his eyes. "That's not the same as you telling me yourself."

She'd been dreading this moment. "I left you a voice mail this morning."

His expression lightened up a little. Good. She really hadn't meant to hurt his feelings, but she'd already faced off against her mother over her acceptance of the terms of Uncle Ray's will. She didn't want to have to defend her decision to anyone else.

"It's just that all of this is so sudden, and I'm feeling a bit overwhelmed."

He looked marginally happier. "Are you sure putting your life on hold is a good idea?"

Was that what she was doing? Maybe, but then what choice did she have?

"I'm simply following the dictates of my uncle's will. He didn't leave me any wiggle room on this."

Shawn drew a deep breath. "Somehow I doubt you would've fought the terms regardless."

He was right. "I'm sorry, Shawn. I haven't been myself since all of this happened. Ray's death hit me hard. The semester is almost over, so the dean was pretty understanding about me leaving early. One of the grad students will cover the last few classes for me and give the final."

"That's good. I'd hate to see you jeopardize your career here at the university on a whim."

That wasn't what this was, but Shawn clearly had something on his mind. "Just spit it out, Shawn."

Her comment startled him, his smile a bit rueful. "Okay, here's the thing. I was hoping the two of us could go somewhere together this summer for a few days, maybe a week."

He shifted to look at her more directly. "I'm not picky about where. Heck, we can even go explore some of those dusty, old ghost towns you love so much. I just thought some time away from all of this—" he waved his hand to indicate more than just the clutter in her office "—would be good for *us*."

The emphasis on the last word wasn't lost on her, and perhaps he was right. Some time spent away from their normal surroundings would definitely answer some questions for both of them. They'd had dinner a few times, but she'd been reluctant to take the relationship to the next level.

Obviously, he wasn't.

Part of the problem was the recent resurgence of her nightmares. She'd never shared the story with Shawn and didn't intend to anytime soon. It was the main reason that she'd never invited him to spend the night at her place. Until she could be sure that she wouldn't wake up screaming, that couldn't change.

On the other hand, she had to wonder that if she'd been convinced that there was something special possible between the two of them, would she have trusted him with her secrets? Their friendship was familiar and comfortable. If it was ever going to be more, she needed to resolve the questions that had plagued her for years once and for all.

For now, she had to offer Shawn an answer that he could understand, a version of the truth that he could accept without revealing her real reasons for going back to Blessing alone. Once she'd made peace with her past, maybe she'd know if there was a place for Shawn in her future.

"I plan to spend the time I'm at the cabin on my

research. Things are too up in the air right now for me to make any other commitments."

"Will you at least think about it?"

He wasn't going to give up unless she conceded at least that much. "Yes, I'll think about it, but no promises."

Her effort at a reassuring smile must have succeeded because he gave her an approving nod. "Great. Now I'd better get back to my office. We've both got work to do."

As a fellow college instructor, he knew the constant pressure to publish. She let him think that was what was driving her research, a far more acceptable explanation for her almost obsessive need to study the past.

In truth, the dream that had haunted her for years was the real reason she scoured bookstores and the internet for new primary sources of information on the lost towns of the West, and specifically about Blessing, Colorado.

It didn't help that all she felt when Shawn left was relief. Her mother would be the first one to tell her that she was being foolish. Shawn was educated, handsome and financially secure; in short, everything Rayanne should want in a man. She liked him; she really did. What did it say about her that she'd rather focus her energy on research than on building a relationship?

This wasn't getting her anywhere. A few more minutes of reading and then back to work. As she opened the book, a dank, musty smell wafted up from the pages, but she didn't mind. Books as old as this one were rarely in pristine condition. Besides, it was the words on the pages that were important.

The passage she'd been reading made her smile. It was like having a private conversation with someone who had lived and breathed more than a century ago. The author, Jubal Lane, had clearly shared her interest in the boom and bust of the towns that dotted the landscape in the late 1800s. The only difference was that he'd seen them firsthand.

Jealousy was pointless, but at least she could see those same towns through his eyes. She read slowly to savor Jubal's thoughts and descriptions, pausing periodically to make notes. When she was about to stop, a word at the bottom of the page caught her attention: Blessing.

With her pulse racing, she quickly scanned the remaining few lines. Jubal Lane had actually visited Blessing, the town that had formed the backdrop of the nightmares that had haunted her since she was thirteen years old.

Before that summer, she'd played in the deserted buildings as a child, loving every minute of her visits with Uncle Ray. But that last trip, everything had changed and she hadn't been back since. The memories flooded through her mind.

How ironic that she'd run across a reference to Blessing now when it was too late to share it with Ray.

Rather than letting herself get dragged back into the past, she closed the book and put it in her bag. For now, she had to finish before the shipping company arrived. Most of her things were headed for storage; the remaining few would be shipped to the cabin up on the mountain where she'd need them for her research.

As she sealed the last box, she paused to look around her office. Odd that it felt as if she were leaving for good rather than for the summer. That was ridiculous. Of course she'd be back in the fall. The terms of Uncle Ray's will had only dictated she had to live on the mountain through August, not the rest of her life.

By the end of summer, hopefully, she will have laid the past to rest once and for all. She'd return rested and ready to pick up the pieces of her life here at the university. That was her plan, and she was sticking to it.

Later that night, Rayanne curled up in her favorite chair, ready to learn what Jubal had to say about Blessing. Since no one in her family had ever answered her questions about the town, perhaps she'd finally find them for herself.

Did she really even want to?

As a rule, she did her best not to think about the solitary man who wore a black duster and carried a rifle. After all, he and the others only existed in her imagination. But if that were true, why had she continued to be plagued by such vivid, horrifying dreams about them?

Worse yet, why had she secretly compared every

man she'd met to a nameless man with black hair and blue eyes?

She'd spent years searching for even a mention of Blessing with no luck until now. With a mixture of trepidation and excitement, she opened the book to the last page she'd read and started over at the top.

When she reached the lines where Jubal mentioned his next stop was to be Blessing, she took a deep breath and turned the page. His words drew her back into the past. He described the valley where the town sat with near-perfect detail, enough to convince her he was talking about the one on Uncle Ray's mountain.

Jubal said most of the townspeople had moved on to greener pastures after some tragedy had occurred. He also alluded to a gunslinger who had met his fate in the street outside the saloon, his tone implying the man had gotten no less than he'd deserved.

Rayanne stopped right there to give herself time to process what she'd just read: there really had been a gunfight in Blessing. Did Jubal have more to say on the subject? With her pulse pounding in her head, she drew a deep breath and turned another page.

"Whoa, this can't be!"

But it was. Not only had Jubal written more about the shootout, but he'd also included a picture. As the reality sank in, her hands shook so badly she dropped the book. She picked it up again.

Nothing had changed. Even in the faded tintype, it was easy enough to recognize the man who'd haunted her dreams for fifteen years. He wasn't wearing a hat, but the hair was the same. So were the intense, pale eyes that stared up at her from the page. She bet they were blue. In fact, she knew they were.

The gunslinger had a name—Wyatt McCain.

He was real.

He'd lived and died right there in the dusty streets of Blessing.

For years, her family and the shrink they'd dragged her to had insisted that she'd made it all up. Her mother had blamed her father for filling Rayanne's head with stories about the Old West. In return, her father had blamed her mother for leaving their impressionable young daughter alone with her nutcase brother. The shrink had blamed it all on her parents' constant bickering and its effect on their daughter. Idiots.

None of them had even considered the possibility that it had all been real—the people, the gunfire, the blood and, most of all, Wyatt McCain.

Had Uncle Ray known? Was that why he'd come to her in the dream to say goodbye? He'd mentioned a gift they'd shared. What had that been about?

Now that she had a few facts to go on, she wouldn't rest until she'd learned everything she could. Once she had her arsenal of evidence, the facts would free her of the nightmares from her past. Even if no one else ever knew the truth, she would.

A real man had died that day in the streets of Blessing, one who haunted her dreams a hundred years after his passing. She would tell his story—her story, too. Her purpose clear, she set the book aside and started a list of what she needed to take care of before she left for the mountain.

Chapter 2

The road leading up to Ray's cabin was in far better condition than she'd remembered, but otherwise it all looked the same. Funny, it felt as if the cabin had been patiently waiting all these years for her return, but this time as owner rather than guest.

Rayanne eased her car around a slow bend to the right, her pulse picking up speed even if the car didn't. After fifteen years, she was about to catch her first glimpse of the chimney that marked the location of her new home. The trees had grown taller, but she could just make out a glimpse of gray stone.

Tension had been riding her hard ever since she'd learned of Ray's death. All the arguments about her decision to take a last-minute leave of absence from her job and move to the mountain hadn't helped. But as she neared the cabin and the freedom it had always represented, the muscles in her shoulders and neck eased, and her mood lightened.

"Well, Uncle Ray, we're almost there."

Wouldn't her mother freak out to hear Rayanne carrying on a one-sided conversation with her uncle? Well, not him, exactly, but the pewter urn that contained his last remains. One of the sidebars in his will was a request that Rayanne scatter his ashes on the mountain. He'd left it up to Rayanne to pick the time and place.

But until she carried out his wishes, she found comfort in the notion that her uncle was riding shotgun and could actually hear her. Maybe she was losing her mind just like her mother had said when she learned Rayanne had willingly accepted the terms of the will without a court fight.

Not that her mom's opinion mattered. The mountain and the town that had haunted Rayanne for years was now hers, lock, stock and belfry. That is, provided she moved there and stayed through the entire summer. Come September, she was free to stay on or move back to the city. But if she didn't follow the dictates of her uncle's will to the letter, the entire estate would pass to a distant cousin. She couldn't bear the thought of that happening.

It hadn't been a surprise that Shawn had agreed with her parents. However, if there was any hope of a future for the two of them, she needed to find the answers she'd been looking for.

"I'm sorry to have to tell you this, Uncle Ray, but I don't plan to live up here for the rest of my life."

A stab of guilt had her giving the urn a remorseful glance. "But I will stay long enough to find answers to questions that my folks would never let me ask. And with luck, I can find enough information about the short history of Blessing itself to write a paper."

Her mouth curved in a wide smile as she considered the possibilities. If she didn't have enough information for a scholarly paper, there was another option. She loved historical romances, and she already knew the time period inside and out. Surely she could come up with a story line that fit the few facts about Blessing that she'd been able to uncover.

The ideas twirled and danced through her head. A beautiful schoolteacher for the heroine would be just the ticket. And the hero would be the sheriff, strong and valiant and handsome. She could picture Shawn in the role, his arm around her waist as together they defied the bad guys.

But then a vision of a gunslinger dressed in black shoved that picture aside, replacing it instead with a man who moved with predatory grace and had a killer's ice-colored stare. Wyatt McCain. Rayanne flushed hot and then cold. A woman would have to be a fool to think a man like that could be anyone's hero.

The excitement died just that quickly.

Finally, the last of the trees faded into an open meadow. Her breath caught in her throat as the cabin came into sight. She hit the brakes, bringing her car to an abrupt halt, needing time to adjust to the onslaught of emotions threatening to overwhelm her. It was almost impossible to sort them all out—relief, trepidation, remembered joy and a great deal of pain that Uncle Ray would never be waiting there to greet her again.

She put the car back into gear and slowly pulled up in front of the cabin. The sun was already sliding down the far side of the sky. If she didn't hurry, she'd be unpacking in the dark. The idea worried her more than she'd expected it to.

She pulled out the ring of keys that the attorney had given her at their last visit. Each one was carefully labeled in Uncle Ray's familiar scrawl. She picked up the urn and stepped up on the porch.

As the door swung open, Rayanne stepped back through time. Her uncle hadn't changed a thing since she'd left all those years ago. Maybe there were a few more books stuffed in the shelves and the sofa was a bit more worn, but that was all. She set the urn down on a small table in the corner and got busy settling in.

Bedtime always came early on the mountain. As Rayanne brushed her teeth, she studied her image in the mirror. Uncle Ray's hair had been a little curlier than hers, but the color had been the same, a shade somewhere between blond and red. They'd also shared a tendency to freckle during the summer and the same bright green eyes. In a lot of ways, she'd resembled her favorite relative more than she had either one of her parents. Once again, the thought of him had her eyes stinging with the threat of tears.

It was definitely time to crawl into bed. Would coming here intensify her nightmares? She sure hoped not. The past several nights she'd slept without incident, a huge relief. She stepped across the threshold into her bedroom, happy that her childhood sanctuary had remained unchanged.

She turned down the quilt that had covered the bed for longer than either she or Ray had been alive. Trailing her fingers over the familiar patches of fabric, she wondered again about the people who had worn the various bits and pieces of cloth in shirts and dresses.

Had they been happy in their lives? She closed her eyes as she caressed the cloth, worn smooth and soft by the years. Maybe another girl had slept under this very same quilt, tucked in by loving hands with a kiss and a wish for sweet dreams or maybe the quilt had been a wedding gift for a bride about to start her new life as a wife.

She doubted she would ever know the real answers, but it didn't matter. The warmth of the quilt gave her a connection to the past, one that appealed to her deep interest in history. Stretching out on the narrow bed felt like heaven. A huge yawn surprised a giggle out of her as she turned onto her back to watch the sweep of the stars and moon through the skylight overhead. Just as she had as a small girl, she fell asleep counting the stars twinkling in the night sky.

A new energy had arrived on the mountain, altering the patterns and drawing his attention toward the cabin. Ray's niece was back. He recognized her even though she'd grown into a woman with long legs and ridiculously short hair.

Drifting closer to the porch, he stared up at the open window high up near the peak of the roof. The man's room had been on the other side. He'd always kept his window closed and the doors locked against the perils of the darkness, real and imagined.

But the girl had her window open to the night. Would she continue to keep it that way if she found out about him and the others? A grim smile crossed his face briefly. Hell, even the others knew to steer clear of him. They certainly recognized bad news when they saw it; maybe the girl would, too.

The light in the window winked out. He lost interest in his vigil and moved away, back toward town. Folks still called it Blessing. What a joke that was, one he doubted the others appreciated. But then he didn't give a damn what they thought, any more than they cared about him.

He passed through the trees, startling a doe and her fawn. As quietly as he moved, he was surprised they even noticed him. But after one look in his direction, the wary beasts bounded away, covering a lot of distance with each graceful leap. He paused to watch them disappear into the shadows, enjoying the sight. God knew there was little enough that he took pleasure in these days.

His thoughts drifted back toward the cabin and its sole occupant. The redhead had been there before. It had been a long while since she'd last visited the man, although time had become too fluid over the years for him to be sure how long it had been. An uneasy feeling churned in his stomach as vague memories stirred about this girl, now a woman. Used to be, she'd come and run wild through the woods and the town, only to leave right before it all unfolded.

All except that last time.

Damn it to hell and back, how many months had slipped past him unnoticed? If she was on the mountain, it could be almost time. Again. No wonder the deer had fled his presence. He didn't blame them one bit for running. Canny creatures that they were, they knew when death roamed free on the mountain. He turned his back on the cabin and faded into the shadows, alone and wishing he could stay that way.

A cool breeze drifted through the open window, carrying a fresh, woodsy scent with it. Rayanne drew a deep breath and smiled without opening her eyes, still caught up in the fading memory of a dream, a good one this time. Instead of fearing Blessing, she'd been walking through the town hand in hand with a handsome man.

That he bore a striking resemblance to Wyatt McCain came as no surprise. After all, he'd dominated her thoughts ever since she'd discovered his picture. Only in her dream world, he seemed less grim, younger and more carefree. She woke up smiling with the sound of his laughter echoing in her mind.

What an interesting start to her day!

The telephone started ringing. Cell phones couldn't get reception this high up, so Ray had run a telephone line to the cabin. No doubt it was her mother calling to check on her.

Rayanne sat up, hoping if she moved slowly enough the woman would give up. No such luck. As soon as the phone quit ringing, it started right up again in the time it took for her mother to hit redial.

Rayanne reached for the receiver. Figuring on a long call, she stretched out and made herself comfortable.

"Hello, Mother."

"Well, I guess you made it safely since you're able to talk on the phone."

Nothing like a snide remark from a parent to start the day off on a low note. Why couldn't the woman just admit that she'd been worried?

"By the time I got settled in last night, it was too late to call."

A small exaggeration perhaps, but it would've been rude to admit to the truth, that she'd never even considered calling.

"I can't believe that you're really up there." Rayanne could picture her mother leaning against the kitchen counter, with a nonfat double latte in her hand.

"Of course, I never understood the appeal of the great outdoors. Seriously, Rayanne, I know you loved my brother, but you don't have to exile yourself up there just to prove it. I should've put my foot down about this."

As if that would've done any good. Maybe someday the woman would accept the fact that Rayanne had grown up and could make her own decisions, even ones her mother didn't approve of.

Especially ones she didn't approve of.

"I'm fine, Mom. I'm safe. I'm happy."

Please let it go at that. She really didn't want to start the day off rehashing old arguments.

"That's good for you. But what about Shawn? Is he happy?" Her voice clearly indicated she was playing her trump card.

She was wrong. "My relationship with Shawn is not open for discussion."

Mainly because she wasn't all that sure they still had one. He hadn't spoken more than a dozen words to her after she'd announced her decision to leave school early and move to the mountain.

"Your father isn't pleased to hear that you're back up there."

Okay, that got Rayanne's attention. "Since when are you and Dad on speaking terms?"

Her mother's voice turned frosty. "He deserved to know what you were up to, especially when your last visit ended up such a disaster."

"Mom, that was years ago. I'm here to do research, nothing more. You shouldn't have gotten Dad all worried for nothing."

She'd give her mother another thirty seconds and then pretend that her reception was failing.

"If I don't hear from you every day, I will be calling the authorities to report you missing or something. Whatever it takes to get someone up there to check on you."

Oh, brother. Rayanne counteroffered. "I'll call you once a week and no more than that."

Rayanne's hand ached from gripping the phone so hard.

"That's not enough." Her mom was going into full martyr mode now. Tears wouldn't be far behind.

"It's my best offer, Mom." And just to make sure her mother got it straight, she repeated it. "Once a week or not at all."

After a long, painful silence, her mother conceded defeat. "Fine, Rayanne. Be selfish. Once a week will have to do."

"I love you, Mom." She did, really, even if the woman drove her crazy most of the time. "I'll call you on Saturday. Bye."

She disconnected the call before her mother could think of something else to argue about. With that behind her, Rayanne headed for the shower, anxious for the day to begin. It was going to be a good one; she could just tell.

Chapter 3

He wasn't sure why he'd returned to the clearing. Curiosity wasn't something he normally indulged in anymore, but it had drawn him back to the cabin. There was no smoke coming out of the chimney. Either the woman must not mind the morning chill or else she wasn't up yet.

When he reached the door of the cabin, he sneered at the lock. As if that flimsy bit of steel could keep him out. Once inside, he looked around. Had he been in the cabin recently? He couldn't remember. Most of the time he'd watched the man from the cover of the woods or where the shadows deepened to near black by the porch at night.

Ray had usually sensed his presence, even though he'd rarely said anything. Maybe it was because what

Ray had seen in the war had been so much worse. Either way, there had been real strength in the man right up to the end. The former soldier had always been silent but content in his own skin.

Unless his demons were riding him hard. Then Ray would stalk the woods, muttering under his breath. Sometimes he stood at the edge of a cliff and screamed out the names of men who'd never set foot on the mountain except in his mind.

But Ray was gone now. They'd come with flashing lights and carried his body back down the mountain. Now someone else, the woman, had come to the mountain to live. He hated having his routine disturbed, but he'd have no choice but to adjust to her presence.

She'd seen him once. Did she remember?

A noise from overhead caught his attention. She was talking to someone, even though he knew full well that she was alone. No one passed through his territory unnoticed. A few minutes later, the shower came on, warning him that his time was limited. He needed to leave before she walked down those steps, although it was tempting to linger long enough to get a closer look at her.

But for the moment, he had time to poke around a bit. He moved toward the kitchen where she'd dumped a few things on the table the night before. He studied the clutter, trying to make sense of the stuff. It wasn't worth the energy it would take to dump the bag out. Besides, he wasn't there to drive her away, just to learn more about the woman who would be sharing his mountain and town.

A paper caught his attention. Careful not to disturb anything, he gently reached out to touch it. Would she remember if she'd left it faceup or facedown? He didn't care. Hell, what was life without a few risks?

Laughing at his own joke, he turned the paper over. Shock rolled through him as soon as he got a good look at the picture staring up at him, leaving him unable to do anything but stand and stare down at the image.

Where the hell had she gotten that?

So caught up in the memories that came flooding back, he failed to notice the silence from upstairs. The shower was no longer running. Before he could react, one of the steps behind him creaked. Hellfire and damnation, the woman was coming down the stairs.

The hot steam had washed away the last bit of tension from talking to her mother. Eventually, maybe she'd long for the company at the other end of the phone line but definitely not today.

About halfway down the stairs, a weird shiver started at the base of her spine and danced its way right up to her head. Even the hair on her arms stood up, as if lightning were about to strike. Had the late spring weather taken a sudden turn for the worse?

No, sunshine was streaming in through the skylights overhead.

Rayanne couldn't shrug off the feeling that something wasn't right. As a city girl born and bred, maybe she wasn't ready to face life alone on the mountain. However, she wasn't about to admit that her mother had been right all along. No, it was only a matter of adjusting to the quiet murmurs of nature outside the window rather than the jarring cacophony of city noise.

That was when she heard a sound that had nothing to do with any four-legged beast that lived on the mountain: human footsteps. She swallowed, trying to get her heart out of her throat so she could breathe. The silence felt frozen now, as if in anticipation of the next sweep of cloth against cloth. It wasn't long in coming.

"Who's there?" Her voice echoed hollowly.

No answer. To her surprise, that made her mad. She came down two more stairs, hoping to find evidence that it was only her imagination running wild. This time the steps were more definite and headed right for the door. Should she remain cowering on the stairs forever or take control of the situation?

This was her home; she would not be a prisoner of her own fear. Besides, if the intruder had meant her harm, he'd had ample opportunity.

Bracing herself for the worst, she charged down the last few steps, determined to give someone a piece of her mind. The bottom few stairs curved down into the kitchen near the door. One glance told her that the door was still bolted but that didn't mean much. If someone had broken in, it could have been through a window, instead. But if so, why hadn't she heard anything?

Nothing in the kitchen looked disturbed, but then she sensed a movement off to her right. Time slowed as her mind scrambled to make sense of what she was seeing. She made a grab for the wall as her knees gave way. Surely this was some kind of joke.

"Who are you?"

Her question was little more than a whisper, but the man heard it all right. There was no mistaking the temper in those ice-blue eyes, not that she really needed him to answer her. His outfit matched the one he'd worn in the picture he held clutched in his fist: scuffed boots, a faded shirt, dark trousers and a worn duster. It couldn't really be him, but every cell in her body screamed that it was.

"Wyatt McCain?"

His name was the last thing she said as the floor rushed up to meet her.

Cool. Smooth. Hard.

Slowly, the fog in Rayanne's mind faded and awareness of her surroundings returned. Right now, her cheek was pressed against something flat and cool to the touch. Her eyes refused to open; instead, she concentrated on moving her right hand and then her left.

Her fingertips felt just the slightest grittiness to the surface, like a hardwood floor that hadn't been swept recently. She slowly processed all the data, because the side of her face was pounding. Finally, she arrived at the obvious conclusion that she was sprawled on the floor, most likely in the kitchen.

Why?

Flashes of memory played out in her head. Shower. Brushing her teeth. Sweats rather than jeans. All of that made sense. What next? She'd started downstairs to fix her breakfast. Halfway down she'd heard something.

No. Someone. Wyatt McCain. Well, not him, but someone who looked just like him, down to the faded blue shirt and scuffed boots. Thanks to her dream, his image had been the first one she thought of.

Her eyes popped open, and she found the strength to push herself up to a sitting position. Ignoring the fresh wave of dizziness, she scooted back until she bumped up against the nearest wall. It offered support but no comfort as she surveyed her surroundings.

From where she sat, she could see the entire ground floor of the A-frame cabin. She was alone. Gradually, her pulse slowed to somewhere near normal, and the pain on the right side of her face eased up enough to allow her to think straight.

The deadbolt on the front door was still firmly in place. No broken windows. No back door, so no other exit. Adding up all the facts, she had to think that she'd imagined the whole thing. Whatever she'd heard had to have been just the wind or a tree limb brushing against the cabin in the wind.

The side of her face was tender to the touch. Obviously, she'd tripped and fallen, landing hard enough to bruise. Nothing that a bag of ice and some aspirin wouldn't cure. She slowly pushed herself to her feet, taking care not to move too quickly.

She rooted around in the cabinets until she found a

small plastic bag and filled it with ice. After zipping it shut, she wrapped it in a thin dish towel and pressed it to her cheek. The cold burn stung but gradually numbed the pain. Next up, the painkillers.

She always carried some in her purse, which she thought she'd left here in the kitchen. Where was it? Hadn't she set it down on the counter when she'd first come in last night?

It wasn't there now. She was sure she hadn't taken it upstairs with her, so that left the living room. Before she'd gone two steps, she spotted the strap of her purse sticking out from underneath the microwave cart. She bent down to pick it up, wincing as the motion exacerbated the throbbing in her face.

How had her purse gotten down there? It wasn't anywhere close to where she'd landed on the floor, so she hadn't knocked it off the counter. Another mystery with no answer. Rather than dwell on it, she dug out the small bottle at the bottom of the purse and took out two pills. She swallowed them with a drink of water.

Next up, caffeine and lots of it. The few minutes that it took to set the coffee to brewing kept her too busy to think about the things that didn't quite add up.

Such as the noise she'd heard, and how her purse came to be under the cart. While she waited for the coffee to perk, she leaned against the counter and studied the room to see if anything else was out of place.

Her computer pack sat right where she'd left it on the kitchen counter. She frowned. Something was different, though. Last night, one of the last things she'd done was look at the picture of Wyatt McCain that she'd printed out. She smiled. Uncle Ray would've gotten such a kick out of what she'd learned about Blessing when the town had been alive.

But now the picture wasn't where she'd left it.

She searched her pack in case she'd put it back. No dice. Nor was it in the living room or anywhere in plain sight. She'd found her purse under the cart. Had the picture fallen there, too?

Only one way to find out. She tugged on the cart, wheeling it out of its usual position. The only thing she uncovered was a wadded-up piece of paper, obviously not the picture of Wyatt. Uncle Ray must have missed the trash can with it.

She bent down to pick it up. Before throwing the paper away, she'd make sure it wasn't something important. As she smoothed it out on the counter, her pulse kicked right back into overdrive. Okay, so she'd been wrong. Uncle Ray hadn't thrown this paper away. He couldn't have for one important reason: he'd never seen it. Wyatt McCain's piercing pale eyes glared up at her, the wrinkled paper doing nothing to dilute the intensity of his gaze.

This was the picture she'd brought with her, but she hadn't been the one to crumple it up. Chills washed through her as she looked around the room. She had proof positive right there in her hands that she hadn't imagined the sound of someone moving around in the kitchen earlier.

She dropped the paper on the counter and hurried

to double-check the lock on the door and the windows. It didn't take long to verify that everything was locked up tight. Even if someone had the key to the deadbolt, they couldn't have fastened the chain from the outside. There was no obvious sign that the cabin walls had been breached.

Surely she would've heard someone climbing to the second floor? Had she left her window open when she came downstairs? She grabbed the nearest weapon she could find, her uncle's rolling pin, and charged upstairs. Sure enough, her window was still open. She knelt on the bed to close it and throw the latch.

She paused long enough to survey the clearing surrounding the cabin. Her past visits had taught her that anyone walking across the meadow while the dew was still on the grass left a visible trail. From what she could see, there was no sign that anyone had passed that way.

She checked the tree line, too. No movement there except for a few birds flittering among the leaves. So it was just her, the bright morning sunshine and the mountain.

From there, she went into the bathroom, but the window in there was too narrow for anyone but a small child to squeeze through.

That left Uncle Ray's room. She hesitated before opening the door. Eventually, she'd have to cross that threshold, but she hadn't planned on doing it so soon. It was Uncle Ray's most private space, his sanctuary from the world outside. Even when she'd visited him, she'd never been allowed inside.

She turned the doorknob but still hesitated before pushing the door open. This was silly. What did she expect to find? She gave the door a soft shove and took a single step forward into the space that her uncle had kept private.

Tears stung her eyes as she realized how much the room looked like her uncle—solid, comfortable, plain. The queen-size bed filled up most of the space. Made from pine, the design was simple, which matched the patchwork quilt and utilitarian blue curtains. The haphazard pile of books on the bedside table came as no surprise. Nor did the closet full of flannel shirts and T-shirts featuring the names of old rock bands.

"Uncle Ray, you sure loved your books and music."

Something else they'd both shared besides their love for his mountain home. She pulled one of the flannel shirts off its hanger and slipped it on. Maybe it was whimsical of her, but wearing the soft cotton felt like one of Uncle Ray's hugs. For the first time since waking up on the kitchen floor, she felt safe.

Eventually, she'd figure out what had happened downstairs. Maybe she'd walked in her sleep; not exactly a comforting thought. And even if it were true, why would she have crumpled Wyatt McCain's picture? Too many questions she had no answers for.

But now that she'd reassured herself that she was alone in the cabin, it was time to do something useful. At some point, she'd have to go through Ray's things and dispose of them. Surely there was a homeless shelter in one of the nearby towns that could make good use of his clothing. Maybe some of his books, too. His extensive music collection, though, she'd keep.

As she walked back out of the room, she rolled the sleeves of the flannel shirt up several turns. Despite being a couple sizes too big for her, the black-and-white-plaid fit her just fine.

At the bottom of the steps, she hesitated briefly. Nothing but silence this time. Good. Where to start? The attorney had gone over the terms of Uncle Ray's will with her in great detail, some of which were odd to say the least. To start with, he'd made the attorney include a message from him saying that he'd loved Rayanne and had known that she'd loved him right back.

Bless the man, those few words had melted away her guilt over not visiting him up here on the mountain. He'd known how she felt about him and that's all that mattered.

Next on the list was the requirement that she had to move to the cabin immediately. If she stayed until Labor Day, the property and everything on it was hers to take care of for her lifetime. She couldn't sell it, rent it, or give it away. Failure to comply would result in the place being left to a distant cousin, and Rayanne and her parents would be banned from ever setting foot on the property again.

He'd also set aside enough money to see her through the summer. Once September rolled around, the rest of Ray's surprisingly substantial estate would also be hers. With care, she wouldn't have to work again.

Meanwhile, the attorney had suggested that she begin by doing a room-by-room inventory of the cabin. The only question was where to start?

The kitchen would be the simplest. Before starting, she picked out some CDs from Ray's collection and put them on to play. His taste was eclectic, but this morning some red-dirt rock and country fit her mood.

With the sound of fiddle and guitar filling the empty silence, she got out her spiral notebook and favorite pen and started to work.

Wyatt drifted closer to the edge of the woods to listen. With the doors and windows closed up tight, he couldn't make out the lyrics. The singer had a smoky voice, the kind that had a man thinking of a pair of lovers breathing hard as they tangled up together in between soft sheets.

After all this time, he had only vague memories of what it had been like to coax a woman into sharing his bed for the night. Closing his eyes, he tried to remember the scent of his last lover's perfume. Something flowery, maybe. He had better luck remembering how silky smooth her skin had been, but nothing at all about what she looked like. Could have been a blonde or a brunette, not that it mattered. She was long dead and buried.

Lucky her.

Rather than continue down that dusty road, he

dragged his thoughts back to the moment at hand. The man had always played music, too. Wyatt hadn't realized how silent the mountain had been since Ray's passing. It seemed odd to know he was gone but that his music would play on beyond his death. It was truly a gift of the modern world, one of the few things Wyatt enjoyed.

Where he'd grown up, music had been a rarity. Sometimes a passing stranger with an old fiddle or guitar would offer an exchange of music for a meal or two. Ma had always thought that was a fair deal.

What was the woman doing now? He hadn't meant to scare her earlier, but then he hadn't expected her to be able to see him at all. When she'd crumpled to the floor, he'd stuck around long enough to make sure she'd wake up on her own. He wasn't sure what he would've done if she hadn't. He'd used up all his energy when he'd wadded up that picture of himself in a fit of anger.

Where had she found that? Why had she brought it with her? Did she remember that long-ago summer? Too many unanswered questions. He'd spent many an hour thinking about her and why she'd been able to see him at all. No one else ever had, not that he knew of.

She'd screamed back then, too, but to warn him about the shooter on the roof. That was the only time he'd shot the bastard instead of taking one in the shoulder himself. It hadn't changed the outcome, just the bullet count. He caught himself rubbing the scar, easing an ache that had nothing to do with the actual shooting.

But music or not, he wanted the woman gone. She'd already disturbed his peace enough. These were his woods and Blessing was his town, even if only by squatter's rights. The law didn't count for much out here. Rules and regulations only held sway when there was authority around to enforce them.

And this morning's encounter was proof enough which one of them belonged here. She had no business intruding on his solitude, especially when he had no way of knowing if she'd be able see him all of the time or if this morning was a fluke. How could he find out without risking scaring her into a fit again?

He hated change almost as much as he hated that nothing ever really changed up here on the mountain.

Time to move on. Maybe see if anyone else was stirring back in town. It was doubtful. Too early in the summer yet. Soon, though. And when the good folks of Blessing put in their appearance, would the woman see them again?

Only time would tell.

For now, he'd check on the town and then rest. Normally, he could hold on to his form most of the time once the days started growing longer. But the encounter with the woman had burned up a great deal of his energy. Even now he couldn't see his feet or feel his hat on his head. If he waited much longer, he'd fade completely. Hating the feeling that he was nothing more than a shadow with no real substance, he preferred to disappear at a time and place of his own choosing.

So for now, he'd just let go. Tomorrow would be soon enough to check in on the woman and see if he could learn when she planned to leave. She wouldn't stay. There wasn't anything up here to hold a woman like her—all modern and independent.

The song faded away, so he did the same.

Chapter 4

Morning dawned sunshine bright and warm. Wyatt preferred the shadows under the aspen trees, but he'd been drawn back to the edge of the meadow. It had been a day since he'd faded out. He rarely paid much attention to the passage of time, but things were different right now. She was still there, for one.

As he'd drifted on the breeze, he'd sensed her movements. He wasn't sure what she was doing, but she'd spent most of the day before banging around in the kitchen. If she'd been hunting for something, he hoped she'd found it. He was tired of the noise, not to mention it disturbed the other residents in the woods.

The deer had moved farther off, the birds were quiet and even the squirrels and chipmunks were nowhere to be seen. Eventually, they'd adjust to the woman's presence, but for now they were being cautious.

Probably good advice if he was in the mood to listen to it, but curiosity won out over caution. Since he'd yet to regain form, it should be safe enough to peek into the kitchen window. One glance and he'd be gone.

He caught a breeze that carried him toward the front porch, the only sign of his presence a faint shadow on the ground below. Nothing a rational person wouldn't put off to a random cloud passing overhead. At the edge of the porch he drifted up next to the wall, keeping well below the level of the window. Once he was settled in place, he rose up slowly.

The kitchen looked as if it had been ransacked by a bunch of wranglers just coming in off a long trail drive with nothing but dust and cows for company. Every inch of counter space was covered with pots, pans and dishes. In all the years Ray had lived there, he'd never once left a mess like that. In fact, the man was obsessively neat, always doing things in the same way on the same days.

Wyatt suspected the habit had given the man some sense of control. When that failed to calm his demons, Ray had walked the game trails for long hours at a time, especially at night. Often Wyatt had followed along, glad for the company, even if Ray had only rarely acknowledged his presence. He'd been too busy trying to outdistance the ghosts of his own past, not the ones who actually shared his mountain home.

Sometimes Ray had also wandered through what

was left of Blessing. Each year more of the old town fell victim to the passing years. Dry rot had left most of the remaining buildings unsafe for humans to explore. Sometimes Ray did small repairs, like when he'd replaced that missing step in the church.

Had he hoped the girl would come back to visit again? Well, she hadn't. Not until it was too late to do her uncle any good.

A movement inside caught his attention. She was headed for the door, holding one of those little things Ray used to talk into. A telephone, Wyatt knew. He had no idea how it worked, but then he didn't understand a lot of things these days.

He flattened himself against the cabin wall as she stomped out onto the porch. Her voice rang out over the meadow, loud and full of frustration. Her free hand waved around in the air to emphasize whatever point she was trying to make, not that the person she was talking to could see it. Or maybe he could. In this ever-changing world, anything was possible.

Eavesdropping was rude, but it was one of the few pleasures Wyatt had anymore. He settled in to listen.

"No, Dad, I won't be leaving here until the first week of September. I told Mom that before I came up here, and nothing's changed."

She listened a few seconds, rolling those expressive green eyes and biting her lower lip, probably trying to hold back her temper. He didn't know what her father said next, but she immediately cut in.

"Dad, don't *Now, Rayanne* me. I'm an adult, even if you and Mom have a hard time remembering that. I'm using the time up here to do research. I can work here just as well as I could from my apartment. Which, I might add, I've already sublet to a grad student for the summer semester."

She listened some more, her fair skin flushing with frustration.

"Look, I understand why you're worried, but I'm doing fine. Don't show up here without calling first because I don't like being interrupted when I'm working."

Wyatt grinned. In the bright sunshine, her hair looked more red than blond, and she sure enough had a redhead's temper. He almost felt sorry for her father, but maybe the man deserved the sharp edge of her tongue.

Her voice softened. "I do love you, Dad. Talk to you soon."

She disappeared inside with the phone but immediately returned to lift her face up to the sun as if needing its warmth. He could still see the gawky girl she'd been the last time she'd come to the mountain, but she'd matured into a beautiful woman. Were those waves of red-gold framing her face as soft as they looked?

He drifted closer, careful to make sure the breeze wouldn't push him into her. She might not notice anything other than a brief chill, but she'd already surprised him with her ability to sense his presence. Even in his current scattered state, it was hard to resist the sweet warmth of her life force. She positively glowed with it.

Hellfire, he wanted a taste of that. What he wouldn't give to kiss his way across that scattering of freckles on her cheeks. He bet she hated them, but he'd always had a weakness for freckles. Did she have them anywhere else? No way to tell with what she had on.

That old flannel shirt of Ray's did little to hide the female curves underneath. He preferred a woman to dress like a woman with lace and petticoats. He'd always loved the challenge of peeling off one layer at a time before he reached all that silken skin underneath. On the other hand, her dungarees certainly showed off the sweet curve of her backside in enticing detail. She certainly didn't need a bustle to draw a man's eye.

Suddenly, she shook her head and smiled. He didn't know what she was thinking about, but he had to wonder if that lush mouth would taste as tart as her words had sounded. And why did he care? It wasn't as if he'd ever know. He wanted her gone. That's all that mattered.

After a few seconds, her smile faded, and she drew a deep breath that she let out in a soft sigh.

"Uncle Ray, I don't know if you can hear me, but thank you for this gift. I need this time up here on the mountain, even if Mom and Dad don't get that."

Her smile was back and she laughed. "Well, Ray-anne, you've only just gotten here, and already you're talking to yourself. Time to get busy."

Rather than heading back inside, she stalked off toward the woods. So now he knew her name—Rayanne. Seemed only fair since she knew his, even if she didn't realize he was around. After all, no matter how he felt about it, it appeared they were destined to be neighbors for a while.

He waited until she reached the edge of the trees before following her. Where was she headed? And why did he care? He couldn't remember the last time he felt curious about much of anything, but he wanted to see for himself where she ended up. He was betting on the old church belfry.

Besides, he had nothing better to do.

No matter how determined she was to not let anyone ruin her time on the mountain for her, it was hard. Why couldn't they just leave her alone? Yeah, like that was going to happen. Her parents meant well, but it freaked her out to have them joining forces against her. It was the first time they'd put up a united front since their divorce.

She understood their concern. As her father had rudely pointed out, they'd spent a lot of time and a ton of money dealing with the aftermath of her last trip to Blessing. Not that it had helped. After months of counseling and arguments, she'd simply given up and spouted whatever the shrink wanted to hear. He'd marked her down as another success on his scorecard, and her parents' guilt had eased. Whoopee, everyone won except her. All she'd done was learn to keep the nightmares to herself.

Even Shawn hadn't bothered to disguise his own displeasure in her decision to accept Uncle Ray's legacy. Did they really think she didn't know her own mind?

Well, she wasn't going to let them ruin her good mood. She was proud of what she'd accomplished so far, even if she'd made a total wreck of the kitchen. She'd washed out all the drawers and cabinets. After she walked off her frustration, she'd replace the shelf paper and put everything back. Tomorrow she'd start on another room. Or not.

Her decision. No one else's.

She stepped into the shadows of the trees. The old game trail looked unchanged from her last visit. At least this time she was wearing the right kind of shoes for hiking over the uneven ground. The faded scar on her shin was just one other reminder of that fateful day.

Here under the trees and out of the direct light of the sun, the day wasn't as warm as she'd thought. Even with Ray's flannel shirt, there was a bit of a chill in the air. As long as she kept moving, she'd be fine. If memory served her right, the far side of these woods was less than half a mile away, at best a ten-minute walk. From there, it was only a short distance to where Blessing sat nestled in a small valley.

She'd keep today's visit short, just a quick trip to reacquaint herself with the general layout of the town. Her plan was to do a complete survey of Blessing, measuring each of the remaining buildings and marking them on a map. When that was complete, she'd follow up with a photo survey.

Once she finished that much, she'd make a trip to

the county courthouse and see if there were any re-
cords of the town still on file. Maybe one of the local
newspapers would have archives that went back far
enough to tell her something. Who knew? Wyatt Mc-
Cain's death might have warranted a column or two.

Slowly, step by step, she hoped to complete the picture. By then, she should have a feel for whether her
work would justify a book on the subject or if she'd
submit a paper to one of the professional journals. Either of those choices would be the sensible thing to do.

Or she could just say the heck with being sensible and try her hand at writing a historical romance
based on what had happened there in Blessing. She
grinned up at a squirrel, which was chattering at her
for disturbing his afternoon.

"Sorry, guy. Didn't mean to encroach on your territory. I promise I'm just passing through."

She laughed and kept walking. The trees came
to an abrupt end just past the next bend in the trail,
giving way to the valley below. The bright green of
the grass sprinkled with early-blooming wildflowers
stole her breath away. How could she have forgotten
how pretty it was?

Somehow the beauty had been overwhelmed by
the darkness in her nightmares. No wonder Uncle Ray
had found some peace of mind living up here. She'd
often wished there had been some magical way she
could have known the man he'd been before the war
had changed him. It was clear that Ray had come
back from Vietnam a different man, one far different
from the older brother her mother had grown up with.

Rather than dwell on the past, Rayanne started down the slope toward the edge of town. She'd like to think her pulse was picking up speed because of the workout she was getting from the walk, but there was no use fooling herself. This first trip back to Blessing was bound to stir up a few bad memories.

Keeping to a slow pace, she walked through the middle of town. In its heyday, Blessing had boasted a population of nearly two hundred people, but there was little evidence left of most of the houses. At least the old church looked much the same, as did the saloon. It was ironic that those two polar opposites survived.

It didn't take long to reach the far end of town. Turning back, she had the oddest sensation that she was being watched. She did a slow turn, looking in all directions, but the only movement came from the breeze brushing across the grass and wildflowers. Obviously, her imagination was running hot.

There wasn't much left of Blessing except faded boards and failed dreams. But maybe, just maybe, with hard work and the right words she could bring the town back to life. Through her, others could get a real glimpse of what life had been like here. She liked that idea. Maybe she could figure out a way to lay out the bare-bone facts of the town's history and then make them come alive through the eyes of a fictional resident. The wife of one of the miners might be fun.

As she considered the possibilities, a glimpse of the town alive and thriving suddenly superimposed itself over the deserted street. She stared in horror at a scene straight out of her nightmares. That the vision had no more substance than did her dreams made it no less frightening. She had the awful suspicion if she were to look behind her, she'd see those gunmen riding into town with death in their eyes.

She rubbed her eyes and looked again. Everything was back to normal. The experience was disconcerting, but perhaps her ability to see what had been would stand her in good stead when it came time to write her book.

She'd already been gone longer than she'd planned, but she had one more stop before she left. If she was going to face her personal demons, it had to start with where it had all happened. She'd climb the steps to the church belfry, take a quick peek around and then head back to the cabin.

She entered the church through the front door just as she had before. The first thing she noticed was that Uncle Ray had replaced the missing step. Since she was the only other person who ever visited the church, he'd done it for her. She brushed her fingers over the unfinished board and smiled. He'd always done his best to take care of her.

She put her full weight on the step, enjoying its solid feel beneath her feet. Then one by one, she climbed the rest of the way up the stairs, noticing he'd also reinforced a few more of the cracked and worn boards while he was at it. The door to the roof swung open on well-oiled hinges. No more loud creaking to warn her if someone followed her out onto the roof like the gunman in her dream. She shivered, but shoved that thought out of her mind.

A few short steps carried her across to the railing. She kept her eyes firmly focused on her feet, telling herself she was keeping an eye out for rotted boards that could give way beneath her weight. The truth was she wasn't quite ready to risk looking down at the street below.

Would she see weeds growing up between the wooden sidewalks or the townspeople going about their daily routine? There was only one way to find out. She latched on to the faded railing with both hands, locked her knees to make sure they'd support her, took a deep breath and cast her gaze outward.

Her relief at seeing nothing but a ghost town was palpable. Another major hurdle cleared. As she started to turn back toward the door, a movement below caught her eye. How odd. The batwing doors on the old saloon were swaying as if someone had just passed through them.

She glanced around, realizing for the first time that the breeze had picked up and white puffs of clouds she'd noticed earlier now covered most of the sky overhead in an angry gray blanket. One of the first things Uncle Ray had taught her was that storms could roll in with little notice. Getting soaked in an early-summer rain wouldn't kill her.

A lightning strike might.

A deep rumble of thunder echoed down the valley, sending a shiver through her. Time to get the heck off the roof of the tallest building in town. Ignoring

the grumble of a few of the boards, she hustled back
to the door and breathed a little easier when she was
back inside. She wasn't out of the woods yet.

She smiled at the image. Actually, she had to reach
the woods first. They'd shelter her from the storm
well enough. Once the worst of it was past, she could
make the final run for the cabin. At least the day
was still warm enough that she didn't have to worry
about hypothermia setting in if she did get soaked
along the way.

She cursed herself a fool for setting off so ill prepared. She knew better or at least she used to. Ray
had laid out the rules for her the very first time she'd
come to visit. He'd written them out in big block let-
ters so she could read them on her own. Then he'd
ordered her to study the rules until she knew them
backward and forward.

When she'd recited them to him, he'd handed her
a pen. Once she'd scrawled her name on the paper,
Uncle Ray had presented her with her very own backpack filled with emergency supplies: granola bars,
bottled water, a first-aid kit and even a rain poncho.
It had been one of the proudest days of her life.

"Sorry, Uncle Ray. Guess I need a refresher course."

She wouldn't make the same mistake again. On
her next trip to Blessing, she'd bring emergency supplies and stash them inside one of the buildings. For
now, though, she had a long way to go to reach the
slope leading up to the timberline. The dust kicked
up by the wind stung her eyes, and another crash of

thunder warned her that the storm was moving faster than she was.

Okay, so maybe she'd be better off waiting out the storm back in town. She reversed course and took off running for the nearest building. The church might be sturdier, but right now she couldn't afford to be picky. The saloon would have to do.

The darkening sky flashed bright with another bolt of lightning. The resulting thunder followed right on its heels, warning her the storm was now centered right over the valley. Big, fat drops of rain splashed down on the dusty road as Rayanne ran. She kept a wary eye on the ground in front of her to avoid stepping in one of the wagon-wheel ruts still visible after all these years. The last thing she needed was to twist an ankle.

After another crack of thunder, the rain poured down even harder, instantly turning the dust into mud so that her shoes made a sucking noise as she ran. It was too late to worry about staying dry. Finding shelter was paramount. The wooden sidewalk outside the saloon creaked in protest when she put her full weight on it, but it held. After shoving through the swinging doors to the dim interior, she bent over, hands on her knees as she waited for her lungs to catch up on oxygen.

When she could breathe, she slipped off her flannel shirt and wrung it out as best she could. She reached for the hem of her T-shirt, planning to do the same with it, when the memory of watching the saloon door swaying in the breeze popped into her head. She froze and looked around to make sure she was alone.

What was she thinking? No one ever came up here uninvited. Of course the room was empty. She peeled off her T-shirt and twisted it until the rainwater dripped down onto the dusty floor. When it was as dry as she could make it, she slipped it back on, figuring her body heat would dry it out eventually. She hadn't bothered with a bra, so at least she didn't have to deal with the discomfort of wet lace and elastic while she was stuck here.

One of the old chairs looked sound enough to sit on, so she dragged it over toward the front window and made herself comfortable. The weather would change for the better soon, and then she'd head back to the cabin where a mug of hot chocolate with her name on it would be waiting.

Hellfire and damnation, did that woman have to follow him around?

Earlier, Wyatt had drifted into the saloon out of habit, not because he remembered the place where he'd had his last drink with any particular fondness. All those years ago, knowing full well he might die, he'd tossed back one last shot of good whiskey, kissed Tennessee Sue full on the mouth and walked out the door.

Nope, he didn't have any good memories of this place, even back when it was in its heyday. But thanks to what he was witnessing at the moment, old Bert's saloon had just become Wyatt's favorite place in the whole damn world.

With the thunder crackling overhead, the woman had bolted through the doors, already stripping off her flannel shirt. Thanks to the rain, the white shirt underneath stuck to her like a second skin, outlining her curves in considerable detail. One thing for sure, Rayanne was a damn sight more appealing than Tennessee Sue had been.

It would've taken a lot nobler man than Wyatt to look away, especially when he realized Rayanne wasn't wearing anything underneath the shirt. Her plentiful breasts swayed gently with each move she made, their dark tips faintly visible through the clingy cloth.

What he wouldn't give to test their weight with the palms of his hands. And damned if she wasn't reaching for the hem of that shirt, too. Surely she wasn't going to— No, she stopped and looked around suspiciously.

Had she sensed his presence? He wasn't visible; he knew that much. But even her late uncle had an uncanny knack for realizing when Wyatt came near. He'd nod in Wyatt's direction and then go about his business. Maybe his niece had inherited the same talent.

But then she went ahead and stripped her shirt right off in front of him. The storm outside had nothing on the one raging inside him right now. He moaned. Her skin was all peaches and cream. He loved the sprinkle of freckles across her shoulders and the dusky peach of her nipples. He sure enough wanted to kiss those freckles and suckle her pert nipples and watch them pebble up. Hell, he just plain *wanted*.

Incredible. He hadn't felt anything this powerful since the day he died. No hunger, no pain. Dread, yeah. Fear, even knowing how things would play out again. But no joy, no peace, no thirst, no hunger.

But by gosh, he hungered now. Unable to help himself, he drifted closer to where Rayanne stood, trying to squeeze some of the rainwater out of her clothes. If she didn't cover herself soon, he wasn't sure what would happen. In this state, his ability to interact with his surroundings was extremely limited. If he brushed against her bare skin, she might feel a chill or a buzz. He might not feel a damn thing.

If she was aware of him, he might have tried it. But a man didn't sneak up on an unsuspecting female. He was no hero, but he had enough black marks on his soul. With that in mind, he needed to put more distance between himself and temptation before he weakened and reached out to her.

He directed his focus toward the back wall to give her a chance to cover herself decently. The white shirt still left too little to the imagination, but it was better than all that peach-toned skin screaming out to be tasted and touched. Once the storm passed, he was sure she'd make her way back to the cabin. Good. He wished she was already gone, back to where she belonged, preferably off his mountain.

Taking her peaches-and-cream complexion and all that temptation with her.

Frustration with the whole situation left him wanting to break something. But if he let his temper slip its leash, he'd do something stupid. Like materializing right here in Bert's place to start breaking up the few pieces of furniture still left intact.

How would she react? She'd already fainted once at finding him in her kitchen. He bet she'd already twisted and turned the facts of yesterday morning to convince herself that she'd only imagined the whole incident. If for one second she'd believed he'd really been there, she wouldn't still be up here on the mountain by herself. He tried to imagine her pelting down that switchback road back to wherever she came from. The picture wouldn't come into focus.

Most folks would cower in a corner while nature raged outside. Instead, she'd dragged a chair right over to the window to watch. Even now, she sat forward, trying to see better through the filthy glass. She sure had gumption; he gave her that much.

If he'd been solid, he realized he would've been smiling. Even in his present state, he felt lighter, more buoyant. That realization scared him. He didn't want to feel lighter, didn't want to *feel* anything.

He needed to get out of there. There was plenty of energy to be had right outside the door. If he was careful, he could absorb enough to let him resume standing guard in the woods. The time was coming when others started prowling the mountain, gathering close. He'd need to make sure they kept their distance from the woman.

He wasn't sure how much harm they could do,

but they all grew stronger as the time grew near. He drifted closer again, this time feeling protective rather than lustful. He might not want her there, but neither did he want her hurt or scared.

Damn, why did she have to be there at all?

For now, she was safe enough. She could find her own way back to the cabin once the storm passed. Far better that their paths crossed as rarely as possible.

Better for him, anyway.

With that, he slipped through the doors and out into the street. The storm had weakened considerably already, the dark clouds having dumped most of their rain before moving on wherever the wind would carry them. The air felt clean as he drew on the natural energy it carried.

Slowly, he moved on out of town, growing more solid as he neared the timberline. By the time Rayanne followed him into the woods, he stood hidden in the shadows, solid from his hat to the soles of his boots.

The rain had brought out more curl in her hair, framing her pretty face and drawing attention to how young she was. But Rayanne moved with the kind of strength and purpose as another woman in his life had. He was surprised he hadn't noticed it sooner.

It wasn't as if he could forget about Amanda, the one woman he'd tried to be a better man for. The one he died trying to protect and succeeded only in destroying them both. He'd always wondered if they would have gone beyond simple friendship if things had played out differently for the two of them. No way to know now.

He followed after Rayanne, preferring her unknowing company to the darkness of his memories. For a second, she hesitated, stopping to look around. She frowned and rubbed her hands up and down her arms, clearly feeling a chill. Whether it was from his presence or from the dampness of her clothes didn't matter.

It was tempting to step out into a small circle of sun to see if she could see him at all and how she would react. But no, that wouldn't be smart. Besides, it was too late now. She was already back in motion, quickening her pace now that the cabin was almost in sight. He didn't blame her. Dark and dangerous things prowled these woods.

He should know. He was one of them.

Chapter 5

Rayanne was finished in the kitchen. Everything was stowed away, and she'd put a fresh shine on the counters, appliances and even the floor. She wasn't ready to face the living room yet.

It had soaked up so much of Uncle Ray's essence, for the lack of a better word. The wear on cushions of his favorite chair showed the outline of his body and carried the scent of his aftershave. The shelves lining the walls were filled with his favorite books, most dog-eared from multiple readings. Bits and pieces of the man, but not the whole.

She missed him so much. Had been missing him since long before he'd actually died.

No, she wasn't ready to sort through all those memories. Not yet. Cowardly, maybe, but she couldn't help but feel that she was intruding on Ray's privacy. Instead, she'd get started on her work in Blessing. The day was sunny and clear, perfect for taking pictures.

She'd made a list of the things she'd need for her survey as well as the emergency supplies she wanted to stash inside the church. That would require a trip down to the small combination grocery store, gas station and post office located at the base of the mountain.

She wanted to get back in time to start on measuring out the streets of Blessing, so she grabbed her purse and stepped out on the porch. Locking the door seemed a bit silly considering she was the only one around, but city habits died hard.

Besides, she never quite lost the feeling that she wasn't alone here on the mountain. Crazy, she knew, and the last thing she'd admit to anyone, but it felt as if someone was out there watching over her. She liked to think that some part of Uncle Ray had remained tethered to the mountain after all the years he'd spent taking care of it.

Her parents would never understand why she'd find that thought comforting, but she did. She stared in the direction of the trail to Blessing, fighting the whimsical urge to roll down the window to yell that she'd be right back.

Then she cranked up the stereo and sang along with the music all the way down the mountain.

"Where's she off to now?"

Not that it mattered. Rayanne would be back because she hadn't taken anything with her other than her purse. Probably going after supplies. Too bad. It would be better for both of them if she'd packed her suitcase and left the mountain.

He'd been spending way too much time lurking near the cabin, hoping to catch even a glimpse of her. All he could think about was the color of her skin, the fullness of her breasts and the way she would have smelled of rain and woman. He'd felt guiltier about that, but it wasn't his fault that she'd revealed all the creamy skin right in front of him.

What would she do if he were to return the favor, even fully clothed? She'd seen him twice before, once as a young girl and on her first morning back. He took off his hat and ran his fingers through his hair in frustration. Would she faint again or finally realize that he was more than a figment of her imagination? Thanks to that god-awful picture she had of him, she had to know he'd been real at one time.

No one in the hundred-plus years he'd been stuck here, straddled between life and death, had ever done more than caught a glimpse of him, except when he lay dying in the dusty street of Blessing. He suspected it was like catching a movement out of the corner of your eye, just a hint of something being there but just out of sight.

A sound deeper in the woods drew his attention away from the clearing and back toward town. Something was stirring or maybe someone. By his reckoning, it was far too early in the summer for most of the townspeople to put in an appearance. That left two people most likely causing the disturbance, the ones responsible for his being in Blessing at all.

Sometimes Amanda, the schoolteacher, and her son, Billy, showed up early with no warning. They never stuck around for long, leastwise not until later in August, right before the whole nightmare started up again. Even when they were there, they only rarely acknowledged his presence. For some unknown reason, he was the only one who truly haunted the mountain year after year. Maybe because it was all his fault.

But even if Amanda and Billy didn't speak to him, he'd seek them out, anyway. Even just a glimpse of Amanda gave him a sense of belonging, a belief that he wasn't truly alone. Her boy, Billy, served as a reminder of the price paid for innocence lost.

Wyatt watched as Rayanne drove out of sight before making his way back toward Blessing.

On the way, he stared up at the sky and muttered, "Someone up there has a hell of a sense of humor. I've got one woman who shouldn't be able to see me but can, and another who should be able to, but can't. Where's the sense in that?"

He paused for a second, tilting his head to the side, hoping against hope this time would be different and someone would answer. Instead, he got the same response he'd always gotten whenever he begged, pleaded or just plain asked for some kind of explanation for this ongoing hell he lived in: absolute silence.

* * *

The old general store hadn't changed much since the last time Rayanne had been there. A few different brands on the shelves, but the same old, faded sign out front advertising gas, groceries and postage stamps.

She grabbed a basket on the way in and made her way up and down the three aisles, picking up the items on her list and a few impulse purchases, as well. For the moment, she was alone in the store. If Phil, the proprietor and postmaster, didn't make an appearance by the time she was done, she'd ring the buzzer by the register to summon him from the small apartment attached to the back of the building.

More than once she and Uncle Ray had been invited back there for a lunch of grilled cheese sandwiches and root beer floats. Ray enjoyed the occasional game of chess with his old friend and hadn't minded her hovering over his shoulder while they played.

She smiled, grateful for another happy memory of her time on the mountain.

The shuffle of feet announced Phil's arrival. She snagged an extra pack of gum off the shelf and tossed it into the basket before making her way to the register. The passage of fifteen years had added a few wrinkles to Phil's face, and his hairline had receded a bit more, but she would've known him anywhere.

She coasted to a stop just short of the counter, waiting to see if he recognized her. It didn't take long. His welcoming smile brightened considerably as his faded blue eyes crinkled at the corners, leaving little doubt about her welcome. He charged back around the counter to sweep her up in a huge hug.

"Rayanne, girl, it has been too damn long. We've missed your pretty face up here on the mountain."

Tears stung her eyes as she hugged her uncle's old friend back. "I should have been here for him, Phil."

Phil held her out at arm's length. "Now, listen here, missy. Your uncle understood that your life was down in the city. He knew you loved him just like he loved you. If you don't believe anything else, believe that."

His words, spoken with such quiet authority, eased the knot in her chest enough so that she could breathe again.

"I'd like to think so, Phil. Thanks for saying so."

"It's no less than the truth." His own eyes looked a bit shiny as he held out his hand for her basket. "Let's get this stuff rung up for you. Have you had lunch?"

"Not yet." And realized she hadn't eaten already because she'd been subconsciously hoping Phil would make that offer.

"Great! We'll have cheese sandwiches and root beer floats, just like old times."

A shaft of sharp grief shot through her chest. Just like old times except that Uncle Ray wouldn't be there. But his memory would be, and that would suffice.

Phil was still talking. "Don't let me forget that I've got a package I've been holding for you. If you hadn't come in today, I would've brought it to you on Sunday when the store's closed."

Really? Her local post office had said it could take

a week or more for her mail to catch up with her. She wasn't expecting any more book deliveries, either. She knew better than to rush Phil. He did things in his own way and at his own speed.

At least he made quick work of her groceries. He added the last can of soup to the bag and then hit the total button on his old-fashioned cash register. "That'll be fifty-five dollars and forty-seven cents."

She handed him the cash and then took the bag with her perishables and stuck them in the cooler at the back of the store. Another habit she'd learned from Ray. With that done, she followed Phil into his apartment.

Two hours flew by as he caught her up on all the changes in the area since her last visit. A few old-timers had passed on; some new folks had moved in. All the usual gossip, only the names changed. She didn't mind hearing about people she didn't know, not if it made Phil happy to talk about them.

Finally, she finished the last of her float, enjoying the combined flavors of vanilla ice cream and root beer. She'd have to live on lettuce for a few days to make up for the calories, but the guilty pleasure of the sweet treat was worth the penance.

"Thank you for lunch, Phil. That really hit the spot. Nobody makes a root beer float like you do."

His smile was tinged with sadness. "It wasn't anything special, Rayanne. Nothing fancy like what you probably have all the time down there in the city."

She reached across the table to put her hand on his,

noticing for the first time how knobby his knuckles had gotten. Her friend wasn't getting any younger. Who would run the store when he was gone? She didn't want to think about it.

"Fancy doesn't make it special, Phil. Having lunch with you and Uncle Ray right here at this same table are some of the best memories I have."

He blushed a bit but looked decidedly happier. "I'll get that package for you. Ray brought it down to me about the time the doctors told him his heart was plumb worn out. He asked me to keep it until you moved into the cabin."

Interesting.

"So he was sure I'd come?"

Phil stared up at the ceiling for a second before answering. "I was sure. He hoped."

Okay. Before she could ask Phil to explain, he was up and heading for his bedroom. She could hear him rummaging around and muttering under his breath. Finally, he returned with a shoebox sealed shut with duct tape. Whatever was inside, Uncle Ray had wanted to make sure it was safe from prying eyes.

Phil handed it to her. "No idea what's in there, but I figure it had to be important because he made a special trip down to bring it to me."

Wow, a special trip. Ray had been a man of habit. He only came down to Phil's on the first and fifteenth of every month to pick up his mail and supplies. Only the worst of weather kept him from his appointed rounds.

"I wonder why he didn't just leave it in the cabin for me to find."

"He didn't say." Phil shook his head. "Who knows, maybe he just wanted to make sure it didn't fall into the wrong hands. You know how he was about protecting his privacy."

The box felt heavier somehow, as if knowing Ray had driven all the way down to entrust it to Phil's care gave it more weight. She was tempted to rip the tape off now instead of waiting until she got back to the cabin, but that didn't feel right.

No, she'd wait until after dinner and curl up in Ray's favorite chair to open it. For now, she needed to get moving. She had work to do up on the mountain.

She set the box down long enough to give Phil another hug. "Thanks for lunch, Phil, and for keeping Ray's package safe for me. I'll let you know what's in it next time I come in."

He shook his head. "No need. If Ray wanted me to know, he'd have told me himself."

Phil pointed to the mountain that dominated the view from his living room window. "I chose to live here because I like things quiet and simple. Your uncle, though, he needed to be up there on the mountain. Ray never talked about what it was that held him there all these years. He was a man who kept his secrets, that's for sure. Years ago I asked him one time why he didn't move down here where he could be around other people instead of living up there with that ghost town."

Then he nodded toward the box she held in a white-knuckled grip. "I figure the answer to that question is in that there box."

There wasn't much she could say to that. She had her own special reasons for spending time in Blessing.

Driving back to the cabin, she kept glancing at the box sitting in the passenger seat. It sat there like a homemade time bomb ready to explode the minute she peeled back the tape.

An uncomfortable thought, but that didn't make it any less true. Somehow she just *knew* that the secret truths it would reveal were going to change her life forever.

Rayanne was back. Even if Wyatt hadn't been watching for her, he'd have figured it out from all the racket she'd been making. It had started with her slamming the door of her car and then doing the same thing with the door of the cabin, both going and coming out again a few minutes later.

From the way she was marching along on a straight line toward the trail through the woods, something sure enough had her worked up. He grinned as she stubbed a toe on a root and turned the air blue with an impressive string of cuss words. That temper of hers was something to behold, that was for damn sure.

He drifted after her, making sure to stay far enough away so she wouldn't pick up on the fact she wasn't alone. Not really, anyway.

As soon as that thought crossed his mind, she froze and slowly looked back in his general direction. Her eyes narrowed, leaving no doubt that she was staring

right at him. Actually, considering he was currently
nothing more than a cloud of energy, she was staring
right through him.

What had he done to draw her attention? Most
likely nothing. Obviously, she'd inherited more than
her uncle's eye color. Rayanne clearly sensed him
on some level. He hovered right where he was, waiting for her to move on. In the future, he'd need to
maintain more distance if he was going to follow
her around.

Finally, she hobbled on down the trail, her gait
smoothing out as her foot quit hurting. When she
was out of sight, he cut straight through to the far
side of the woods, moving far faster than Rayanne's
human legs could carry her. Then he skirted the edge
of the woods to approach Blessing from the other
side of town.

First things first. He made a quick trip up and
down both sides of the street, reaching out to see if
there was anyone else around. Earlier, Amanda and
her son had passed through. He'd called out their
names, waved his hands and even stomped his feet,
but failed to draw their attention. All he'd done was
use up all of his power for the day, leaving him nothing but a mist on the wind.

Even if it was too early in the summer for them to
really be there, he hated to be ignored. He might not
feel the heat of the summer sun or the bitter cold of
the winter snow, but he could feel lonely.

But not right now. Rayanne had finally caught
up with him. She came around the far end of town

headed toward the church as usual. At the last minute, she surprised him by veering off course into the saloon, instead. Interesting. What was she doing in there?

Only one way to find out. He drifted close to the door, keeping low and moving slowly to avoid drawing her attention again. She'd already dragged an old table over beside the chair she'd left by the window. When she had it right where she wanted it, she tested its strength. Thanks to one leg being shorter than the others, it wobbled like crazy. Resourceful woman that she was, she used a scrap of wood from another broken table to shim it up.

Satisfied with her efforts, she unloaded one of the packs she'd carried with her. Paper. Pencils. Ruler. Those things he recognized. She pulled out another item, something shiny and new-looking. What was that? There were so many things in the world that he knew nothing about. Then she pulled on a small tab and ran out a short strip of metal as she looked around.

"Might as well start in here."

The device's purpose became clear as she used it to mark off distances in the room and jotted them down on paper. Why was she measuring the room? Who would care how big a saloon was, especially one that hadn't served a single drink in a hundred years?

He edged through the door, moving slowly. She was so intent on her ciphering to take note of his presence. Inside, he drifted up toward the ceiling to stay out of her way. She'd finished marking down the size of the floor and had moved on to the old bar and even the table she was working on.

It made him tired just watching her.

On the other hand, he wasn't about to complain about the view. Right after she'd started working, she'd stripped off her oversize flannel shirt, another one of Ray's old castoffs. The shirt she wore underneath would've scandalized the good folks of Blessing back in his day. It was dark blue with no sleeves and a neckline that plunged low enough to offer a tantalizing glimpse of those freckles he liked so much. Memories of yesterday's storm had him smiling.

He didn't know when women took to wearing trousers, but he had to admit he could get used to how that well-worn denim hugged her feminine charms. She'd been bent over, checking the number on that measuring device when she abruptly straightened up. Her hand moved up to rub the back of her neck as she slowly glanced around the room. After a few seconds, she walked over to the door to look outside. Finally, she turned back to face the bar and slowly lifted her eyes up to the corner where he was.

"Okay, so I'm imagining things."

No, she wasn't, but he'd just as soon hope she didn't figure that out. The last thing he needed was a hysterical female on his hands. He drifted back outside. On his way, though, he used a small spurt of energy to set the doors swinging. His efforts were rewarded when Rayanne charged out onto the sidewalk right behind him, her hands on her hips as she glared up and down the street. He couldn't help but laugh at her frustration.

Besides, why bother haunting the place if he couldn't have a little fun with it?

Chapter 6

Dinner was done, and the few dishes Rayanne had used were washed and put away. She'd run out of excuses for avoiding the shoebox she'd left sitting on the coffee table in the living room. Right now she was heating water for a pot of tea. She'd picked a blend that was supposed to soothe the nerves.

She hoped it worked because she'd been jumpy as heck ever since she'd left Phil's place. She'd never minded being alone; most of the time she preferred it. No parents and no would-be boyfriends questioning her every decision.

What she didn't like was the creepy-crawly feeling that someone had been staring at her both in the woods and a little while later in the saloon. Silly, probably, but then there was that swinging door. Not exactly a smoking gun, but it was the second time it had started swinging while she was in town.

Granted, the first time was when the storm was moving in, and she'd written that time off to the wind. However, today when she'd been plotting out the saloon, there hadn't been even a hint of a breeze.

Her uncle had told her often enough that people didn't stick around long when they came to visit him because they weren't welcome. Lord knew her mother and father had hated the place. She'd always thought what he'd really meant was that she was one of the few he didn't mind sharing his space.

Now she had to wonder. Was it possible that it was the mountain itself that didn't like intruders? As soon as that thought crossed her mind, she shook her head and laughed. Maybe she should write a fantasy story with a sentient mountain complete with a ghost town. She even had the perfect dark hero, the same one who'd haunted her dreams last night.

She studied the picture of Wyatt McCain that she'd smoothed out and stuck on the fridge with a magnet. Those pale eyes followed her wherever she went. Had that straight slash of a mouth ever softened into a smile? And why did it matter? He'd been dead and buried a hundred years before she was born.

Enough about Wyatt. He'd already claimed too much of her thoughts lately. Time to open the box. She put the old teapot on a tray along with her favorite mug and the cookies she'd picked up at the store. Then she added a box of tissues.

Just in case.

Ray's favorite chair was the perfect spot for the great unveiling. She dug out the old pocketknife he kept in the drawer of the end table and used it to loosen one edge of the sticky, gray tape. When she had enough to grab hold of, she stripped off the first layer of tape. It took her a solid ten minutes of careful work to finally get down to the cardboard.

Before lifting the lid, she took time to drink a cup of tea and nibble on one of the cookies. Maybe some music would help. She reached for her iPod and turned it on. Better. Out of excuses, she removed the lid and set it aside.

Inside, a stack of leather-bound books were nestled in a bed of wadded-up newspaper. A white envelope was stuck inside the top one with her name on it written in Uncle Ray's handwriting.

She left the books in the box and set it aside for the moment. Using the same knife, she slit open the sealed envelope and pulled out folded papers. They had ragged edges, looking as if they'd been torn out of a spiral notebook.

As she spread them out, she closed her eyes and took a deep breath.

Dear Rayanne,
If you're reading this, well, we both know why. Even before the war, I was never much good with words, spoken or otherwise, but I'm going to give this my best shot. I knew you'd accept the terms of my will although I figure your mom and dad probably gave you hell about it.

Sorry about that, but they never did understand the mountain and how it called to you just as it did me.

There's a reason for that, Rayanne. This is no ordinary mountain, and Blessing is no ordinary town. I regret like hell how things went down on your last trip up here. I hope you can find it in your heart to forgive me for letting you get caught up in something you were too young to handle. I tried to tell your folks, but they wouldn't listen. No surprise there.

But not all of the story is mine to tell. When Great-Aunt Hattie left the place to me, she gave me the bottom two books to read. The next one is mine. Read them in order, starting with the one with a brown cover, then the black one, and finally the blue one. I bought the green one for you.

All that I would ask is that you not tell anyone about what you've read. First off, they'll think you're crazy. Secondly, the mountain likes to keep its secrets. You don't want a bunch of crazy outsiders up here trying to prove you right or even wrong.

Remember that I love you. Even if you decide to live down below, keep an eye on the place for me. When it comes time for you to pass the place on to the next generation, choose your successor well. I know I did.

Love,

Ray

Okay, that was strange. But when she lifted the
four books out of the box, she could have sworn she
felt a jolt of energy that left her fingertips tingling.
She set all but the brown one aside and opened to
the first page. The lines were covered with a decidedly feminine handwriting that gradually grew more
shaky toward the end of the old journal.

Feeling as if she were about to take a step off a
precipice, she turned the lamp up a notch and began
reading aloud, her voice echoing through the cabin.

*"My name is Amanda Green, and I live here in
Blessing in the state of Colorado. There's not much
left of the town now, but I have nowhere else to go.
This is my home, and the people I love are buried
here, my husband, William, and my son, Billy. The
mine took William, and Billy died the day of the Great
Incident. Someday I will sleep beside them out there
on the side of the valley."*

Rayanne read aloud until her voice grew hoarse;
then she read on in silence. Even though Amanda had
thought to live out her life alone, eventually she did
remarry and start a second family.

As interesting as that was, it was Amanda's vague
references to the Great Incident that kept Rayanne
turning pages long after she should have been in bed.
Details. She needed details even if she wasn't sure
how she felt about finding out that her great-great-
grandmother had actually known Wyatt McCain.

For sure, it was a relief to find out he'd been real,
but she was also just a little jealous of Amanda's relationship with the man. And wasn't that a little bit

crazy? Even so, for the first time she felt a real connection with the woman, who until then had only been a fading name in the family Bible.

Finally, Rayanne set the book aside, her eyes too tired to make sense of the spidery handwriting. The lack of detail about the day Amanda's son died was frustrating. Wouldn't a day that significant warrant more than a handful of vague references? The passage in Amanda's journal made it sound as if Billy might have been another casualty in the streets of Blessing the day Wyatt McCain had died.

Tomorrow she'd pick up where she'd left off and see if the rest of Amanda's journal held the answers to Rayanne's questions. If not, perhaps Great-Aunt Hattie had been more forthcoming.

Upstairs, Rayanne climbed onto her bed and opened the window to let in the night air. She stared up at the stars overhead. Reading the journal had left her both exhausted and yet too wired to immediately fall asleep. Sometimes making mental lists helped her to relax.

She'd start off with the normal routine—shower, breakfast and getting dressed. Next, she'd head back to Blessing to map out another building. The old mining office should keep her busy for a good part of the day. Maybe she'd take the journals to read when she needed a break.

Perfect. Having everything planned out, she snuggled down under the quilt and drifted off to sleep, secretly hoping she'd dream of a certain gunslinger with those startling blue eyes.

* * *

Rayanne was in town again. Evidently, she was done in the saloon because she'd spent the past hour or more poking around in the old mining office. Measuring out the saloon was a waste of time, but the mining office was even more so. Hell, the mine had been pretty much played out shortly after Wyatt had breathed his last. What possible use was it to her?

Wyatt would be better off wandering in the woods than watching her from across the street. All it did was aggravate him, and he didn't need that. From the way she kept wiping her forehead with the back of her hand, the weather must be hot. He couldn't tell one way or another. No matter what the temperature was, winter or summer, he felt the same. Good thing, too, considering he'd been wearing his duster that last day.

Rayanne stepped out on the porch and stared up at the sun. Once again, her attire had him wondering how modern men managed to keep their hands to themselves. She was wearing another one of those formfitting shirts with no sleeves and no modesty. But today, instead of her usual dungarees, she had on short pants. Very short pants.

Were her shapely legs as smooth to the touch as they looked? Wouldn't do him much good if they were, but a man had the right to wonder about such things when they were put on display like that.

Now what was she up to? She'd dragged her pack outside and then sat down on the porch, leaning up against the side of the building. She pulled out a bottle of water and a sandwich, obviously her lunch.

After the first couple of bites, she reached back into the bag and brought out a book. He frowned. It looked familiar. Before he could figure why, Rayanne opened it to somewhere near the back and read a short passage out loud as if to make better sense of it.

"I hear voices sometimes. See shadows that should not be there. They move through the trees as if blown about by the wind, even though the leaves hang still on the branches above. Today I swear I heard my Billy calling for me.

"That's when I realized that it was that time of year again. I used to love the heat of the summer sun. Now it only reminds me of all that I lost on that hot August day. Does a mother's love carry on beyond the grave? I think it must. That's the only reason I can think of that would allow me to hear Billy's laughter on the breeze.

"I've learned to keep to myself in the safety of my cabin. Too many strange things happen here when summer draws to a close. I won't speak of them here. Not yet. Not until I come to terms with what it all means. Could it be that they were all trapped here, just as I am even if I yet live and they don't? For years my grief has consumed my every breath. Only now, with Billy's laughter echoing in the woods, have I started looking beyond my own selfish pain and wondering about theirs. Is there nothing to be done to ease their burden and let them find peace at last? Could it be that my grief keeps them anchored here? I shudder to think that could even be possible."

Rayanne's voice carried well in the quiet, but then

she went back to eating her sandwich and reading silently. That was all right. She'd read enough for him to realize who had written those words—Amanda. It had to be her journal, and the reason it looked so familiar was because he'd spent a lot of nights watching her write in it. He'd never wanted to pry enough to see what words she'd written on all those pages.

Had she mentioned him? If so, it was doubtful that it had been anything good, and he was right sorry about that. Amanda had good reason to hate him, though, so he could hardly blame her. He ought to go wander around somewhere else but couldn't resist trying to get a glimpse of Amanda's words.

But before he managed to slip close enough to peek over Rayanne's shoulder, she closed the book. Damn. Now he'd never know what the book contained.

She stuck it back in her pack and pulled out another book. It was probably Hattie's. She'd been the first one to live on the mountain after the town had dried up completely. She'd gone about her daily chores without paying much attention to him. If she'd known he was around, she'd never said.

On the other hand, after her first summer on the mountain, she'd packed up and left the mountain for two weeks every August. He had to think she'd known more about what went on in Blessing than she'd let on. Cantankerous old biddy, he'd missed her when she'd passed on.

He settled against the wall and listened as Rayanne started reading aloud again.

"My kin thinks me addled for living up here by my-

*self. If I ever told them I was never really alone be-
cause a certain handsome man haunts these woods,
they'd come drag me down to see some city doctor.
But Wyatt's here. I know it even if they don't."*

Well, damn, so Hattie had known he was there.
Did she know about the others? The next sentence
answered that question.

*"I know it's cowardly of me to leave in August,
but I watched Wyatt die once. I have no desire to do
so again, not when I can't do a thing to change what
happened to him or Aunt Amanda's first son. There
are others around, but I don't know their stories or
why they're still here."*

The words hung heavy in the hot summer air. Rayanne slammed the book closed and scrambled to her
feet, staring up and down the street, looking as if
she'd seen a ghost. But then, she had. She'd probably convinced herself that the gunfight had all been
a dream, a nightmare, something she'd conjured out
of the clear mountain air. Then there was that first
morning in the cabin.

It had to shake her up some finding out that she
wasn't the only one in her family who'd seen that day
play out again and again over the years. She thought it
was scary seeing ghosts. How did she think it would
be to feel your body torn apart by a hail of bullets only
to wake up trapped in a never-ending hell?

Disgusted with the whole situation and even more
so with himself, he had to get away from Rayanne.
Right now. Before he did something stupid like pull-

ing himself together out here in the bright sunshine just to see if she'd see him this time.

And what she'd do if she did.

He didn't really want to scare her again, not like he'd done before when she'd hollered out a warning at him from the belfry. She'd done her best to save his worthless life. Even though it hadn't worked, he owed her for trying.

As he moved off, she whispered something, a hopeful note in her voice. He tried to tell himself he'd misheard her, but then she whispered it again.

"Wyatt? Are you here?"

Should he answer? Even if he did, would she hear him? Before he could make up his mind, she laughed and walked back inside the mining office, shaking her head and muttering something about an overactive imagination and crazy talk.

Rather than prove her wrong, he decided it was time to make himself scarce. More scarce, actually.

He'd barely crossed the street, heading for the saloon, when he heard a crash followed by a scream.

"Rayanne!" he hollered and charged back to the mining office, latching on to the blazing heat of the summer sun overhead to pull himself back together. By the time Wyatt hit the front porch, his body was rock solid and the sound of his boots landing on the old wood rang in the air.

Old habits die hard, so he drew his gun as he charged inside to see what kind of trouble Rayanne had gotten herself into.

Chapter 7

Rayanne scrambled for something to hold on to, anything to avoid slipping any farther into the hole that had opened up in the floor. One of the old boards had shattered with no warning when she'd put her weight on it, sending her lurching to the side. Her foot slipped down the old wood to get wedged in the tangle of broken timbers and the floor joist below. If the ground was only a couple of feet down, she wouldn't be worried, but there was a good eight-foot drop down into an old cellar.

And something was stirring down there. She didn't want to know what. At best, it was a varmint of some kind. At worst, rattlesnakes were known to seek out cool, shady places.

Right now every move she made only made mat-

ters worse. Trying hard not to panic, she supported
her weight with her arms as she considered her options, none of which were good. Finally, using her
other foot, she kicked the broken board as hard as she
could to loosen its hold on her ankle. Her first attempt
failed, but the second one did the job and then some.
Not only did that board give way, but so did the one
she was sitting on.

She yelped again as the floor beneath her collapsed,
sending her slip-sliding down toward the jagged timbers below. As she toppled off the edge, her trapped
foot came free, and she managed to brace herself long
enough to stop her fall. Fear tasted bitter, and her pulse
was running hot.

What now?

"Son of a bitch, woman!"

A pair of strong hands grabbed hold of her arms
just before another piece of the floor cracked wide
open. With her heart banging around in her chest, she
was left dangling over the gaping hole in the floor.

The same deep voice growled. "Are your feet hung
up on anything?"

She wiggled them slightly to make sure. "No."

No sooner had she answered when the mystery
man heaved her up and out of the hole, carrying her
toward the edge of the room. From there, he dragged
her through the door into the other room and then
straight out onto the porch where he dumped her in
an undignified heap. Not that she was complaining.
Without his help, she could've been badly hurt or
even killed.

The mountain was unforgiving when it came to the careless or the unlucky. Her mysterious savior disappeared back into the mining office, returning a few seconds later to drop her things on the sidewalk beside her. He'd left her sitting, facing the street, and even now he stood in the doorway out of her line of sight.

"Are you hurt?"

She'd already done a quick survey. A few bumps, a bruise or two and a scrape on her knee. "Nothing serious. My ankle hurts, but all things considered, I'm not complaining."

He snorted in disgust. "That's what you get for poking around where you don't belong."

Okay, she was willing to cut the guy some slack for coming to her rescue, but who did he think he was to tell her she didn't belong here in Blessing? She owned the place and had the paperwork to prove it. The land had been in her family for four generations now. Feeling decidedly at a disadvantage sitting on the ground, she gingerly pushed herself back up to her feet.

When she turned around, the doorway was empty. Where had he gone? She hobbled a couple of steps to peek in, but the room was empty. She wasn't about to go any farther inside, not with the floor as rotten as it was.

"Mister? It's not safe in there."

"Not for you," he said in the same deep voice.

She jumped when he answered from behind her. How had he gotten past her? She got her answer when she spun around to face him. For a brief second, her stomach lurched as if the sidewalk had just done a roller-coaster dive. Rayanne stumbled backward until her back was pressed against the side of the building. Locking her knees kept her upright, but just barely.

"Who? You? How?"

Okay, her babbling only made her rescuer even angrier. Rather than continue, she stared down at her feet and concentrated on taking a slow, deep breath and then a second one. Finally, when she thought she could string together a coherent statement, she looked up again and tried to put all the puzzle pieces together.

There he stood, still wearing that same blue shirt, hat and duster he'd had on fifteen years ago. His steel-blue eyes stared right back at her, his mouth set in an angry snarl. Maybe if she hadn't spent much of the past twenty-four hours reading Amanda's and Hattie's journals, she might have convinced herself that she'd knocked her head hard enough to scramble her brains.

But if she hadn't, though, then this was really happening. What had Hattie said? Something about once she let herself accept that it was possible, then it was. Once she believed Wyatt McCain haunted the mountain, he'd become real to her. Rayanne got that now as all the pieces of the puzzle finally fell into place. The why or how didn't matter.

It was easier to fall back on good manners than it was to ask for explanations. Especially when she wasn't sure there were any.

Rayanne drew a deep breath and stepped toward him on legs that still wobbled. She thrust her hand out toward him. "Mr. McCain, thank you for saving me."

He immediately backed away, his eyes flicking briefly to her hand and then back up to her face. Then the air crackled and shimmered as he faded from sight.

"Wyatt?" she whispered.

Silence again. She looked up and down the street, looking for some evidence that she hadn't just imagined the whole thing. That was stupid, though. If he hadn't just rescued her, how had she ended up out here on the sidewalk instead of the cellar floor? Who else would've left those boot prints in the dust?

She took a tentative step forward and thrust her hand into the spot where he'd been standing. Nothing of substance although the air felt several degrees cooler. Did that mean he was still there? Just in case, she jerked her hand back.

"Sorry. I didn't mean to…" To what? Touch him?

Suddenly, it was all too much—the near disaster and the even more shocking rescue. She grabbed up her pack and started for the far end of town and the trail back to her cabin. Maybe there would be something in either Aunt Hattie's journal or Uncle Ray's that would help her make some sense of things.

Walking as fast as her sore ankle would allow, she made her way back toward the woods. It was a constant battle to keep from glancing back over her shoulder, but she needed to watch where she was going. She allowed herself one look when she reached the trail through the trees. Staring back to where Blessing sat baking in the summer sun, she shivered.

"Well, that gives a whole new meaning to the term *ghost town.*"

It was a poor joke, but she laughed, anyway. She'd come to the mountain to find answers to the questions she'd been living with all too long, and today she'd definitely made progress. But staring down at the twin sets of bruises forming on her upper arms where Wyatt had grabbed her, she had to wonder if the truth might not be even scarier than her worst nightmares.

With that worrisome thought, she stepped into the shade of the trees and followed the narrow trail back to the cabin. Before she went inside, she hesitated in the doorway. Had he followed her? Had his efforts to rescue her hurt him in some way? Was that why he'd disappeared right there in front of her? God, she hoped not.

But just in case he could in fact hear her, she called out, "Thank you again, Mr. McCain. I hope to see you soon."

She meant that, but not right now. Not until she could get her mind around what had just happened. Looking back to that first morning at the cabin, it was obvious now that a locked door wouldn't keep Wyatt McCain out if he was of a mind to come inside. Even so, she set the deadbolt and fastened the chain.

And if she laced her tea with a medicinal shot of Uncle Ray's favorite brandy, who was to know?

Wyatt hurt. It didn't make sense, but it felt as if he was coming down off a three-day drunk that had involved a fistfight or two. He wasn't sure how he'd managed to haul Rayanne to safety, but he had. A good deed. Who would've thought it possible?

All he could remember was hearing her scream and reaching out for every drop of power he could grab. For a few minutes, he'd been rock solid, almost human again. For the first time in a hundred-plus years, he'd felt the heat of the sun, the pull of air into his lungs and the sour taste of fear.

Not for himself. For Rayanne.

Hellfire, that woman needed someone to shake some sense into her. What did she think she was doing, risking her life like that? If he hadn't been there, hadn't been able to pull off that miracle... No, it didn't bear thinking about. The mountain had already claimed enough lives.

An even bigger surprise was the connection he'd felt when she'd looked him straight in the eye, recognizing both who and what he was. Rather than run screaming down the road or fainting as she had when she'd seen him in her kitchen, she'd stood her ground.

He hadn't expected that. It had been almost a relief when his last bit of energy had burned up, leaving him fading back into oblivion. He couldn't believe that she actually stuck her hand out again to see if she could find him that way. He grinned or would have if he'd been solid again. From the way she'd jerked her hand back, she must have felt the chill that he'd heard Ray and Hattie complain about once in a while.

What was there about Rayanne that affected him so strongly? This was the second—no, make that the third time she'd seen him clearly. Even when she couldn't, she obviously sensed his presence. She'd looked straight at him in the woods that time and again in the saloon when she'd been caught in the rain. That had him wanting to grin a second time. Would she eventually figure out that he'd been watching when she'd stripped off her wet clothes?

He bet she'd pitch a fit if she did. He'd sure enough gotten an eyeful, but that wasn't his fault. After all, he'd been there first. If he floated on this mountain for another hundred years, he wouldn't forget how she'd looked. He should be ashamed of himself for thinking about it so much, but too bad. What else did he have to do?

At least she'd had the good sense to pack up her stuff and hightail it back to the cabin. He had little doubt that she'd had a big enough scare to keep her barricaded inside for the rest of the day. He hoped so, because he was in no shape to ride to her rescue a second time.

He was so scattered right now that a good breeze might tear him apart for good. Probably not, but he sure enough felt like hell. Slowly, he gathered himself back together piece by piece, although it did little to ease the pain. When he'd patched himself together enough to move, he drifted out into the sun, hoping the combination of heat and light would seal the rifts that had been ripped in his ghostly hide.

Ah, yes, the warmth gradually soothed the aching until once again he felt…nothing. Back to normal.

Rather than drift aimlessly around town, he headed

straight for the cabin. Once he knew the woman had made it back safely, he'd prowl the woods. Come sunrise, though, he might just show up at her door and see what happened.

Rayanne sipped her morning coffee and skimmed a few more pages of Hattie's journal. Eventually, she'd go back and read it more carefully and take notes. Much of the time Hattie had written about her day-to-day activities: gardening, knitting, mending, cleaning. Interesting to Rayanne as a historian, but right now her focus was on something else. Actually, someone else.

She ran her finger down the page, searching for even the vaguest reference to Wyatt McCain, Blessing and the events of August 23, 1883. More and more, she was convinced she'd witnessed a replay of the gunfight on the anniversary of the original events.

She marked the passage where Hattie talked about believing making it real. Right now it was the only proof Rayanne had that she wasn't just imagining things. After reading over it one more time, she moved on.

A few pages later, she found another passage that had her pulse racing.

He was watching me today. I sensed his presence even though I couldn't see anything but shadows under the trees. I suppose I should simply ignore him, but that seems rude. I'd wave at any other neighbor. Why not him?

No response, but then I didn't really expect one.

I went back to hoeing the garden. At the end of the row, I stopped to rest. Enough weeding for the day. Before I could quit, though, I needed to haul water for the potato plants.

When I started toward the well, something knocked me stumbling backward. I didn't fall, but it was a close call. What had just happened? Then I saw a movement in the grass right where I'd been about to step. A snake. Most were harmless, but that one sure wasn't.

I froze, unable to move. Despite the heat of the sun, I shivered from the close brush with death. Against all logic, I knew who had just saved my life. Looking around, I finally spotted a bit of shadow that was darker than the others. Maybe I was imagining things, but I swear that shadow had substance. I could just make out the shape of a man's hat and maybe a hint of broad shoulders.

"Thank you, Wyatt. Much obliged."

The shadow faded away, but I know he heard me. There were those who never had a good word to say about Wyatt McCain. But I figure if he was such a coldhearted bastard, he wouldn't have lifted a finger to help me.

I waved one last time and headed for the cabin. The potatoes would just have to wait until tomorrow for that water.

When Rayanne reached the last page, she closed Hattie's journal and ran her fingers over the cracked leather cover. What an amazing story! So she wasn't the only one who'd been rescued by their phantom neighbor. She set the book aside and reached for the next volume in her family's history of life up here on the mountain.

She found herself reluctant to read Uncle Ray's story. He'd been such a private man, and she hated intruding. On the other hand, he wouldn't have entrusted the three journals to her care if he didn't want her to learn what was in them.

But rather than delving into his, maybe it was time to start her own. She poured herself another cup of coffee before taking the journal and one of her spiral notebooks out onto the front porch. She settled into one of the old Adirondack chairs and set her coffee on the table. Chewing on the top of her favorite pen, she tried to decide where to start.

At the beginning seemed to be the logical choice, which for her was fifteen years ago. Yeah, that felt right. Rather than start writing in the leather-bound journal, she'd take notes first in the spiral notebook. That felt less scary, less serious. If she was going to hand her journal down to another generation, it was important to get it all right.

Closing her eyes, she thought back to that summer and how awful the tension had been at home. Her parents had been too caught up in the downward spiral of their marriage to pay much attention to how it was affecting their daughter.

It had been such a relief to leave all of that tension and anger behind to come visit her uncle. The memories came so fast and furious that it was hard to get it all down on paper.

After about ten minutes of writing, she stopped
to stare out into the distance, her thoughts turned in-
ward, lost in the past. Gradually, she realized that she
was rubbing the back of her neck again. That same
eerie feeling of being watched was back. She sat up
straighter and studied her surroundings.

The meadow was empty except for a few but-
terflies making the rounds of the wildflowers. She
cocked her head to the side as she listened. Nothing.
No cars coming up the drive, no voices. That left the
woods. She scanned the shadows under the closest
trees and worked her way outward.

After the first pass, she started back across again,
going more slowly this time. There, off to her right,
next to the trunk of one of the bigger pines. It was
almost, but not quite big enough to disguise the man
standing behind it.

She rose to her feet, panic nipping at her nerves.
She didn't want to think Wyatt McCain was any kind
of threat. From this distance, she couldn't even be
sure it was him. Did she even want it to be? It was
rare than anyone happened to pass through Blessing
and the meadow, but it wasn't unheard of.

She stepped down off the porch, unwilling to go
any farther until she knew more about the intruder.
Whoever he was, he had to realize he'd been spotted.
Should she go inside and get Ray's old twenty-two?
He'd made sure she knew how to use it, but she had
no desire to shoot at anyone.

Her mysterious guest stepped out from behind the
tree, leaving little doubt it was Wyatt McCain. Even
from a distance, she recognized his profile, although

he was too far away for her to make out his facial features. Besides, how many men would be wandering around this area wearing that exact style of duster?

Finally, he started toward her. Her pulse kicked it up a notch, and she felt an odd rush of heat watching him walk with such predatory grace. Breathing became difficult as if the air around her were too thick to breathe.

Even as she struggled for control, she wished she had her camera or even her cell phone. Anything to snap a picture of the man now skirting the edge of the woods but definitely heading her way.

Doing her best to act casual, she returned to her chair, grateful for its solid support. Keeping one eye on the approach of her reluctant visitor, she picked up her pen and scrawled a note, this one about her current situation.

He's coming toward me, his hat pulled low, making it impossible to read the expression on his face. He looks unchanged by yesterday's events. Where did he go? Will he speak this time? If I touch him, will my hand go through him? If he's able to talk, will he answer my questions? Should I offer him a cup of coffee?

She waited until he was within a few feet to look up again. As soon as she did, he stopped. Unsure of the etiquette, she stood up, nervously wiping her sweaty palms on the seat of her jeans. There was a stillness about the man that gave her the courage to abandon the high-ground position the porch afforded her.

"Mr. McCain?" she asked with a tight smile as she walked down the steps.

His lips moved, but no sound came out. She thought he had tried to say his first name, but she couldn't be sure.

"I'm sorry, I didn't quite catch that. Did you say I could call you Wyatt?"

Her smile felt more genuine when he nodded. "I'm Rayanne Allen, Ray's niece. You know that he died."

She winced. Dying might be a touchy subject given Wyatt's current situation. She plunged on. "He left me this place in his will. I'll be here until after the first of September."

Okay, the one-sided conversation was definitely awkward. She didn't know about him, but she needed to sit down again. "Would you like to come up on the porch and sit for a while?"

Without waiting for him to respond, she led the way back to the two chairs. She assumed he wasn't interested when she only heard her own footsteps crossing the porch. When she turned around to see what the hang-up was, he was right there behind her. She squeaked in surprise and dropped back down in her chair.

"Don't creep up behind me like that!" she snapped, more embarrassed than angry.

Wyatt stepped past her to settle in the other seat. He wasn't exactly smiling, but his expression had softened just enough to let her know he'd found her reaction amusing. She was amazed how silently he moved, especially for such a big man. The old wooden chair didn't protest at all as he sat down.

She picked up her coffee again. It had grown cold, but her mouth was cotton dry.

"I'm going to get more coffee. Would you like a cup?"

There was a definite twinkle in his eyes as he reached out to touch her coffee cup. His hand went straight through it. She stared at him, her mouth moving but with no words coming out.

Finally, she sputtered, "Right. I'll be back."

Inside the house with a stout door between them, she grabbed on to the counter with both hands as her world shifted on its axis as she struggled to come to terms with a new reality. Not only had she seen a ghost, he was sitting out on her porch, his boots propped up on the railing as if he'd settled into staying awhile.

Right now another shot of brandy sounded pretty appealing, but she needed her wits about her. She poured a fresh cup of coffee and headed back outside to entertain her very special guest.

Chapter 8

Wyatt couldn't remember the last time he'd actually laughed. But, by damn, it was pretty entertaining to watch Rayanne Allen act like having a ghost come calling was an everyday occurrence. Especially after the way he'd spooked her when she hadn't noticed him standing right next to her.

Spooked. Exactly the right word for it. He chuckled again. Maybe he shouldn't take such pleasure in her discomfort, especially because she was the first person he'd actually spoken with in over a hundred years. At least the first live one. The others who'd taken note of his presence had mostly done their best to ignore him, pretending he wasn't real or that they didn't know him.

Rayanne was definitely different, though. Yeah,

she'd fainted that first day, but since then she'd dug in her heels and refused to cower. She'd not only sensed him watching her from the woods, she'd stood her ground when he'd come strolling right up to her front porch.

Amazing. For such a little bit of a thing, she had courage.

What was taking her so long with that coffee? Had the reality of what was going on finally hit her? He started to get up to peek in the window when he heard the turn of the doorknob. As she stepped back out on the porch she had her cup in one hand and the telephone in her other hand, its cord stretching back into the kitchen.

When she stepped closer to him, she jerked the receiver away from her ear. Even from where he sat, he could hear the loud crackling that came from it. The noise lessened as soon as she backed away a few steps. Smiling now that the mystery was solved, she kept her distance. Obviously, something about him interfered with the stupid thing.

"Mom, it hasn't been a week since we last talked. I told you that's how often I would call, so you're jumping the gun. I'm doing fine, just busy."

Wyatt shook his head and tried to look shocked that she would lie to her mother. Rayanne's mouth quirked up in an unrepentant grin, and she stuck her tongue out at him. He gave up the pretense of disapproval and grinned back at her.

As soon as he did, she backed up another step, an odd look in her eyes as she stared at him. What was going on in that pretty head of hers that put that extra sparkle in those spring-green eyes? He wasn't sure he wanted to find out.

"Look, Mom, I promised I'd keep in touch. I'm sorry I've missed your calls, but I must have been down at the grocery store visiting with Phil. Uncle Ray didn't have an answering machine, but I'll try to remember to pick one up next time I go down the mountain."

After listening for another few seconds, Rayanne was looking a bit ragged around the edges. She turned her back, probably to keep him from seeing how the call was affecting her. Whatever her mother was saying had to be truly awful to upset Rayanne so badly. Judging by how she handled yesterday's near disaster in the mining office, she didn't rattle easily.

Maybe her mother would give up if he got close enough to the phone to cause it to crackle again. He'd have to be careful, though. If he destroyed the phone altogether, her mother might come charging up the mountain to confront Rayanne in person. Before he could decide, she took care of the problem herself.

"That's enough, Mother. I'll tell you everything when I see you at the end of the summer. I promise I'll call you in a few days."

Then she pushed a button and calmly walked back inside. Well, maybe not so calmly. If he wasn't mistaken, that was the sound of something being knocked over, accompanied by a few words that ladies in his day weren't supposed to say. He liked her all the better for it.

She came back out and stood staring off at the trees for a few seconds before resuming her seat with a heavy sigh. "I'm sorry you had to hear all that."

She glanced in his direction and asked, "You can hear me, can't you?"

He nodded, wishing she could hear him in return, but he wasn't solid enough. Not like he was yesterday. He'd spent much of the night puzzling over that whole event. For those few minutes, he'd been there, all of him. Not just the shadow of the man he used to be except for one day a year.

She clutched her coffee with both hands, maybe drawing some comfort from its heat. "You probably figured out that was my mother. She's not happy about me being up here. Nobody is."

Who else was included in that disapproving group besides her parents? He watched Rayanne out of the corner of his eye. He couldn't be the only man who liked the combination of red-gold hair and freckles. Did she have a beau waiting for her down below? If so, he couldn't be much of a man to let his woman go wandering off by herself.

Hell, she'd come damn close to being badly hurt or even killed yesterday. The mountain was unforgiving. There were more ways to die up here than being torn apart by bullets. He should know.

"You're looking pretty angry there, Mr. McCain."

He glared at her. "It's Wyatt."

She stared at his mouth and then repeated herself. "Fine. You're looking pretty angry there, Wyatt."

He spoke slowly, hoping she could make out what

he was trying to tell her. "Your mother is right. Dangerous."

Rayanne's efforts to lighten up the moment faded away. "Yes, it is, and I don't need you to tell me that any more than I need my mother's rantings on the subject."

She picked up her pen and paper. "Tell me, Wyatt, do you remember me visiting my uncle when I was a little girl?"

Where was she going with this? He nodded and held out his hand to indicate how little she'd been when he'd first seen her. She couldn't have been more than five or six, all pigtails and no front teeth.

"I came for the same two weeks every summer."

Not exactly, and they both knew it. He waited to see what she had to say next.

"Except for the summer when my parents split up. Dad thought Mom would come back for me, and she thought he would. Dad called to say he'd been delayed, and I'd have to stay a few days longer."

Her voice sounded more distant, as if they were both being dragged back to that hot summer day. He didn't want to go there, not with her, not now. But she kept right on talking, totally oblivious to his growing agitation.

"I was fine with it." She lifted her face up to the sun, its warm light bathing her creamy skin. "I knew Uncle Ray was unhappy, but not why. I thought he was tired of my company or something. He got so agitated. I was scared, too. Not of him, but for him."

Her silence was telling; her pain obviously still

raw after all these years. After all, why would a mere uncle want her if her own parents couldn't be bothered to come back for her on time? Wyatt wanted to take a bullwhip to the lot of them. Instead of taking care of the one person who had needed them the most, they'd left her up here on the mountain to get caught up in his nightmare.

"Do you remember seeing me that summer?"

It was time to go. Even if she could hear him, he had no interest in rehashing the past, not when he had to relive it again in a few weeks. He stood up, planning on walking away. But Rayanne leaped to her feet to plant herself right in front of him. She stood close enough that he could have counted the freckles scattered across her nose and cheeks.

"Move," he mouthed, making sure she could understand his order.

She didn't budge. "I asked you a question, Wyatt."

That didn't mean he had to answer. He arched a brow and said, "So?"

She not only saw him, she saw too much. "You do, don't you? Remember me and what happened? On that day when I was up in the belfry?"

She kept her eyes pinned right on his mouth to read his response. It was clear she wasn't going to give ground until he answered. Instead of giving her what she wanted, he stared down into her upturned face, at her lips, liking the way the lower one was a bit too full. Damn, he bet she'd taste sweet. Before he realized what he was doing, he'd leaned down far enough that all that separated them was his ability to resist temptation.

What would happen if he actually kissed her? Would she be able to feel the press of his lips against hers? He had no business even thinking such thoughts. She'd quit demanding answers and stared up at him in silence. He got lost in her eyes and the possibilities, imagining the slight sizzle and burn if her lips were to actually touch his.

Then they did. Had he closed that gap or had she? He didn't know. Didn't care.

The tingle he'd expected surged hot and hard, as her mouth softened beneath his. He canted his head to the side, to find the perfect fit between them, as he slowly lifted his hands to tangle his fingers in the soft silk of her hair.

It was the first good thing that had happened to him in a lifetime of loneliness spent on this godforsaken mountain. But then it all went to hell when Rayanne's eyes flew open and instantly filled with fear or maybe it was horror. She staggered backward, putting the full width of the porch between them, rubbing her lips with her fingertips. Was she trying to erase his taste, his kiss? Her whole body shook far worse than it had the day before when the floor had caved in beneath her feet.

What had he done wrong? She'd been right there with him, kissing him back. He might have been a century out of practice, but he knew when a woman was enjoying a kiss. Her head whipped back and forth. What was she looking for?

"What's wrong?"

She turned to stare out at the woods. "Wyatt, where did you go?"

"Damn it, I'm right here."

Fury and frustration had him reaching out to her, but when his hand passed right through Rayanne's body, he jerked it back to his side. Hellfire and damnation, he'd poured everything into that kiss and now there was not enough left of him to be seen or even felt. Maybe he was wrong about that last part because she was rubbing her arms again, which were covered in goose bumps.

She stared right at his chest, although he knew she couldn't see him. "Wyatt? What happened? Are you all right?"

"Hell, no, I'm not all right. I'm dead," he bellowed right in her face, even though she clearly couldn't hear him.

Unable to answer her with words, he resisted the urge to touch her again, not when all he had to offer was the cold chill of the grave. He'd always thought being caught up in this never-ending cycle of death and more death had been bad. But knowing what he was missing, how Rayanne felt in his arms, how she tasted and not being able to act on it, was hell itself.

He had to get away, back to the darkest shadows where he belonged. Wyatt floated past her, careful to keep his distance, and on across the meadow without stopping, even though she called his name twice more.

When he reached the sanctuary of the trees, he looked back one last time. The porch was empty, and Rayanne was gone.

* * *

Rayanne paced the length of the kitchen and back. Okay, what was she going to do about what had just happened? What could she do?

She'd kissed a ghost. What could be crazier than that? Well, enjoying it that much also ranked pretty high on the crazy charts. Was he still out there watching? As she peeked outside, she brushed her fingertip across her lips, remembering that last millisecond before Wyatt's mouth had claimed hers. It wasn't just her mouth that had been left aching, needing far more than a simple kiss.

Who was she fooling? There had been nothing simple about the whole incident. From the second he'd touched her, she had melted, craving the press of his hard body against hers. If he'd been human, their embrace wouldn't have ended out there on the porch, but upstairs in her bed. Her wayward mind tried to imagine what it would be like to have his ice-blue eyes staring down into hers as he surged over her, in her.

Enough of that. There were other things to think about. God knew the metaphysical and scientific implications alone were mind-boggling. She lived in the here and now while Wyatt existed trapped somewhere between this world and the next. Even so, there was no denying the very real connection between the two of them.

Over the short time she'd been dating Shawn, how many times had she kissed him? A half a dozen times? And never, not once, had she experienced anything like the burn of desire that she'd felt kissing Wyatt McCain.

What did it say about her? She didn't want to think about it, but she could imagine what her parents and that idiot shrink they used to drag her to would have to say on the matter. She'd be lucky if they didn't have her court ordered into a hospital for a psych evaluation.

Maybe the only good thing that had come out of the experience was that she now knew she had to tell Shawn that things were over for them. It was only fair to let him go. He deserved better than a woman who preferred a ghost from the past to a real-live man.

This one-sided discussion was getting her nowhere, and she had work to do. She wanted to snap a few more pictures from the front door of the mining office and then move on to the old mercantile. Building by building, she'd learn everything Blessing had to teach her. She packed up her gear and headed to town.

The woods were quiet and cool as she passed through them. She paused more than once to simply listen to the breeze and the rustle of leaves overhead. So far, she didn't sense anyone watching her. She was too new at all of this to know whether that meant Wyatt wasn't around or if she simply wasn't picking up on his presence.

Maybe he'd returned to Blessing. When she reached the road through town, she headed straight for the saloon where she'd set up her makeshift office. Inside, she looked around. Again no sense that she was anything but alone. Ignoring her disappointment, she pocketed her tape measure, camera, pencil and notebook.

"I'm going back to the mining office, but I won't go inside."

She pitched her voice loud enough to carry some distance, refusing to be embarrassed that she might be only talking to the mountain. Photographing the mining office went without incident. Moving on from there, she headed toward the building that had served the town as general store and post office. Inside, she took a few cautious steps, testing the feel of the floor beneath her feet.

The whole building was in much better condition than the mining office, maybe because it had been built better to begin with. It was pretty much intact with only the faded gray color of the wooden walls and the floor showing the building's true age.

There were still a few glass jars on the counter. Had they held candy? Crackers? No way to know for certain, but it didn't matter. She picked one up to study it. Maybe she'd take them back to the cabin and wash them clean of the cobwebs and dust. They'd make a nice souvenir from her time here in Blessing. Or not. There was so little of the town left now. She didn't want to contribute to its disappearance.

She started with her usual rough sketch of the room's layout. Once she was done, she measured the floor and then the windows, jotting the numbers down on the sketch. Next, the remaining counter and shelves.

Behind the counter she found several rows of cubbyholes, obviously designed for sorting the mail. Had Phil ever been up here to see this? She'd have to ask him because she thought he might like seeing the similarities between this old place and the store he ran today.

She snapped a few close-ups from different angles for her study but also to show him on her next trip down the mountain. Meanwhile, she was done with the interior of the store. If the light was good, she'd take a few outside shots before heading back to the saloon for lunch.

The day had grown warm enough to take off her chambray shirt. Did she want to eat inside or out on the porch? She studied the saloon, sensing it was empty except for her. That made the decision for her.

She carried her chair outside and made herself comfortable in the shade of the overhang. Propping her feet up on the railing, she slowly ate her sandwich and apple. Anything to linger here awhile longer.

Where was Wyatt? Was he all right? She hoped so. She let her eyes drift closed, trying not to think about their heated encounter, concentrating instead on the details of the man himself. On impulse, she made a trip back into the saloon and grabbed her sketch pad and pencil.

She pictured how he'd looked as he'd strolled across the meadow toward the porch. He was a shade under six feet tall and built along lean lines, all muscle and sinew without an ounce of extra fat on him anywhere. The calluses on his hands came from a

time when men worked with their hands, his skin
weathered and tan.

What had he done besides use those guns he wore
with such casual ease? So many questions and no way
to get answers. Instead, her pencil flew across the
paper as she struggled to get the shape of his cheek-
bones and mouth just right. Next, she filled in the
details of his clothing. His shirt had a double row of
buttons down the front, his trousers were black and
a bit faded. And thanks to that duster, he'd cause a
heck of a stir in the female population at the university if he were to go strolling through the center of
campus. The thought made her smile.

When that picture was done to her satisfaction, she
started another one, this time just of his face and how
angry he'd looked the day before when he'd rescued
her. Next, she drew him in Uncle Ray's kitchen. And
finally, how he'd looked right before he'd kissed her.
She'd come full circle.

Sighing, she looked up and realized her light-
ing wasn't quite as bright and the temperature had
dropped a few degrees. Where had the day gone? It
was definitely time to be heading back home.

No, not home. She couldn't let herself think of it
that way. All of this was temporary, a chance to do
some firsthand field research. Come fall, she'd return to her life down below, picking up where she'd
left off. Well, sans Shawn and most definitely sans
Wyatt McCain.

Only one of those last two things hurt.

There was no use in hauling everything back to the
cabin every time, so she left it all spread out on the

table in the saloon. She'd be back early in the morning to pick up where she left off.

As she started out of town, she stopped and looked back one last time. "Wyatt, I hope you're all right. Stop by anytime."

The breeze kicked up a small dirt devil, the only movement anywhere. Feeling a bit foolish, she turned her back on the town and walked away.

Chapter 9

Wyatt rolled his shoulders and stretched his arms out to the side. A tentative step forward and then another went without mishap. Everything was back in working order, such as it was. He patrolled the town, checking every building as he made his way down one side of the street and then the other. No changes. No new gaping holes in floors. No broken and bleeding bodies anywhere.

If he still breathed, he would've sighed in relief. Rayanne had managed to avoid any new disasters while he'd been wherever the hell he'd been. The same thing happened to him every year when the bullets tore into him. He felt the pain, tasted his own blood in his throat and then nothing. Gradually, he would become more aware of his surroundings, and then he'd find himself standing back in front of the saloon right where he'd died.

As he headed for the saloon, the last spot on his tour, he skirted the patch of dust where he always spent his last few seconds before it all went down. How many quarts of his blood had soaked into the ground there over the years? Too damn many. How many days had passed by since that morning on Rayanne's front porch?

Several, if he had to guess, but no more than that. Most times he lost the rest of the summer after the gunfight, reappearing when the trees were dressed in their fall colors. He didn't know how all of this stuff worked, but with the gunfight looming on the horizon, it was doubtful he'd been gone long.

Had Rayanne missed him? He smiled at the thought.

He wandered into the saloon and looked around. Rayanne had cobbled together another couple of tables out of the bits and pieces of furniture left in town. Judging by the piles of papers scattered on their surfaces, she'd been busy.

Curious, he studied the ones on the top of the pile. He recognized the layouts of the mercantile and the mining office. So that's what she was doing. Another was only a rough sketch, clearly a work in progress. Cocking his head to the side, he decided it was the shipping office.

The next table was covered in photographs, all done in exquisite color. Obviously, cameras were another device that had come a long way since his time.

He'd only had his picture taken once. He couldn't even remember the occasion or who the photographer had been, but the picture was the same one he'd found in Rayanne's kitchen that first morning.

The third table was covered in pencil drawings. All things considered, he liked them better than the actual photographs. Rayanne had a real talent. Somehow she'd looked at the town and seen past the scars and damage to the way Blessing had been in its prime. She'd even included a few of the old places that had been torn down and scavenged for their wood. The only thing missing in her sketches were the people.

Or maybe not. There was a boot and a bit of a leg showing on a piece of paper sticking out from underneath the top layer of sketches. He tried to pull it out from the stack, but his fingers slipped right through the paper. On a good day, he could sometimes move something a little, like when he'd made the saloon door swing.

Considering he'd only just pulled himself back together again, he shouldn't risk trying any harder to dislodge the paper. He couldn't bring himself to walk away, though, not when there was something about that boot that stirred his curiosity. Finally, he decided to risk it.

Concentrating all of his energy into his right hand took longer than usual. Using the tips of his thumb and forefinger, he grasped the paper and tugged and then tugged again. At first the paper stubbornly stayed right where it was, but then it gave way and flew out of the stack, scattering papers all over the place.

He let it drift back down to the table and waited to see if he'd overextended himself again. His fingertips faded out of view for a few seconds but then snapped back into focus. Good. No real harm done.

Now that he knew he wasn't headed for oblivion again, he moved around to get a better look at the paper. What the hell? She'd drawn him, not just once, but half a dozen times. No wonder that boot looked familiar. He'd been wearing the damn thing for longer than he'd been dead.

He leaned in closer, wishing he could hold the picture up in better light. If that's how she saw him, it was a wonder she'd let him get within spitting distance of her. He'd spent much of his adult life earning his livelihood with his guns. That amount of killing showed in a man's eyes, and he recognized the look in his own. He should. He'd crossed paths with enough killers in his time.

But then he looked at the last picture she'd drawn. It was different than the others, although at first he couldn't quite put his finger on the reason. Then it hit him. In the others he looked angry, cold, determined. In this last one, he looked hungry, his eyes reflecting his desire for Rayanne. This was what she'd seen in his face right before they'd kissed.

Memory of that moment wrapped him in warmth, making him smile, something he'd rarely done even in life and almost never since he'd started dying on a regular basis.

"Wyatt?"

His hand automatically went for his guns, but he managed to stop short of drawing them.

He yanked off his hat and slapped it against his leg in frustration. "Damn it, woman, don't sneak up on a man like that!"

Rayanne hovered in the doorway, neither in nor out. He waited for her to make up her mind which way she was going to go. When she stepped inside, he suspected what he was feeling was relief.

She nodded toward his guns. "Would the bullets have hurt me?"

An image of her stumbling backward, a circle of red blooming on her chest, filled his head. Even the idea of something hurting her that badly made him want to howl. His voice felt like gravel when he spoke. "I don't know, but do you really want to find out the hard way if they can?"

She'd started out watching his mouth, but then she looked up in surprise. What was wrong now?

"What?" he mouthed slowly so she'd understand.

"I can hear you." She took a cautious step toward him. "Why? What's different?"

How the hell was he supposed to know? It's not like anyone ever gave him a book of rules that explained how any of this stuff worked. She could see him when no one else did. That she could also hear him at times was just more mystery.

"I don't know. I wouldn't count on it lasting."

The bright green eyes studied him for the longest

time before she finally spoke again. "I've been worried about you. Where have you been?"

He didn't know how to deal with her first statement so he focused on the second. "Something else I don't know. One minute I was there by the porch and then I was gone. Not sure where I go when—" he waved his hand around to indicate the town "—I leave here. Nowhere, maybe. Eventually, I'm back with no idea how I got here."

She nodded, chewing on that full lower lip. "So what we did shorted you out somehow."

What did that mean? "I'm no shorter. I'm always the same."

A bit of humor sparked in her eyes. "Sorry, I forgot they didn't use electricity much in your day. What I mean was that when we, uh…"

Her cheeks turned a bit rosy. Cute. He finished her sentence for her. "When we kissed?"

Looking exasperated, she rolled her eyes. "Yes, that. Maybe somehow it was like dumping boiling water into a cold glass jar, making it shatter. Everything inside pours out, leaving it empty."

He shrugged, although it was as good a description as any. "That's sounds about right."

"So we should avoid physical contact, not if there's a chance you wouldn't make it back next time."

Was that disappointment in her voice? He hoped so, because he wasn't all that happy about the idea himself. They'd been in the same room for less than five minutes, and she already had him thinking about how it had felt to touch her. For those precious few seconds, he'd been a man again, not this shadow who haunted a dead town.

What choice did he have? "Agreed."

There was a sadness in her pretty face that hadn't been there before. Could one kiss have meant that much to her? If so, either modern men were idiots or she was picky about who she kissed. He liked both of those possibilities.

Time to move on. "You've gotten a lot done while I was gone."

"I've had a week without interruptions to concentrate on my work."

Okay, he wasn't sure he liked being referred to as an interruption. A distraction, maybe, but it was enough to know that he bothered her as much as she did him. He nodded in the direction of the tables.

"What is all of this for, anyway?"

She moved past him and picked up the sketch she'd started of the shipping office. "I'm doing a detailed survey of the town, starting with how it is now. Once I've finished with the existing buildings, I'm going to look for evidence of the ones that are gone. I figure there might be corner posts left in the ground, bits and pieces of dishes and things."

"You want to look for trash? Why would you waste your time doing something like that?"

Rayanne lowered the paper she'd been studying to frown at him. "It's not trash, Wyatt. It's evidence of how people lived. I'm a history professor with a specialty in the American West. If I can gather enough information, I'm hoping to write the history of Blessing."

He understood that she was excited by the prospect, even though he didn't understand why. From what he could see, modern people had it so much better than people had back in his day. But if helping her find what she was looking for meant spending more time in her company, he'd do it even if the last thing he wanted to do was relive his past.

It hadn't been that good the first time around, and now it just reminded him of everything that had gone wrong. Even so, for the first time he had someone who could see and hear him. Talking about the past wasn't nearly as painful as drifting through the hours and days alone.

"I didn't live here in Blessing, not for long, anyway. But I can share what I remember about the place."

His begrudging offer was rewarded with a huge smile. "I was hoping you'd say that."

"You might not always be able to hear me or even see me, but I'll try to let you know when I'm around."

"Sounds great."

She picked up the sketch of the shipping office. "Well, I should get started."

Then she frowned. "What happened over here?"

Rayanne bent down to gather up the papers he'd accidentally sent flying when he got curious about the sketch of the boot. His boot.

"Maybe a breeze caught them. I noticed them on the floor but couldn't pick them up."

Luckily, she was too busy straightening her art-

work to question his explanation. Those sketches were
on the table farthest from the door, so it would be unlikely a breeze would send them flying and leave the
other two tables undisturbed. When she picked up the
sketches of him, she blushed again and shoved them
to the bottom of the stack.

He pretended an interest in the floor plans she'd
drawn out. What would her family think of her work?
It was clear that her mother had disapproved of Rayanne's decision to spend the summer in Blessing. He
could only imagine what the woman would say if
Rayanne ever told her about him.

"That smile is a tad scary, Mr. McCain."

He toned it down. "I was just thinking about that
history you're planning to write. How would people
down below react if they found out you'd gotten some
of your facts from the likes of me?"

She picked up her pack and headed for the door,
making sure not to brush against him on her way out.
"Let's just say that I'm going to make darn sure they
don't find out."

"That's what I figured."

He followed her out into the sunshine. Stirring
up old memories wasn't going to be any fun, but he
couldn't find it in him to walk away.

Three more weeks had flown by. Other than a
quick trip down to Phil's for supplies and the answering machine she'd promised to buy, Rayanne
had spent every possible minute with Wyatt McCain.
They'd wandered the streets of Blessing together as

he pointed out everything he could remember about the town. With his help, she'd been able to fill in a lot of the empty spaces on her hand-drawn map.

She wasn't sure how she was going to explain to anyone else how she knew where the schoolteacher lived and that some of the miners had lived in tents pitched outside the edge of town. She also had a list of names to research, ones she had no way of knowing other than that Wyatt had told her.

Wyatt stayed with her as much as he could, but there were times that he simply melted out of sight with no warning. The first few times had startled her. One minute they'd be having a conversation, and the next she was talking to herself. Evidently he only had so much energy to expend, and maintaining visibility ate it up pretty quickly.

Right now, he was nowhere to be found. She shivered despite the heat of the day. Common sense said she should be a bit scared to be up there alone with no one but a ghost for company, but she wasn't. But then Wyatt was more real to her than any other man she'd ever known.

She lived for the odd moments when he found something amusing, and the rough sound of his laughter would ring out over the streets of Blessing. From the little he'd told her about his past, the man hadn't had much to laugh about. The one thing they never talked about was the gunfight that had claimed his life.

She couldn't blame him, but his story was an integral part of the history of Blessing. Her work wouldn't be complete without it. But anytime her questions skirted anywhere near the subject, he'd fade right out of view.

"Good morning."

His deep voice slid over her skin like warm honey, making her think about things she shouldn't. The trouble was, that particular subject was never far from her mind since that single kiss they'd shared. For both their sakes, she hadn't mentioned it since the day he'd reappeared. That didn't mean her days, and especially her nights, weren't filled with dreams of how things might have progressed beyond that first kiss.

And a few of those moments had been incredibly intense and real, as if somehow the two of them were connecting in her dreams in a way they couldn't in the real world. It was unsettling, to say the least.

For a lot of reasons, it would be far smarter to keep herself firmly grounded in the present, her focus on her work. Although she appreciated Wyatt's companionship, if even the slightest touch damaged him, they needed to keep some distance between them.

Which was easier said than done, especially when she seemed to be hyperaware of him at all times.

She loved the way he moved, all power and confidence. It was hard not to stop and stare when he appeared at the end of the street and walked toward her. Maybe she could get past it and see him just as a friend, but it was obvious the attraction ran both ways.

He might not think she noticed the way he stared at her backside whenever she bent down to take measurements. Then there was the day she'd worn a halter top to town. He'd been unable to tear his eyes away from her chest for the longest time, his pale eyes glittering with a delicious hunger. That the weight of his gaze had left her nipples pebbled up hard and achy hadn't helped the situation.

"Are you all right?"

His question sounded amused rather than worried, a clear sign that he'd picked up on the direction her thoughts had taken again. She'd also failed to answer his greeting.

"I'm fine. I was just thinking about what I want to do next."

Wyatt didn't even try to hide his smirk, but at least he didn't push it. "You still haven't surveyed the church."

No, she hadn't. What's more, she had no explanation for her reluctance to do so. Right now, it was just a blank square on her map of the town, and she hadn't set foot in the place since her first day back on the mountain. No photos. No diagram. All because she associated it with Wyatt's death. Not going into the building wouldn't change anything, but—

Wyatt was no longer looking at her. Instead, he was staring off in the direction of the woods, his expression dark.

"What's wrong?"

His eyes were chilling as he shoved his duster back to rest his hands on his guns. "Someone is coming up the mountain."

She didn't doubt him for a minute, but still she had to ask, "How do you know?"

He'd also moved to stand between her and the perceived threat. "The energy changes."

It was unlikely that whoever was making the long drive up the mountain had done so by mistake. That narrowed the field of possibilities to a handful of people. Best-case scenario, Phil had taken her up on her invitation to come for lunch sometime, but she wasn't holding out much hope for that. He'd said he'd call first.

None of the other options were good, but she'd never find out standing here in Blessing.

"Well, there goes my morning's work."

She shouldered her pack. "I'll be back after I deal with this."

Wyatt still radiated a whole lot of tension. "I'm coming with you."

"That's not necessary."

He just stared at her, clearly unwilling to budge on the issue.

Heck, if it was her mother who'd decided to drop in, Rayanne would need all the moral support she could get. "Fine, but it's your funeral."

As soon as the words slipped out, her hand flew up to cover her mouth. "Oh, Wyatt, I can't believe I said that. It's just a saying. I didn't mean anything by it."

His expression softened a little. "Rayanne, you don't have to watch what you say around me. I know I'm dead. Nothing's going to change that."

She started to reach out to touch his arm, but

stopped herself just in time. "I know, but I'm the one who forgets sometimes. Don't you?"

The sadness in his handsome face hurt her heart. "I wish I could."

He stared past her, toward the far end of town. "We need to get moving. That car will be here soon."

The two of them walked through the woods in silence. The closer they got to the cabin, the bigger the knot in her stomach grew. She was in no mood to fight with her mother, and confronting her father wouldn't be any picnic, either. Together, well, she'd rather bang her head on the wall.

But then it wasn't her mother's car rolling into sight. Oh, no, nothing that simple. She coasted to a stop.

"Well, rats. What's he doing here?"

Especially uninvited and unannounced. Her temper flared hot. Yeah, Shawn had mentioned wanting to visit her and to see the town that was holding her captive for the summer. His words, not hers. She hadn't wanted to hurt his feelings by telling him that he wasn't welcome up here on the mountain, but she'd made it clear that she was too busy to entertain guests.

Wyatt stared at the man climbing out of the SUV parked next to hers. "Who is he?"

The deep rumble of Wyatt's voice startled her, not that she'd forgotten he was standing there. "His name is Dr. Shawn Randolph. He teaches at the same college that I do."

"Somehow I doubt he drove all the way up here just to check on a colleague." Wyatt's eyes were ice cold as he moved up to stand between her and the clearing. Doubt dripped from his every word. "I'm guessing he's more than that. Is he your lover?"

Honesty had her saying, "No, but he wants to be."

With that, she stepped around Wyatt and marched off to greet Shawn, already counting the minutes until he left.

Chapter 10

"Shawn."

Her smile felt brittle, but her guest didn't appear to notice that Rayanne's greeting lacked something in the enthusiasm department. Maybe that was a good thing. He set his overnight bag down at his feet and started right for her, his smile bright and his arms held out for a hug.

She let him enfold her and reluctantly hugged him back. After all, they'd been friends long before they'd started dating. It would be a shame if they couldn't find their way back to that. At this point, she wished they hadn't taken their relationship in that other direction at all. With Wyatt around somewhere, she was relieved that Shawn didn't try to kiss her.

Instead, he held her at arm's length and smiled

approvingly. "You're looking good, Rayanne. The mountain air must agree with you, and I like the tan. You're obviously spending a lot of time outdoors."

How else did he think she'd be studying a ghost town? She bit back the snark and aimed for pleasant. "Pretty much. I work in Blessing all day and type up my notes at night."

Wyatt picked that moment to move up beside them, standing where she could see him out of the corner of her eye. He was staring at Shawn with what she called his gunslinger game face on. Clearly he wasn't happy about Shawn being there, but then neither was she. She especially wasn't happy about his showing up, suitcase in hand. The question was, what spurred Shawn to make the trip in the first place?

Time to play hostess. "Why don't you come on inside and tell me why you're here."

As if she couldn't guess. While they made their way to the porch, she glanced back to check on Wyatt, but he'd disappeared. Somehow she doubted it was one of those times when his energy had run out or whatever it was that caused him to blink out of existence for a while. Where the heck was he?

She unlocked the door and stepped back to let Shawn walk inside. "Set your bag down anywhere and have a seat in the living room. I'll fix us a couple of cold drinks and join you in a second."

He dropped his suitcase on the steps that led to the bedrooms upstairs. "Sounds good."

She filled glasses with ice and grabbed a couple of soft drinks from the refrigerator. Shawn stood in front of the picture window, staring out at the meadow and the trees beyond. He turned to face her just as she set his drink down on the coffee table.

"That was lucky timing that you happened to be coming back to the cabin right when I drove up."

"Yes, it was. I usually stay gone most of the day."

She sipped her drink, stalling until she came up with a good reason why she would've needed to return just then. Somehow she didn't think Shawn would believe her if she told him the truth, that her friendly neighborhood ghost had sensed him approaching.

"I've been taking measurements of all the buildings left standing in Blessing, but I forgot my tape measure this morning."

She automatically headed for Ray's favorite chair, leaving Shawn no choice but to take the sofa. An odd look crossed his face, but it was gone before she could read it accurately—maybe disappointment or even frustration. Did he expect her to cuddle up next to him?

If so, too bad. She wouldn't have felt very comfortable doing that before she'd left to come up on the mountain. Now that they've been apart for a while without her calling him even once, she felt the distance even if he didn't. She didn't want to hurt him, but she felt nothing for him beyond the ordinary friendship between two colleagues.

When the silence dragged on too long for comfort, she asked, "So, what brings you up here?"

Shawn immediately sat up straighter and set his glass down hard enough to cause the pop to slosh over the top. Obviously, she'd hit the wrong button with that question.

His expression went completely flat, yet his barely controlled anger was obvious. "You promised to consider spending some time together, Rayanne, but obviously you're set on spending the whole damn summer up here. That left me no choice but to surprise you. I thought maybe we could take off for a few days, do some sightseeing and stay at a nice hotel somewhere."

She hated to disappoint him. "I really wish you'd called first, Shawn. You do know that I'm working up here, not vacationing. I've made good progress, but I still have a lot left to do. Once I get my survey done, I want to get a good start on writing. I also need to finish going through my uncle's things. I've barely started on that."

If he was aiming for charming her into giving in, he failed miserably. "Oh, come on, Rayanne. You can afford to take a day or two off. It's not like that ghost town is going anywhere."

She prayed for patience. "You're welcome to stay for dinner and spend the night. I'll even show you around Blessing this afternoon if you're interested in seeing it before you go."

"Fine, then," Shawn snapped, not backing down. "I'd love to see what it is about this place that's kept you fixated on it since you were thirteen."

Okay, that did it. "And who told you about that? Never mind, don't answer that. It had to be my mother. When did you two become so friendly? As far as I knew, you two had only met that one time she stopped by my office last semester."

He flushed guiltily. "Uh, yeah, the subject might have come up when she called me at the college to see if I had heard from you recently. She was concerned about you being up here all by yourself and suggested I surprise you with a visit."

Before she could decide how to respond, a wave of cool air washed through the room. Great, Wyatt listening in on the conversation was just what she needed right now. She took a slow look around. No sign of him, but he was there. She'd bet money on it.

Finally, she set her drink aside. "Shawn, I'm sorry you made the trip up here for nothing. I appreciate your concern, but I'm doing fine. I've waited my whole professional life to work on a project like this, and, thanks to my uncle, now I've got the chance. As I said, you're welcome to spend the night so you don't have to risk driving down the mountain in the dark, but it would be better for both of us if you left in the morning. The offer for a tour still stands."

She stood up. "I ate breakfast really early this morning, and lunch is sounding good to me. How about I make us each a sandwich?"

"If you're sure it's not too much trouble."

She ignored the sarcasm. "Not at all."

As she gathered the makings for a quick lunch, she struggled to regain control of her temper. Maybe Shawn did have the right to assume she'd be glad to see him. It wasn't as if they'd parted on bad terms.

He followed her back into the kitchen. "So tell me

how your work is going. Have you decided what the focus of your paper will be?"

Slowly, the tension between them faded away, and it felt like old times as she described what she'd accomplished. Over the past couple of years, they'd often spent hours discussing each other's research projects, colleagues supporting each other. The whole time they talked, she remained all too aware they might not be alone. But if Wyatt was still in the cabin, she couldn't feel him.

As she and Shawn carried their lunch out onto the porch, she studied the trees. Finally, she spotted her ghostly companion standing deep in the shadows. He raised his hand to acknowledge her and then faded out of sight. Her own hand automatically raised to wave back. Realizing what she'd been about to do, she acted as if she were brushing away an insect. At least Shawn didn't appear to have noticed.

For the next few minutes, the two of them concentrated on finishing their lunch. Once they were done, she'd show Shawn around Blessing that afternoon so that he could get an early start in the morning. She didn't want to hurt Shawn's feelings, but she wanted him gone so she could get back to work.

But if she was going to be honest about it, that wasn't the real reason. Sitting here with Shawn felt like she was cheating on the other man in her life— Wyatt McCain.

If that made her crazy, so be it.

Wyatt headed back to where he belonged, leaving Rayanne to entertain her gentleman caller. After all,

Blessing was his home, such as it was. He let himself fade out of sight and made his way back to town. Where to next?

He had no interest in hanging out in the church. Right now the saloon held no real appeal, but it was better than drifting up and down the street with no purpose. He pushed through the doors, deliberately setting them to swinging, a reminder to himself that he had substance, that he was a little bit real. Inside the saloon, he automatically drifted toward the work Rayanne had spread out all over the place.

Her handwriting was neat and precise. She found even the smallest bit of information he could share interesting. When they'd unearthed an old pitcher underneath a pile of old lumber, she'd cradled it in her hands with a look of utter wonder on her face. He loved the way she took pleasure in such simple things.

She'd covered the wall with sketches of the individual buildings and then of the town as a whole. She had a real eye for detail. It spoke to how strongly that day in the belfry fifteen years ago had affected her that she could draw the missing buildings with uncanny accuracy. He hated that for her. Getting drawn into his world was the last thing he wanted for anyone, but especially her.

The only pictures missing were the sketches she'd done of him. What had she done with them? He smiled, remembering how she'd blushed when she'd picked them up and shoved them under a stack of files. He didn't expect her to spend any more time here on the mountain after she finished her research, but he hoped that she kept the picture of him.

It would be nice to be remembered by someone.

He froze, listening to what the wind was whispering. People were coming his way. It had to be Rayanne, which was fine. The question was why she was dragging her unwanted guest, Shawn, along with her. He doubted the man had any real interest in Blessing. No, it was the heat in Shawn's eyes whenever he looked at Rayanne that was the driving force behind his feigned interest in her research.

Wyatt had disliked Shawn on sight, and he didn't want the man anywhere near Blessing or Rayanne. What kind of man showed up at a woman's home, dragging his luggage on the assumption he'd be welcome to spend the night? Maybe things were different in the world beyond this mountain, but Wyatt thought he should be horsewhipped for such an outrage.

It was a damned shame that Wyatt's guns only worked reliably one day a year. With lightning-fast reflexes, he drew both of his revolvers, taking aim, pretending Shawn was in his sights. Yeah, he'd love to run that son of a bitch right off the mountain. For Rayanne's sake, he'd refrain from hurting him, but he'd make damn sure the cad didn't come sneaking back up to her cabin again anytime soon.

The temptation to shoot off a few rounds was strong. If he were alone in town, he might have tried it. But Rayanne was only down the street. If he'd become so real to her, would his bullets always be real, as well? While he wouldn't mind putting a scare into Shawn, he wouldn't risk frightening her. Not again.

They were almost to the saloon. Should he fade away and allow them some privacy?

Hell, no.

He hurried across the room to stand behind the old bar where it would be unlikely that Shawn would run into him. He might not be able to see Wyatt, but he would likely feel the cold that surrounded him. For Rayanne's sake, he'd do his best to avoid direct contact with her friend.

That is, unless Shawn made any kind of move toward Rayanne. It had been hard enough to watch him hug her earlier. Anything beyond that and he'd— No, he stopped right there. The truth was, he couldn't do anything at all. Besides, Shawn could give her everything that Wyatt couldn't. If he weren't such a selfish bastard, he would even encourage her to spend time with the man. With that happy thought, he faded to invisible.

Rayanne came through the door first. Before inviting her companion inside, she glanced all around the room with a worried expression on her face. As she panned the saloon, her eyes swept past him but then snapped right back to where he stood. She stared at him for a second, her eyes narrowed in suspicion.

So much for hiding. He gave up and pulled himself back together. Shawn wouldn't be able to see him, anyway, and obviously there was no hiding from Rayanne. It would be interesting to see if she could ignore him while she showed her friend around. He crossed his arms over his chest and leaned back against the counter behind the bar, meeting her frown with a smile.

"Come on in, Shawn. You can see what I've been working on and then I'll show you the rest of the town."

Her companion followed her inside. Shawn removed his dark glasses and blinked several times to adjust his eyes to the dim interior. Rayanne led him over to the cluster of tables and explained what he was looking at. Wyatt hated the way Rayanne chewed on her lower lip as she waited for her friend to pronounce judgment on her work.

After studying her line drawings of the interior of the buildings still standing, Shawn wandered over to study her side-by-side sketches of the exteriors now and how they would've looked a hundred years ago.

"I sometimes forget what a talented artist you are. You've definitely taken the skeletons of the buildings and brought them back to life in these."

Finally, he moved on to the pictures she'd drawn from memory along with Wyatt's assistance. After a few seconds, Shawn frowned. "I know I haven't seen the whole town, but it didn't look as if there were this many buildings left standing."

"There aren't. I drew those from memory."

Rayanne obviously regretted letting that slip out when Shawn shot her a questioning look. "From memory? When would you have seen them?"

She jammed her hands in the front pockets of her jeans and shot Wyatt a quick look. "I should have said memories. I pieced them together from descriptions in books where Blessing was mentioned and from photographs of similar buildings in other towns. My uncle also left me journals written by a couple of relatives who actually lived here in Blessing."

Shawn looked surprised. "I didn't know you'd found any family journals. I'd love to read them sometime."

Wyatt frowned. Why hadn't Rayanne talked about what she'd learned from Hattie's and Amanda's journals with him? She'd had plenty of opportunity during the hours they'd spent together roaming through town.

Hattie had been a young girl when the town died out. By that time, a good part of Blessing had already been torn down, so it must have been Amanda who'd described the town in her journal.

He had to wonder what horror stories she'd recorded in the pages of that book. He wasn't sure he wanted to know. His name had come up, though, or else why would Rayanne have kept the stories to herself? He'd have to decide whether to press her for answers. Right now, he planned on sticking close as she showed Shawn the rest of the town.

She shuffled her friend out the door, pausing in the doorway to shoot one last look in Wyatt's direction. Clearly, she wasn't happy about him eavesdropping on their conversation. He waited long enough for them to put some distance between them and the saloon before joining them out in the warmth of the afternoon sun.

As they walked along ahead of him, Shawn put his arm around her shoulders, pulling her close to his side. The casual familiarity had Wyatt gritting his teeth and wanting to reach for his guns again. But within only a few steps, Rayanne did a sidestep that took her out of Shawn's reach to point out something of interest. Wyatt smiled at the other man's frustrated expression, but Shawn was quick to paste a smile back on his face.

Wyatt moved closer to keep an eye on the situation. It was obvious that Shawn wanted far more from Rayanne than mere friendship. That was fine. It showed that the man had good taste. But if he tried to press the issue in a manner that upset Rayanne, Wyatt would do his damnedest to intervene. With that in mind, he checked the slide of his guns in their holsters and followed his lady down the street.

Rayanne's jaw ached from grinding her teeth. It was bad enough she was having to fend off Shawn's clumsy attempts to reassert himself as her boyfriend. She didn't need Wyatt following their every move as if he were some ghostly chaperone. She was an adult, perfectly capable of taking care of her own problems.

She shot Wyatt a dirty look when Shawn wasn't looking, but Wyatt didn't back off. If he thought that innocent look on his face was working, he was sorely mistaken. Finally, he brushed past her to join Shawn on the porch outside of the mercantile. The jerk! He knew she couldn't even say anything without confirming her mother's worst fears, and Rayanne had little doubt that Shawn would carry tales right back to her parents.

Rather than let Wyatt know how mad she was, she carefully schooled her features to look interested in Shawn's impressions of Blessing. But as the two men stood nearly side by side, it was difficult not to draw comparisons and note that one came out the clear winner—Wyatt McCain.

Although close in height, their builds were noticeably different. Shawn prided himself on his efforts to keep fit, but he lacked the rock-hard muscles built from years of hard labor. There was a softness about Shawn that didn't fare well standing next to Wyatt's lean strength.

Both men were good-looking. Shawn's blond hair and dark eyes combined with an engaging smile attracted women of all ages. Charm came easily to him, maybe too easily. Wyatt's face was more sculpted, all hard edges with the story of his life etched there in harsh lines. Rayanne's inner woman was definitely drawn to the classic alpha male, but that wasn't the deciding factor.

It came down to how each of the two men viewed her. Wyatt's starkly blue eyes saw too much, but Shawn only saw what he wanted. In the end, it was no contest.

Wyatt might not understand her passion for studying the past, but he'd done everything he could to help her. Shawn seemed to be jealous of her work, as if she should put it on the back burner to pay more attention to him. Maybe she was wrong to resent Shawn's intrusion, especially if he really did have strong feelings for her.

But what if those feelings were only for the woman he wanted her to be? It bothered her a lot that he was such a perfect fit for her mother's vision of the kind of man Rayanne should want in her life. She might have been able to get past that, but his unexpected alliance with her mother didn't help his cause.

The creak of wood snapped her out of her reverie. While she'd been lost in her thoughts, the two men had moved on. Realizing Shawn was about to walk into the mining office, she took off running, yelling his name.

"Shawn! Stop! That building isn't safe."

He froze and quickly backed out of the doorway. "Thanks for the warning."

She joined him on the porch, all too aware of Wyatt standing only inches away. "Didn't mean to startle you, but the floor inside this particular building is rotten."

Shawn held on to the door frame and leaned inside to get a better look. "Whoa, the whole back half is caved in. Pity the poor sucker who found out the hard way that it wasn't safe."

"Wait a minute." He took a cautious step forward. "Those breaks look fresh."

They were. She just wished he hadn't noticed. "Yes, I discovered the boards were weak. I haven't been back inside since. I haven't decided yet whether to hire someone to patch the hole and reinforce the support from underneath. There's a cellar under the building that would give easy access for any repair work."

When Shawn turned to face her, it was clear he wasn't buying her matter-of-fact description of the incident. His eyebrows snapped down to frame the anger in his eyes.

"Let me get this straight. You walked in there and fell through the floor?"

He moved closer, crowding her into backing up. He followed her step for step, using his superior height to intimidate her. That so wasn't going to work. She stopped retreating and planted her feet, her hands clenched in fists at her side.

"No, I did not fall through."

Her stomach lurched at the memory of how close she'd come to doing exactly that. She carefully schooled her expression and went on. "A couple of boards broke when I stepped on them, but I caught myself in time to avoid falling through. No harm, no foul. End of story."

His response was one note lower than an all-out bellow, his alarm over the situation all too clear. "Damn it, Rayanne, you could've been badly hurt in that death trap. What if you'd broken something? You would've lain there for hours or even days! You could have died!"

One of them needed to remain calm to ramp down the tension, especially with Wyatt standing right next to them, his right hand on his gun. She took a long, slow breath before speaking.

"Come on, Shawn. Clearly, I wasn't hurt." She did

a slow spin, holding her arms out to prove her claim. "I now make a habit of checking to see if any of the other buildings I enter have a cellar or if they're built right on the ground."

He wasn't backing down. "Your mother is right. This whole place is a death trap. You can't stay here alone."

Okay, that did it.

"I hate to sound like a four-year-old, but you're not the boss of me and neither is she. I'm an adult and a professional historian. Thanks to Uncle Ray, this property and the town itself both belong to me. I can and will stay here as long as I darn well want to. If you don't like it, that's too damn bad."

He jerked back as if she'd slapped him. "Be reasonable, Rayanne. You've got to admit this place is nothing but a disaster waiting to happen. You've got plenty of pictures and measurements. There's no reason you can't complete your research and write up your findings from your condo or your office at the college."

"No, I can't." She spaced the words carefully, injecting as much conviction into each one as she could. "Not that it's any of your business, but the terms of my uncle's will dictate that I live here until the first of September to finalize the transfer of the deed to my name. If I leave before then, I forfeit my inheritance. I'm not going to let that happen. Blessing belongs to me."

He looked thoroughly disgusted. "Your mom told me about your uncle's crazy stipulations. No wonder she's been talking to an attorney to see what it would take to break the will. He thinks she has a good shot at it."

"On what basis? She's not the heir. I am."

Shawn's mouth snapped shut, as if he realized just how far out on a shaky limb he was. She waited him out, making it clear she wasn't going anywhere until he spit it out.

"On what basis?" she repeated.

Finally, he caved. "On the basis her brother was mentally unstable."

Well, that certainly came as no shock. She didn't know if her mother was really worried about Ray-anne or if she was jealous because her brother had skipped over his sister to leave his home and money to his niece, instead.

"That's a crock. He had post-traumatic stress dis-order as a younger man, but he was doing fine. Be-sides, his attorney, who is now mine, as well, assures me that the will is ironclad. Uncle Ray clearly ex-pected my parents would have issues with me in-heriting Blessing because he took the precaution of having one of the top law firms in the state draw up his will to make sure the documents were airtight. They even included two different psych evaluations, stating that he was of sound mind when he signed the paperwork."

She looked past him at the town she'd come to love and the ghost who had his own space in her heart. "I'm sorry my mother put you in the middle of this, Shawn. I know you're trying to be a good friend to me, but I'm staying."

Then she turned on her heel and marched off, not caring if Shawn followed or not. He could find his own way back to the cabin. About halfway to the end of the street, she stopped and turned back. No matter how mad she was at the whole situation, she wouldn't leave him standing in Blessing, especially with a pissed-off ghost hovering right behind him.

"I'll tell you what," she said, forcing a small smile. "I don't want to fight on your only evening here. Let's go back to the cabin. It's been a long day already, and I'm ready for some downtime. I've got lasagna in the freezer that I can heat up for dinner, and then we can watch a movie if you'd like."

His charming smile was firmly back in place. "That sounds great, Rayanne, and then tomorrow maybe we can—"

"No, Shawn, don't go there. Come morning, you need to leave."

When he started to say something, she held up her hand to stop him. "Alone, Shawn. I'm staying here."

This time, when she walked away, he followed her. With his longer legs, he could have caught up with her easily. That he didn't spoke volumes.

Chapter 11

The lights blinked out, leaving Rayanne's cabin bathed in moonlight. Lucky for Wyatt, he was at home in the darkness, his vision as sharp in the shadows as it was in sunlight. But right now, none of his senses were telling him anything.

He hated questions without answers. Always had. But when those unanswered questions were about Rayanne, they left him edgy and trigger-happy. Maybe he should head back into the woods to do some target practice but rejected the idea. He wasn't sure if Rayanne would hear his gunfire if they weren't in close proximity. More and more often, he felt solid and real when she was right beside him, but not always. Either way, if she was asleep, he didn't want to disturb her.

He stared up at her bedroom window hoping like hell she was sleeping alone there. It was none of his business if she'd decided to forgive Shawn's attempts to bully her into leaving the mountain. Their relationship was a puzzle, that was for damn sure. The man acted as if he'd staked a claim on her, but one that Rayanne didn't accept.

On the other hand, it clearly pained her to fight with the fool. Had they been more than friends down below? When they weren't striking sparks of temper, it was clear they knew each other well and even enjoyed each other's company.

Which brought him back to the question he'd been pondering. Where in that cabin had the city man bedded down for the night? Ray had never minded Wyatt wandering inside once in a while. Sometimes he'd lurk in the corner while Ray watched that box with moving pictures in it. Rayanne's uncle had a fondness for what he called Westerns even though most only had a nodding acquaintance to reality.

Wyatt had never ventured upstairs in the cabin, but knew Rayanne's bedroom was at the front of the house overlooking the meadow. Ray's was at the back, looking toward the woods. No light had come on in Ray's old room all evening. So either someone was sleeping on the couch downstairs or else Rayanne had invited Shawn into her bed.

And damned if the very thought didn't give Wyatt an even stronger urge to chase the bastard down off the mountain.

The not knowing was driving him crazy. He'd be better off wandering the woods and town looking to see if any of the others who came to life in Blessing had shown up yet. Most only flickered in and out of existence, gradually staying longer as the time grew closer.

He hadn't mentioned anything to Rayanne, but he'd already spotted half a dozen or so of the townspeople over the past few days. Considering she could see him, would she also be able to sense whether others were around? Old Hattie certainly could. She'd pack up and leave for most of August because she didn't like being bombarded by ghostly images. She'd told him so once.

Rayanne, stubborn thing that she was, wouldn't budge a step off the mountain between now and the day it all played out again. He knew that without asking. It was too important for the adult she'd become to face down the demons from her past.

But with Shawn planning on carrying tales back down the mountain to Rayanne's mother, she'd be lucky if they didn't come boiling right back up to drag her back down to their world. If he had any decency left in him, he'd do whatever he could to make sure that she left with them.

She didn't need to watch him die, cut down in a hailstorm of bullets. What's more, he didn't want her to learn what he'd done there right at the end—something so terrible that he was still paying the price after more than a century of penance.

He cared what she thought of him. Considering how he'd lived his life, he wasn't sure what to make of that. True, he'd tried to do the right thing by Amanda and her boy, but look how that turned out.

It was time to go. Not knowing about Shawn's role in Rayanne's life had him too wound up to simply stand there. He studied her window one last time, ready to retreat. Before he turned away, though, he caught a movement in the kitchen window. He moved closer to get a clearer look.

It was Rayanne. He took two slow steps toward the cabin, hoping to draw her attention. She raised her hand in a small wave and pointed toward the cabin door. If his lungs still worked, he would've held his breath in anticipation. A few seconds later, she stepped out onto the porch.

She didn't stop there but headed straight for him. He wanted to hold out his arms, to pull her close to his chest, to kiss her long and hard. Anything to mark her as his. None of that was going to happen. It couldn't.

Rayanne had that sweet look a woman had when she was fresh out of bed with her hair all tousled and her eyes sleepy. She had on a white shirt over plaid short pants that barely covered her backside. Not at all proper attire for a lady, but he wasn't about to complain, not when they allowed him to admire those long, tanned legs.

"What's the matter? Couldn't you sleep?" he asked, despite never knowing when she'd be able to hear him or not.

She nodded as she stretched her arms over her head and yawned. The movement drew the soft, white fabric tight across her chest, drawing his attention to the soft curve of her breasts. From the way they moved, it was clear that they were once again unbound.

He'd give anything to be able to cup them in his palms, to feel their weight, to coax them into stiff peaks right before he took them in his mouth. Right before he took her, hard and slow. Had he ever wanted to bed any other woman this much in his life? He didn't think so. Yes, he'd been attracted to Amanda, but nothing had ever come of it. She'd still been in mourning for her late husband, and then there was her young son underfoot all the time.

"I'm sorry you had to hear all of that between Shawn and me earlier."

Even in the dim light of the moon, Wyatt could see the echo of anger mixed with pain in her eyes. All the more reason for her houseguest to depart at first light.

"I wanted to punch him." He softened the comment with a small smile.

Rayanne tipped her head to the side and grinned up at him. "Me, too."

They both laughed, savoring the moment. He couldn't remember ever enjoying a woman's company so much. Or anyone's, for that matter. He could've spent all night standing in that one spot and staring down into her pretty face.

She shivered, a reminder that she was standing out there wearing next to nothing.

Rubbing her arms, she said, "I forget that even in summer the nights are chilly."

"I'd lend you my coat if I could. You'd better get inside and try to get some sleep." He walked her back to the cabin.

She climbed the steps to the porch and turned to look back down at him. "What do you do all night?"

Watch her cabin and wonder what it would be like to share her bed up there. That wasn't something a man said to a lady, especially when he had no right to want her that way.

"Wyatt?"

He realized he'd never answered her. "I wait for you."

She drew in a sharp breath and took a half step forward, her hand lifting as if to touch the side of his face.

Before she could do so, the door behind her opened and Shawn stepped out on the porch. "Rayanne, what are you doing out here? I thought I heard you talking to someone."

Wyatt retreated. He'd said enough. Too much. He'd wait to make sure she didn't run into any problems with her houseguest and then go. She kept her back to her friend when she spoke.

"Sometimes I come out here at night to look at the stars. You can see so many more than back down in the city." Then she smiled. "I like that there's always something special waiting for me."

Wyatt couldn't find the words, so he simply nodded. Message received. Then he faded into the night.

* * *

Rayanne reluctantly followed Shawn back inside. She poured herself a glass of milk. She held up the carton. "Want some?"

Shawn leaned against the kitchen counter. "I'm good."

She sipped her drink and waited to see what Shawn had to say. It was obvious he had something on his mind. She just wished he'd picked a more convenient time to decide he wanted to chat.

Finally, he drew a deep breath. "Rayanne, I've been lying awake upstairs and thinking about how badly I've handled this whole situation. I should've called first, but honestly, I was afraid you'd say no. I also shouldn't have let your mother's concerns blind me to how important all of this is to you."

For the first time since his arrival, Shawn sounded like the man she both liked and respected. "Thank you for that, Shawn. I appreciate it."

He sidled close enough to tug the glass from her hand and slid his arm around her shoulders. "I still think we could share something special if you'd give us a chance. I know I sprang this visit on you, and I'll leave in the morning if you still want me to. But how about this? Why don't I come back in a few days, even a week from now so you have time to get your ducks in order so you can leave Blessing for a few days. We'll go somewhere nice, just the two of us, and then I'll bring you back up here."

No, that wasn't happening. He'd heard what she'd said earlier, but he hadn't really listened. She tried to step away, to put some distance between them again. "I don't think that's a good idea."

"Why not? At least give us a fighting chance."

If his tone had been an accusation, she would've walked away. Instead, he was trying to coax her into letting him try to convince her that there was a spark, a possibility of something more than what they'd shared so far. He leaned closer, going slowly but obviously still determined to kiss her. She didn't fight him, her own curiosity kicking in.

His lips brushed across hers and then settled more firmly against her mouth. She had to give Shawn credit for giving it his best shot; it was a far more impressive kiss than they'd previously shared.

Then he broke it off, his dark eyes staring down into hers for a second. Then he shook his head and leaned his forehead against her, his smile rueful.

"This really isn't going to work, is it?"

When he stepped away, she should have felt regret. All she felt was relief. "I'm sorry, Shawn. I know it sounds clichéd, but I hope we can still be friends."

His laugh had little to do with happiness, but at least he didn't press the issue. "The jury is still out on that, Rayanne. Right now all I can promise is that we can try. Tell me, though, is there someone else or is it just me?"

What could she say to that? Telling him she preferred a dead gunslinger to a live college professor wasn't going to help. Even so, she couldn't help glancing toward the picture of Wyatt still hanging on the refrigerator door.

It was too much to hope that Shawn wouldn't notice. A brief flash of temper in his expression. "A phantom from the past won't keep you warm on cold nights. I hope you realize that before it's too late, Rayanne."

As if to prove his point, a cold blast of air shot through the room and sent Shawn stumbling backward into the opposite wall of the kitchen. He looked around as if hunting for the source of the draft.

"What the hell was that?"

Rayanne knew full well that it wasn't a *what* but a *who*. However, she wasn't about to tell him that it was the very phantom he'd just mentioned, a man who'd died a century before Shawn had even been born. She ignored her other uninvited guest, hoping he'd behave.

"So you'll be leaving in the morning?"

"Yes," he said, "I guess I should."

As he spoke, another chill rippled through the room. Shawn's hair fluttered as if someone had just run their fingers through it. He shivered as he looked all over the room for the source of the cold touch.

His eyes were a bit wild when he looked back toward Rayanne. "Did you feel that?"

"Feel what?" she asked, trying to sound innocent but failing miserably. "You know how drafty these old cabins can be. Of course, maybe it's haunted. Uncle Ray died here, you know."

"That's not funny, Rayanne. I've never felt anything like it."

Of that she had no doubt. Right now she wanted to kick a certain ghost. She knew he was feeling protective, but she didn't need him fighting her battles for her.

"It's almost sunrise. Why don't I fix us both breakfast while you get packed up and ready to go?"

Shawn finally conceded defeat. "Fine, but I'm guessing your mother's going to want a report. What should I tell her?"

So be it. "Tell her the same thing I do. I'm happy and doing fine up here."

"I'm not sure she'll believe me."

Rayanne had to laugh. "Don't take it personally. She doesn't believe me, either. Now, how do you like your eggs?"

"Scrambled."

"Perfect."

When he started up the stairs, Rayanne waited until she heard the door to her room close before speaking. She'd let Shawn have her room while she'd slept on the couch downstairs. Eventually, she'd have to deal with Ray's room, but she still wasn't ready to cross that threshold.

"Wyatt, are you still here?"

He shimmered into visibility briefly, barely long enough for her to locate him in the room. "Thank you for defending me, but you'd better disappear until he's gone. I can't afford for him to carry tales back to my family."

A cool touch brushed across her skin, sending a delicious shiver coursing through her veins.

"See you later," she whispered, crossing her fingers that was true.

For now, she put the coffee on to brew and started Shawn's farewell meal.

Chapter 12

Rayanne was noticeably absent as her unwelcome
guest tossed his valise in the back of his car and
slammed the lid shut. A few seconds later the car
roared to life. Shawn rolled down his window and
stared at the cabin, his expression flat. Not that Wyatt
cared what the man was thinking. He clearly wasn't
the right man for Rayanne. The car pulled away from
the cabin in a cloud of dust.

Good riddance.

Earlier, Wyatt had reached the edge of the woods
on his way to Blessing when he'd abruptly turned
back. A mix of curiosity and jealousy had made him
slip inside the cabin, determined to see what was
going on between Rayanne and her would-be beau.

Watching the bastard kiss her had been like being

dragged behind a horse across rocky ground. The only comfort was in knowing that Rayanne didn't welcome his advances. Even so, there had been a hint of guilt in her eyes after Shawn retreated upstairs to pack. What was that about?

Hell, if he had her best interests at heart, he would've encouraged her to give the guy a chance. After all, Shawn could offer her everything Wyatt couldn't, including a future.

Now wasn't the time to press her for answers. He'd brushed against her on his way out, but it hadn't been enough. He wished he could wrap her in his arms and hold her, to offer at least the comfort of his touch. On the other hand, he doubted being enfolded in a wave of cold would improve her mood. If only he could find a way to be with her. He could still sense her sadness.

Should he check on her?

Yes.

He drifted back toward the cabin. In his present form, he couldn't knock. He passed through the door, stopping inside the kitchen to listen. Rayanne wasn't there or in the living room. That left the upstairs, the one part of the cabin he'd never been before.

He paused, hovering at the foot of the steps. If he waited for an invitation, hell could freeze over before he got to see where Rayanne slept. Maybe it was wrong of him to want to intrude on her privacy, but it wasn't only lust that had him wanting to see her in bed. He was worried about her.

He drifted upward, still considering his options. If she appeared to be fine, he'd leave, and she'd be none the wiser. But if she wasn't, well, he'd do whatever he could to comfort her.

At the landing, he stopped to listen. The bathroom door was open, so he knew she wasn't in there. The door to the room that had belonged to Ray was closed with nothing but silence on the other side. That left Rayanne's bedroom.

A true gentleman wouldn't cross the threshold into a lady's room uninvited. Good thing he'd never been accused of being one. Her door was open. She stood by the bed, still wearing those skimpy shorts and shirt. In a burst of action, she peeled the sheets off the bed and heaved them toward the far corner. Okay, so Shawn had indeed spent the night in Rayanne's bed, but from her behavior earlier, he'd slept there alone.

The odd thing was that even though Wyatt had never been in this room before, it somehow felt incredibly familiar. He knew without looking that there was a painting of a mountain scene on the far wall and that a matching one hung behind the open door where he couldn't see it.

There'd been long hours during the night where he'd stared up at the window from the meadow below and wondered what it would be like to hold Rayanne in his arms. At times, those moments had been so real to him that he could have sworn her hands had touched his bare skin as he'd made love to her. Probably just wishful thinking on his part. With her usual quick efficiency, she made up the bed with fresh linens. When she finished fluffing the pillows, she tossed them on the mattress.

"Wyatt, I know you're there. The question is why?"

He pulled himself together. The incident with Shawn had burned up a lot of his energy, but he managed to solidify enough that he could be seen.

"I needed to know you were all right."

Rayanne frowned and sat down on the edge of the bed. "Sorry. I didn't quite catch that. I'm guessing that whole mess downstairs took a lot out of both of us."

He nodded.

"Shawn is a nice guy. We've dated a few times. I enjoyed his company, but…"

She stopped for several seconds, staring down at the floor. "I knew he wanted more than I was willing to give. I didn't want to hurt his feelings, but I should have broken it off as soon as I realized all I wanted was a dinner companion while he wanted a wife."

For the first time, Wyatt felt a glimmer of sympathy for the other man. After all, he wanted the same things from Rayanne and was just as unable to satisfy her needs. He wanted to punch something and curse the gods who had condemned him to this nonlife.

He waited until she looked up again and slowly mouthed. "Are you all right?"

This time she understood him. "I will be. Right now I'm tired, so I'm going to go back to bed for a while. Maybe I'll feel like working later, but I'm thinking I'll probably take the day off."

Her smile was anything but happy. "I'll need all my strength to deal with my mother once she hears from Shawn. She won't be happy that I let him leave without me."

Her voice caught on a sob. "I came up here to lay the past to rest. Why can't they understand that?"

Damn, he wished those people would leave her alone. It didn't help that instead of laying the past to rest, she'd gotten tangled up with him. He edged closer, unsure what he could do to make her feel better. Touching her might use up the last bit of strength he had, but it was worth the risk.

She tracked his movement as he came toward her but made no attempt to dissuade him. When he stood right in front of her, he slowly raised his hand, bringing it ever closer to the soft curve of her cheek. The warmth of her life force drew him like nothing he'd ever known before. When his fingertips came to rest on her cheek, her skin felt like living, breathing satin.

She sighed and leaned into the curve of his palm, obviously taking as much pleasure from the small contact as he did. Once again, thanks to Rayanne, he felt solid; he felt real; he felt like a man.

One who hungered.

But the last thing she needed right now was another man pushing her for something she couldn't give. He backed away.

He forced one word, hoping she'd hear him. "Rest."

Then he started to fade away, to leave her alone to recuperate from the strain of the past twenty-four hours.

Her green eyes looked at him with such sadness, the sheen of tears making them shine brighter and even more beautiful. "I wish you and I could… I mean, I feel so comfortable with you, not like when

I'm around other people and have to pretend to be like them. If you weren't… But you are, and I'm not."

She swiped a hand across her cheek to catch the tears. "I'm sorry. I'm not making any sense. Go ahead and go. I'll be more myself later."

He owed her a bit of his truth, too. "I wish we could, too."

Then he dissolved into nothing at all.

Rayanne had slept like the dead. Well, all things considered, maybe that wasn't the best analogy. But at least no dreams had plagued her this time. She sat up on the edge of the mattress, her thoughts sticky with too much sleep and not enough caffeine. The light from outside was dim, meaning she'd lost most of the day.

A shower would help clear out the cobwebs. She needed to be sharp because she had no doubt that there'd be a message waiting for her downstairs from her mother. Coward that she was, she'd turned off the phone to avoid another crisis until she'd gotten some rest.

Twenty minutes later she stepped out on the porch to watch the sunset, her mood vastly improved. No message from her mother or her father. She wasn't foolish enough to think they'd finally decided to back off and let her make her own decisions, but she'd take what she could get.

Out of habit, she scanned the area, looking for Wyatt, but he was nowhere in sight. She'd learned enough about his condition, for lack of a better word, to know that the events of the early morning would have taken their toll on him, as well. For the moment, she'd fix herself some dinner and eat it out on the porch. If he didn't appear before then, she'd take a stroll into Blessing to check on him.

As she put together a salad, she glanced at the calendar and realized she'd lost track of the days. Tomorrow was Uncle Ray's birthday, the day she'd planned to scatter his ashes on the mountain that he loved. It seemed an appropriate way to celebrate his life.

The only question was where she should take him. Maybe Wyatt would have a suggestion. He knew better than she did where Uncle Ray liked to prowl when he'd walked in the woods. Some quiet spot, one off the trail where he'd find peace at last.

But that was tomorrow. Tonight, all she wanted to do was relax. Picking up her food, she headed back outside. To her surprise, Wyatt was waiting for her. Her mood brightened immediately.

"I'm glad you're here. I was going to go into town to check on you if you didn't come back."

He'd tipped his hat back and propped his boots up on the railing, looking content. "I'm fine."

His gaze was pinned on the fading light to the west. That didn't mean his real attention wasn't on her, just as hers was on him. "Thank you again for this morning, Wyatt."

He nodded, but the following silence was comfortable, two friends enjoying the evening air. When she was done with her dinner, she set the plate aside.

"Uncle Ray asked one last favor of me. He wanted

me to scatter his ashes on the mountain. I was wondering if you had any suggestions where he might have had…you know, a favorite spot where he can be laid to rest."

Wyatt sat so quietly, she wondered if she'd somehow offended him. There was a sadness in his expression that she hadn't seen before. Sometimes she forgot that he'd actually died back when Blessing was a bustling town, but he'd remained trapped here on the mountain. Would he ever know peace?

"I'm sorry, Wyatt. I wasn't thinking. I forget sometimes."

He stopped her. "It's all right, Rayanne. It means a lot that you forget what I am, that you treat me like a real man and a friend."

"You are my friend, Wyatt. Never doubt that."

There was a lot of heat in his eyes when he smiled at her, the kind of heat a man felt for a woman he found attractive. She suspected that he could see the same need reflected in hers. Something dark and hungry stirred in the night air between them.

She wanted this man. And what an irony that was. She'd gotten rid of Shawn because he left her cold.

And Wyatt, who carried the chill of death with him everywhere, made her blood run hot. The gods obviously had a perverse sense of humor. The single kiss the two of them had shared had almost destroyed him. Losing him would destroy her.

Damn.

She couldn't sit still, but night had fallen. Too late to walk off her frustration. Rather than stay in one spot, she stood up and walked to the far end of the porch, well aware that Wyatt watched her every movement. When she finally lit in one spot, he joined her at the railing.

"I know a spot Ray loved. I'll take you there in the morning. Pack a lunch. It's a bit of a walk."

"I will. Thank you." She stared at him, drinking in the strength in his handsome face.

"You have something on your mind, Rayanne?"

His voice was a deep rumble that she felt all the way to her bones. She tried to put what she was feeling into words. "I was just wondering about the why of it all. Why you're still here. Why I can see you when even Amanda, Hattie and Uncle Ray only got the occasional glimpse of you and the others. Why I want—"

Oops, almost went too far with that. It's bad enough that she'd developed such an attachment to her ghostly companion without embarrassing both herself and him by admitting that she had feelings for him. Desires the likes of which she'd never known before for any man.

He stared off into the distance. "We'll need to get an early start tomorrow."

She managed a small smile. "Okay. I'll be ready at first light. Thank you for doing this for me, Wyatt."

"Anything within my power."

Once again he raised his hand to her face, but this time the cold made her flinch. He knew it, too, because he jerked his hand back down to the railing.

"I'm sorry."

"Don't be. I like it when you touch me. A lot." Feeling a little embarrassed, she admitted, "I dream of you...of us every night. It's like you're right there with me."

His eyes widened in surprise. "I think maybe I have been." He glanced up toward her bedroom window. "I'd never been in your room before, but I knew exactly how it looked."

"Maybe somehow we find each other in the one place we can be together, but it's not enough, Wyatt. I want to hold you in my arms for real."

As she spoke, she eased closer to him, but he shook his head and stepped away. "As much as I'd like to, Rayanne, we shouldn't. You deserve a man of your own time, a good one. Not someone like me. And I'm not just talking about the fact that I'm dead. If you really knew me, knew what I was capable of, you wouldn't want me."

Tears stung her eyes, but she blinked them away. "I don't believe that. I've seen the kind of man you are. I *like* the kind of man you are."

"You don't know—" he started to say, but then he hesitated. "Look, none of that matters. Nothing will change that I'm not alive. I'm just a fragment of a man caught between here and hell."

She hated the pain in those words, the despair. How had he remained sane after all this time?

But if he wouldn't defend himself, she would.

"Stop that right now. You are not just a fragment, Wyatt McCain." She faced him head-on to make sure he knew she meant business. "I don't know why you're stuck here like this, but I'm damn glad you are. You saved my life that day in the mining office. That makes you a hero in my book, and I won't let you tell me any different."

She didn't know what kind of reaction to expect, but laughter wasn't it. On the other hand, the bright smile across Wyatt's lips took years off his face, reminding her that he hadn't been much older than she was now when he died.

"What's so funny? I meant what I said."

She knew she sounded more than a bit defensive, but at least his laughter had brightened both his mood and his image. Before, the gleam of the porch light had passed right through him. Now he actually cast a faint shadow.

"I'm sorry. A gentleman should never contradict a lady."

His eyes crinkled in good humor as he held up his hands in surrender.

"See, that proves you're smart, too."

This time their shared laughter rang out across the meadow. As the last echo died away, she found herself lost in the wonder of Wyatt's gaze. She could feel the power of it calling to her, pulling her closer, right into the strength of his arms.

She whispered his name as he closed the last bit of distance between them, for once his lips warm and soft against hers. His arms held her so very carefully, as if she were something precious and fragile. She leaned into his strength, learning for the first time what it would've been like to hold this man in her arms when he'd been alive, back when he walked the streets of Blessing.

His tongue swept into her mouth, tasting, touching, exploring, driving her crazy. She shivered, this time with anticipation, not cold. The heady scent of leather and man filled her head. How could this be real?

But it was.

At that moment, Wyatt was right there, solid as a rock, kissing her, holding her, demanding as much from her as she could give. She moaned, wanting so much more.

She broke off the kiss long enough to ask, "Will you come upstairs with me?"

But as soon as she did, he faded, no longer solid, no longer there.

"Wyatt!" she cried as he stepped away from her, staring at his hands as they flickered in and out of sight.

Even so, he smiled. "That was amazing!"

Although his voice was little better than a whisper, his joy remained real. "Did you mean that? About me coming upstairs with you?"

"Yes." She put all the conviction she could into the single word.

More of him was gone now. "I'll try to come to you in your dreams again. Not sure if—"

But then he was gone.

What had he meant by coming to her in her dreams? Only one way to find out. She picked up her dinner dishes and went inside. After locking up and turning off the kitchen lights, she headed upstairs. A long bubble bath, a glass of wine and an early bed-time were definitely in order tonight.

Then maybe she'd find out if dreams could really come true.

Chapter 13

Wyatt stared up at the night sky, watching the moon rise overhead and counting the stars. As beautiful as they were, all of those countless shiny specks combined didn't compare to the bright light of Rayanne's spirit.

A hero. She thought he was a hero. Who would've thought a woman would ever look at him that way? Earlier, her unshakable belief that he'd done something special had been enough to give him substance. If it never happened again, for those few short seconds he'd held her in his arms as a man, not a ghost.

He'd always thought the gods had cursed him, but maybe this was the only way they had of letting him exist long enough to meet Rayanne. If so, he owed them an incredible debt. What a gift it was to hold her, to kiss her, to love her.

And damned if that last part wasn't true. He'd thought he'd felt something special for Amanda, but he'd never once held her in his arms or kissed her. But looking back, his feelings for Amanda paled in comparison to the connection he shared with her granddaughter, several times removed. Just knowing Rayanne soothed the anger he'd carried with him for as long as he could remember.

Amazing.

Right now she was moving around in the cabin. The lights were off downstairs, but he could hear her splashing around in that big claw-foot tub he'd seen earlier. He could imagine how she looked right now—all slick skin, her red-gold hair curling up in the steam, and that lush mouth curled up in a soft smile.

The images flashing through his mind had him hard and hurting. He wished like hell he could join her. First off, he'd work up a lather with his hands and then use them to learn every curve of her luscious body. He'd spread his legs and tuck her in between so that she'd lean back against his chest.

He loved the thought of massaging those pretty breasts while he nibbled his way along her elegant neck. But that wasn't happening. Not for real.

But maybe, just maybe, he could find Rayanne in her dreams. It wouldn't be the same, but it was as close as the two of them would ever share. Was he being selfish? Hell, yes, but after living in this nightmare for more than a hundred years, he deserved one last good dream.

Because eventually, Rayanne would return to her real life, the one down below where she stood a chance of finding a man who could give her everything she deserved and more. Wyatt would do his best to be happy for her when that happened. Really. He'd like to think he was a good enough man to want that for her. However, if he had to spend eternity caught in this endless circle of pain, at least he'd have the memories of one night in her dreams, in her arms, to carry him through.

Now the only light in the cabin came from Rayanne's bedroom. When she stepped in front of the window, he deliberately moved farther into the shadows. Even though he was shrouded in darkness, Rayanne stared right at him and raised her hand in a brief wave. She always managed to find him. He smiled and stepped into the light.

She opened the window and called down. "I'll be waiting for you."

Then she disappeared. A few seconds later, the light winked out. How long should he wait? And where? For now, he'd make himself comfortable on the porch. Somehow he doubted she'd find it easy to go to sleep with him standing beside the bed and looming over her.

As he waited and watched, a family of deer moved into the meadow. The doe watched him with wary eyes until she was sure he presented no danger to her twin fawns. He remained still until they'd eaten their fill and moved on.

He should do the same, but he found himself reluctant to make the next move. What if this didn't work? Telling himself he could try again on another night wasn't much help. Time was running out. He could feel it slipping through his fingers as the anniversary of his death drew near. Soon, he'd be caught up in that same cycle of pain and death again. Rayanne had no part in that tragedy.

But tonight with the full moon overhead and only the two of them on the mountain, maybe they could share something special. With that thought in mind, he pressed through the door of the cabin and took that first fateful step up to the second floor.

He stopped outside Rayanne's room, although she'd left the door open.

For him? He'd like to think so.

The only sound was the soft rasp of Rayanne's breathing, slow and easy. Good. He'd been worried she wouldn't be able to sleep. Normally, his movements were totally silent because his body had no substance, but right now each step was awkward and loud to his own senses.

He froze, waiting to see if his movements had disturbed Rayanne, and then eased into her room. Inching toward the side of her bed, he was stunned by her beauty. The silvery light of the moon spilled through the window right on her pretty face. She looked peaceful with her mouth curved up in a small smile.

One hand lay flung out in his direction, as if she'd fallen asleep reaching out for him.

Her shoulders were bare, making him wonder what, if anything, she wore under that patchwork quilt. He wouldn't peek, not while she was unaware of his presence. If he were able to find her in her dreams, they'd be on equal footing. Right now, she was far too vulnerable for him to take advantage of the situation.

He stepped back and sat down on an old cedar chest and stretched his legs out, trying to get comfortable. Studying his old boots, he wished he could have cleaned up before coming to her, but that wasn't possible. Even if he'd had access to other clothes, he couldn't have worn them. Only the things that he had on, held in his hands, or carried in his pockets had made the transition to this life.

If he'd had his druthers, he'd have bathed, shaved and worn a suit. Certainly his guns had no place here, not with the taint of violence that had soaked into the very metal they were made from.

He dragged his eyes up from the floor and his mind out of the past. While he might not have a future, he had this one chance, and he'd be a fool to waste it. Anchoring himself firmly in this place and this moment, he closed his eyes and sent a tendril of thought toward the sleeping woman who called to his heart.

Gradually, he poured more and more of himself into the effort until at last he saw her. She stood at the edge of a small stream that ran along the far edge of the meadow. Her hair was twisted up in a knot at the top of her head with a few tendrils hanging loose along the back of her neck. She wore a loose-fitting dress that ended just above her shapely ankles. It left her shoulders bare, the only thing holding it up a narrow ribbon that tied at the back of her neck. The pale green suited her coloring well.

He noticed her pretty feet were bare. Funny how that one detail was the one that made him ache to touch her.

In their dream world, he spoke her name. She immediately turned to face him, her smile radiant.

"You came."

He nodded. "I promised."

She held out her hands. "Do you have to stand way over there?"

Now that the moment had arrived, he wasn't sure how to proceed, feeling like a youngster gone courting for the first time, not a full-grown man who knew what he was about. He stepped forward, slowly at first, but then faster, needing to close the distance between them.

He stopped short of where she stood. "I'm not sure what will happen when we touch."

Her smile warmed him from the inside out. "Only one way to find out, Wyatt. You look handsome, by the way. I'm really fond of that duster you always wear, but that shirt really brings out the color of your eyes."

He hadn't noticed that somewhere between sitting on the cedar chest and stepping into this meadow, he'd changed clothes. His shirt was a deep blue and his trousers a dark tan. Even his boots were new. He touched his face, relieved to find he'd shaved.

Rayanne closed the distance between them, near enough that her scent filled his head and her warmth left him edgy and hungry. Slowly, he lifted his hand to toy with a strand of her hair, twirling the curl around his finger.

"You smell like roses."

She looked a bit shy. "I took a bath in rose-scented bubble bath before I went to bed."

"I like it."

His hand found hers and gave it a gentle squeeze. It felt so normal, so perfect. Both of them let out a small sigh of relief. Here, in the dream world she'd created, they were both solid and real.

As much as he hungered for her, he didn't want to rush things or even presume that she wanted more than a simple day in the sun with him.

"Would you like to take a walk?"

Rayanne stared up at him with a temptress's smile. "That depends. How long do we have here?"

"I don't know. I've never done this before, not on purpose anyway."

"Then let's save walking for later. Right now, I'd rather sit down on the quilt I brought with me."

She tugged on his hand, leading him down toward an open area surrounded by a stand of aspens. If he wasn't mistaken, it was the same quilt that covered her bed back in the cabin.

By the time they reached the blanket, his pulse was

racing and his breath was shallow, two sensations he hadn't experienced since the day he died. The combination of anticipation and nerves was a potent one. He felt young and reckless.

"May I kiss you, Miss Rayanne?"

"You may do anything you want to with me, Mr. McCain. And sooner rather than later."

She slid into his arms as if she'd always been at home there, lifting her face to him. God, she was so beautiful.

He kissed her gently at first, thanking her without words for the gift of this moment with her.

Then he kissed her with a promise of what was to come, but making sure she'd know he would treat her with care.

And finally, he kissed her with everything he had. He claimed her mouth with lips and teeth and tongue, loving it when she gave as good as she got. It was a dance, one where their steps matched perfectly.

He broke it off as he carried them both to the ground, glad for the cushion of the soft grass and quilt. Rayanne murmured her approval as he pressed her back and kissed her again, this time letting his hands do a bit of roaming. First he traced the bare skin of her shoulder down the length of her arms and back. He trailed his fingers over her collarbone and back up to her neck. As their tongues played tag, he gave the ribbon that held her dress up a gentle tug.

She smiled against his mouth, well aware of where he was headed next. He owed her a confession.

"That first day when you got caught in the rain, I was in the saloon."

She frowned and then her eyes opened wide. "You were watching when I stripped off my shirt to wring out the water?"

He nodded, his smile feeling a bit wicked. "I did. Liked what I saw, too."

"Really?" She reached for the top of her dress and tugged it down to reveal another inch or two of her silky skin. "Did you only want to look?"

"No, I wanted to touch," he whispered as she gave the soft fabric another tug until the top edge of her areolas showed. "And I wanted to taste."

The minx immediately pulled the fabric back up. "Fine, but take off your shirt first. It's only fair since you've already seen me without mine."

He sent a couple of buttons flying in his haste to finally feel her hands on his bare skin.

"I like what I see, too," she said as she rose up long enough to kiss his throat and run her hands across his chest and back. "Now, where were we?"

This time there were no half measures. Just that quickly, the top of her dress was gathered at her waist, at last giving him free access to the breasts that haunted his thoughts since that first day. He'd been right. They filled his hands perfectly, and their pretty tips begged to be kissed.

Rayanne tangled her fingers in his hair, pressing him closer as he captured her nipple with his lips, working it hard as he squeezed and plumped her other breast with his hand. He loved the sounds she made as he worked them both up to a fevered pitch.

When he tried to tug the hem of her skirt up, it was tangled in her legs. Damn, he wanted it out of the way along with everything else they were both wearing. In a flash, all of their clothes disappeared, leaving only the dappled shade to protect them from the bright light of the day.

His lady grinned, obviously delighted. "Nice trick, Wyatt."

"Thank you," he said as he tugged the pins out of her hair, wanting it spread out on the quilt.

For a few seconds, they both seemed content with a few touches and easy kisses. Gradually, though, they coaxed the embers of passion back into full flame. This was what he'd been looking for. This connection, this mutual hunger, this coming together of two people across time to find each other.

When at last he rose over her, seeing the welcome in her eyes and feeling the sweet way her body and his fit together, he knew he'd finally found heaven.

The grass beneath Rayanne's back was as soft as the bed she slept in. The man who'd just settled on top of her was as hard as steel. She loved the contrast, loved the way he touched her with such care, and flat-out loved him. She'd keep that last tidbit to herself.

The press of his body against hers kept her anchored in this dream, if that was what it was. It was so real, his weight too solid for her to believe it wasn't more. He rocked against her, centered right against her core, a promise of what was to come.

She wanted him to take her, to claim her in this most basic way. "Wyatt, this feels so good, but it's not enough."

He pushed himself up to support his weight on his arms and smiled down at her as he rocked against her again, this time a little harder, faster. "In a bit of a hurry?"

So he wanted to tease, did he? She reached between them to capture his cock in her hand and gave it a squeeze. He moaned and threw his head back when she did it again. She loved having this power over his pleasure; it was only fair since she'd wanted this since the day he'd rescued her and she'd first felt his touch.

He held so still, dragging out the anticipation to the breaking point. Finally, he flexed his hips enough for her to guide him as she opened her heart and her body to him. He slid in deep and hard. Her breath caught in her chest as he growled in satisfaction.

His blue eyes gleamed down at her. "Are you ready for this?"

She brought her legs up around his hips as she caressed his handsome face with her fingers. "I think I've been ready for you my whole life."

He stooped to kiss her again, his tongue mimicking the flexing of his hips as his rhythm picked up strength and speed. She held on, meeting his thrusts, taking him deep and then deeper until nothing existed except the joining of their bodies. He pulled her legs higher up his hips and dropped down on his elbows, bringing the hard planes of his chest back against her breasts. She reveled in the solid feel of their bodies coming together, moving together, saying what she had no real words for. The tension built, second by second, breath by breath, until her whole being stood poised at the brink of exploding.

It was hard to breathe, impossible to think. All she could do was feel. "Wyatt, it's too much!"

His smile was so sweet. "I've got you, honey. Just let it fly."

She dug her fingers into his back, trying to hold on, but his promise gave her the strength to quit fighting and let the climax roll through her. As soon as she did, she took Wyatt with her. He hollered, his whole body rigid as he shuddered in his own release.

She held her breath, hoping against hope that the power of what they had shared didn't throw them out of this perfect moment and back out into the real world. A few seconds passed before Wyatt rolled to the side, taking her with him, holding her close. She breathed in his scent, content to listen to his heartbeat and enjoy these few minutes of peace.

It wouldn't last, it wasn't real, but it was all they had.

Chapter 14

As much as Wyatt loved holding Rayanne in his arms, the same instincts that had saved his hide several times back in the day were telling him they should get moving. He smiled down at his woman and pressed one last kiss on her forehead.

"If we can rustle up some clothes, maybe we could take that walk I mentioned."

Rayanne was cuddled in with her head over his heart. She rose up long enough to look him in the eye as she let her hand wander down his chest and farther south. "And if I like you this way?"

He caught her hand in his and brought it to his mouth for a kiss. "I like you this way, too, and we can get back to it in a while but..."

He broke off what he was about to say to listen to

their surroundings. He'd heard a noise in the distance, but couldn't quite put his finger on what it had been.

The smile faded from Rayanne's eyes. "What's wrong, Wyatt? What are you hearing?"

"I'm not sure."

There it came again. Footsteps, and they were headed straight toward them. How could that be? This was Rayanne's dream, one meant for just the two of them. Who would dare intrude?

"We need to get up and get dressed."

He surged to his feet and then offered her a hand. Just that quickly, he was clothed in the same clothes he'd been wearing for the past century. Rayanne no longer had on the pretty green dress, but instead wore her usual jeans and shirt.

Another sign that the real world was intruding on their moment in paradise.

"Stay behind me until I figure out what's going on."

Now he could hear the murmur of voices. At least two people, maybe more, were nearby.

"There!" Rayanne whispered, pointing off to the left.

Sure enough, two people were moving through the woods on the far side of the creek. For now, they seemed unaware of Wyatt and Rayanne. It wasn't until the pair stepped out of the trees a short distance away that he recognized them.

Amanda and her son.

Son of a bitch, what were they doing there? How could they have found their way into Rayanne's dream?

"We need to go."

He slowly bent down to gather up the quilt, but it was too much to ask that young Billy wouldn't notice. That boy always did have more curiosity than good sense. He tugged on his mother's arm and pointed toward where Wyatt stood. Amanda smiled, but when she spotted Rayanne, it faded away.

Her voice carried across the babble of the water. "Wyatt? What are you doing out here? Who is she?"

How the hell was he supposed to answer that? *Amanda, meet your great-great-granddaughter. You and I never actually...but I'm standing here looking guilty because she and I just did.*

The two of them needed to leave and right now. It was bad enough that Amanda and her boy were there, but now he could see others moving toward them. Was the whole damn town headed this way? And what if Earl and his boys were drawn into this moment, too? They'd been willing to shoot up a town full of innocent people. What if they went after Rayanne?

He whirled around and grabbed her by the hand. "Rayanne, you need to wake up before they get here."

She let him lead her away, but she kept checking back over her shoulder. "But who are all those people?"

He waited to answer her until the two of them had gotten far enough from the creek that he could no longer see Amanda or the others.

"They're like me, but they shouldn't be here in your dream. You invited me in, not them. I don't know what it means or what will happen if they reach us. You need to wake up and right now."

But not before he held her one last time. Who knew if they'd ever have another chance like this? He enfolded her in his arms, savoring her sweet warmth. Holding Rayanne against his heart plain felt so right, as if they'd been born to be together. The moment wouldn't last, though, and he'd feel nothing but the cold chill of death.

And if that wasn't just sad.

He kissed her one last time and then stepped back. "Wake up, Rayanne. I'll be waiting for you if I can."

She started to reach for him. "Wyatt, there's something you should know. I—"

Before she could finish, she shimmered and disappeared, leaving him alone with his fellow ghosts. Time to deal with them. But when he reached the edge of the creek, the woods were empty, and he was more alone than he'd ever been.

The morning sun spilled through the window, its warmth gradually coaxing Rayanne awake. She kept the quilt pulled up, reluctant to leave the comfort of her bed after the best night's sleep she'd had in years. Then she stretched and discovered she had a few twinges in unexpected places.

She bolted upright and looked around. The dream! Had it been real? Some of it must have been or else her body wouldn't be feeling the way it did. She blushed, remembering what it had been like to make love with Wyatt outside under the summer sun. Thinking about the powerful surge of his body moving over hers, moving in hers, had her legs stirring restlessly. Her breasts were tender, and there were other signs that made it clear that the hours she'd spent in Wyatt's arms had been more than her overactive subconscious.

The idea of birth control hadn't even crossed her mind. But then, why would it? Her lover was a ghost and they'd made love in a dream. And if that wasn't all mind-boggling, she didn't know what was.

But back to the problem at hand. Where was Wyatt? He'd promised to be waiting for her, especially because this was the day they were going to scatter her uncle's ashes. Not only was he nowhere to be seen but she couldn't sense his presence anywhere in the cabin.

She hoped he was all right. Everything had been so perfect right up until those other people had intruded. Odd, though, that Wyatt had known them when it was her dream. Shouldn't they have been people she knew?

Their presence definitely worried him. Had something happened after she left? Wouldn't her dream world have ended when she woke up? How was she supposed to know something like that? Only one way to get answers. She'd grab a quick shower, fix something she could eat on the go and head into Blessing. If Wyatt wasn't there, she'd decide what to do next.

Twenty minutes later, she reached the head of the path that led toward Blessing. Before she'd gone more than a handful of steps, she realized something felt off. Someone else was out there in the trees, and it wasn't Wyatt. She would've recognized him whether he could be seen or not.

She backed up to study her surroundings. There. Behind a clump of trees, a flash of dark red moved through the trees. Who was that? She remained still, waiting to get a better look at whoever it was. Finally, a woman strolled into sight, wearing a dress better suited to Wyatt's era than this one.

As she came closer, Rayanne realized the woman moved in absolute silence. What's more, when she walked through a spot of sunlight, she cast no shadow. Okay, so the obvious answer was that she belonged in Blessing of a hundred years ago. Was that what had freaked out Wyatt in her dream? That all those people belonged in his time, not hers?

The woman winked out of sight as quickly as she'd appeared. Before continuing on, Rayanne did a slow three-sixty to make sure that no one else, real or otherwise, was in the area before hurrying on down the path. Wyatt didn't scare her, but the presence of these others did.

It meant the anniversary of the gunfight that had cost Wyatt his life was drawing close. She didn't know if she'd have the courage to see it all play out again, not if it meant watching Wyatt die. There had to be something she could do to change things. Were the events of the past written in stone?

She hadn't seen everything that happened that day, and Wyatt never once spoke of the events that had led up to the gunfight. Clearly, the memories were powerful ones for him, but there had to be some reason he was caught in this endless nightmare. As soon as she found him, she'd start by making sure he was all right.

And then it was time for some long-overdue answers.

She found him sitting on an old bench outside of the saloon. His dusty boots were propped up on the railing, his hat pulled down low over his face. Was he actually asleep? She grinned. Maybe even a ghost needed a nap after the night they'd shared.

But at least he was all right. She'd been worried about the effect the night's vigorous activities would've had on his energy level. Walking as quietly as she could, she stopped in the street right in front of where he was seated. As soon as she stopped moving, he stirred.

Pushing his hat back, he studied her, his pale eyes staring right through to the heart of her.

He asked, "Are you all right?"

She brushed her hair back from her face and mustered up a smile. "I was about to ask you the same question. I thought you'd be waiting in my room when I woke up this morning."

Okay, that came out sounding worse than she meant it to. She'd been more worried than disappointed that he hadn't been there. "I was concerned about you."

His boots hit the porch hard. He stood up and leaned forward on the railing, looking up and down the street. "Sorry, but I had things to check on."

"Like those people who showed up when we were…when we'd finished?"

Okay, now she was blushing. Why was it so hard to just say that they'd made love? Maybe because right now Wyatt looked about as warm and approachable as a grizzly bear.

"Who were they?"

He finally dragged his gaze back to her. "The fine, upstanding citizens of Blessing. I didn't think you'd be able to see them at all, especially under those circumstances."

Rayanne swallowed hard. "I saw another one on the way here—a lady in the woods wearing a dark red dress. She wore her hair braided and coiled around her head."

Wyatt frowned. "Did she take note of you?"

"Not that I could tell. She was walking through the trees, but after a minute she simply disappeared."

"Damn it, I was hoping I was the only one you'd have to deal with. They'll be appearing more often now. It's always this way right before it all plays out again."

He slammed his fist down on the railing hard enough to crack it. "God, I hate this. What the hell do I have to do to make it all stop?"

Rayanne hated the pain in his voice, but all she could do was stare first at the broken wood and then up at Wyatt. "You broke the railing."

He glared at the damage he'd done. "Yeah, so? It's not like anyone hitches a horse to it anymore."

Clearly, he hadn't realized the significance of what he'd just done. She joined him on the porch. "I don't care about a piece of broken, half-rotted wood, Wyatt. I do care that you were able to break it."

She held her breath and stepped closer, slowly raising her hand to brush across the sleeve of his duster. The leather was buttery soft and just a bit gritty from the ever-present dust in Blessing. Wyatt froze, the muscles in his powerful forearm bunching up tight under her fingertips.

"I broke the railing." His eyes filled with wonder and his voice was gravel-rough as he stared down to where her hand had come to rest on his. "Rayanne, I broke the railing."

She smiled back up at him. "You sure enough did."

Slowly, he lifted his hand from the railing, turning it over to mesh his fingers with hers. She didn't blame him for moving slowly. They were treading on unknown territory here. Had the physical and emotional bond they'd forged in their dream world somehow spilled over into this one?

Better to savor the moment rather than risk shorting him out again. Wyatt's skin was warm to the touch, that of a living man, not the usual cool feel of her ghostly lover a hundred years dead. How long would it last? She didn't know the answer to that question, but she knew one thing. She wasn't going to waste a second of this amazing gift.

That didn't mean she wanted to rush things, especially when they didn't know what the rules were. With the lightest of touches, she trailed her fingertips across his lips, then down his jaw to follow the length of his neck and back. He closed his eyes and drew a deep breath as she continued her explorations.

She tested the breadth of his shoulders and the hard planes of his chest. Sliding her hands inside his duster, she basked in the warmth of his lean strength, kneading his chest like a kitten would a soft blanket.

"You feel so good, so real."

It was tempting to ask questions. What had happened that was different? But the wonder in his eyes warned her that he didn't have the answers, only the same terrified joy that they could share even this much.

"My turn," he whispered. His powerful hands were ever so gentle as they settled on her waist and pulled her closer to his body. She sighed with pleasure when he cupped the curve of her bottom and squeezed as he nuzzled the juncture of her shoulder and neck.

"You smell like lemons this time."

He smiled against her hair as he did some more exploring. His fingers trailed up the length of her back. His teasing assault on all of her senses had her body softening, melting into his. She ached in all the right places. Her breasts felt swollen and heavy, and her core had grown damp, preparing for what she prayed was about to follow.

Finally, she grabbed his hat and tossed it onto the bench behind them and tangled her fingers in the black silk of his hair. "Wyatt, kiss me. Please, while you're—"

She didn't get to finish because just that quickly, his mouth was on hers, hungry and demanding, just as it had been during the night. She rose up on her toes, trying to get closer, to hold on that much tighter.

He swept her up in his arms, lifting her legs high around his waist as he carried her inside the saloon. His actions made her giggle. Did he really think they needed privacy in a ghost town? But then he set her on the bar and reached for the tie on her drawstring shorts and tugged it loose.

Okay, the man definitely knew what he wanted. What they both needed. She put her hands on the worn surface of the bar and lifted her hips up long enough for him to peel down her shorts and panties.

"Lean back," he ordered. "And spread your knees."

She'd willingly comply with his orders but not before she issued a few of her own. "Take off the duster and your shirt."

His smile was all male hunger as he tossed the coat aside and reached for the first button on his shirt. He took his time, offering her a slow striptease that had her clenching her knees together, trying to assuage the aching hunger for this man's body.

When his shirt hit the floor, she stripped off her own and flung it in the same direction. Her bra quickly followed suit.

"Now your pants."

Wyatt hopped on one foot and then the other while he yanked off his boots, which hit the floor with a satisfying clunk, another reminder that he was all so solid and real. A heartbeat later, he was shed of his pants and drawers, revealing proof positive of how much he wanted her. On the other hand, he seemed content to stand just out of her reach, watching her with his sexy mouth quirked up in a half smile.

What was he thinking? "Why are you standing way over there?"

"Trying to decide where to start."

Starting at the top of her head, he stared at her with an intensity that felt as if he were stroking her most sensitive places with his hands or, better yet, his tongue.

"Have you figured it out yet? Because I've got some suggestions if you need them." She cupped her breasts and lifted them, hoping he'd take the hint.

He quickly spread his duster on the floor, adding to the rest of his clothing. Then he carried her over to settle her down on the makeshift bed.

He stretched out beside her. "Sorry this isn't more comfortable."

She didn't give a damn about the floor. "I'm betting you can make me forget all about that."

His smile was full of wicked intent. "I'll do my best."

"I know you will."

When his lips settled on her breast and drew her nipple into the wet warmth of his mouth, she arched up off the floor. He held her still with the weight of his leg between hers. She clamped her knees hard, pressing against the strength of his thigh. It helped, but not nearly enough.

When she tried to push Wyatt over on his back, he grinned and offered himself up to her. She straddled his hips, centering her core right over the hard length of his cock. Rocking forward and back gave them a little more of what they both needed.

She kissed that stern mouth and then nibbled her way down his chest and kept right on going. He propped his head up on his arms and simply watched. He was far too calm, especially when she was slowly going out of her mind. Well, she'd see what she could do to shake him up a bit.

Sliding farther down his legs, she stopped at just the perfect position to lean down and kiss the tip of his cock. Wyatt didn't move an inch but he couldn't hide the hitch in his breath, especially when she did it a second time.

"Rayanne!"

He groaned when she took him in her mouth and pleasured him in every way she could think up. Oh, yeah, this was good. From the way he was straining up and murmuring encouragement, he was almost at the breaking point.

She cupped his sac and gave it an easy squeeze. "Like that, do you?"

"Yes!" His eyes glittered down at her. "But you'd better stop now."

She teased him with a little more tongue action. "What if I don't?"

What she should have remembered was that he was a man of action rather than words. Before she knew what was happening, he sat up, captured her in his arms and flipped her over onto her stomach and pulled her back up on her knees. He kept one arm wrapped around her waist as he positioned himself between her legs.

"Wyatt!"

"Hold still." He took a long, slow breath and added, "Please."

When she nodded, he found the entrance to her body and pushed slowly forward. She dropped her head down on her arms and pressed back toward him, taking more of him, asking without words for as much as he could give her.

"Brace yourself, honey. I don't think I can be gentle this time."

Then he cut loose, overwhelming her with the sheer power of the connection between them. She'd thought what they'd shared during the night had been amazing, but both of them had known it was but a dream.

This was as real as it got. The smooth leather beneath her hands and knees. The slick sweat on their skin. The slap of his body against her bottom. The calluses on his fingers feeling so delicious on her breasts and between her legs as he drove them both fast and hard.

The whole world shrank down to the two of them, their bodies joined in a dance with their own unique rhythm. The tension built until first she and then he shattered. She cried his name; he hollered hers as he held on tight as he shuddered out his release deep inside of her.

Then they both collapsed. Wyatt pulled away long enough to ease them both over onto their left side and then spooned behind her. He kissed the back of her neck and held her close.

"Was I too rough?"

She smiled back at him. "You were perfect. Better than perfect."

"Good."

After a bit, he added, "This all seems so unfair to you, Rayanne. You deserve better than a man who can't always be there for you."

The sadness in his words hurt to hear. She rolled over to face him. "Believe me, Wyatt, if that had been any more real, I don't think I would've survived it."

"Thank you for that." He kissed her again, softly this time, offering her comfort rather than passion. "But I can't help but feel that we're running out of time. The day is almost upon us."

A fact that was never far from her mind. Now probably wasn't the best time to push him for answers, but he was the one who'd brought the subject up. She decided to ask, anyway.

"Wyatt, will you tell me what happened that day in Blessing?"

Chapter 15

He'd known this moment had been barreling toward them as much as he'd really prefer to avoid it altogether. But if anyone deserved to know the true story of Wyatt McCain, it was the woman who'd made him feel more alive than he'd been even in his own time.

"Let's get dressed first."

As if clothes would do anything to protect him from the acid-hot pain of the worst day of his life. At least the few minutes required to fasten his pants and button his shirt would give him a chance to pull together his scattered thoughts.

Rayanne quietly slipped back into her shirt and those ridiculous shorts and then went out on the porch to wait for him on the bench. When he joined her outside, she held out his hat. Rather than put it on, he sat down beside her and held it in his lap.

The damn thing had been pretty expensive back in the day, but now it looked as worn and tattered as he felt. There was no way to pretty the story up, to make himself out to be anything better than the gun-for-hire he'd been. The best he could hope for was that Rayanne wouldn't hate herself for consorting with the likes of him.

When he didn't immediately launch into the story, she scooted closer, pressing her body next to his. He put his arm around her shoulders, needing her touch to anchor him in this world.

As the silence stretched on, she started to move away. "I'm sorry, Wyatt. I shouldn't have asked. It's none of my business."

He caught her and pulled her back to his side. "No, you're wrong, Rayanne. You have every right to know, but it's going to change how you feel about me. I did a lot of things that I'm not proud of, but that day was the worst."

She stared across at the old church, reminding him that she'd once had a clear view of the beginning of the events that had condemned him to this existence.

"Wyatt, I know something went horribly wrong that day. I also know that you've spent over a century trying to figure out how to fix it."

She leaned back against his shoulder and tugged one of his hands over into her lap. "I want to help you so maybe you'll finally know some peace. Maybe we both will. The memory of that day has haunted me for fifteen years. I can't imagine living with it as long as you have."

"It should never have been your burden to bear, Rayanne, and I'm right sorry you got pulled into my world like this."

He sat in silence for a few seconds. "What makes you think you can change the outcome? What can you do what I've never been able to do for myself?"

His sharp words made her flinch, but she held her ground. "I don't know, but I know we've got to try. You need to move on, and I need to get on with my life. Besides, I was up there that day and saw what happened. When I shouted to warn you about the shooter in the belfry, you shot him. Did that ever happen before that day?"

"No, and it hasn't happened again since. Other than that one time, he shoots me in the shoulder."

The remembered pain of that rifle shot tearing into his body had him rubbing the old wound with his free hand. "What are you thinking?"

"And no one else has ever seen you as clearly or as often as I have. I've read the journals that Uncle Ray left me. He knew you were here, and so did Amanda and Aunt Hattie, but none of them saw you as often as I have."

"That's right."

She patted him on the leg. "You've never been real like this since that day, either."

All right, he could follow the trail she was laying out. "No, I haven't, which means you're the reason things are changing for me."

"What do you think it means, Wyatt?"

"I wish I knew." He stared down the street, seeing it as it had been all those years ago. "I'll start at the beginning and try to tell you everything. If it gets to be too much, say so and we'll stop."

His throat was dry, making it hard to get the words out. "There was only one thing I was ever good at and that was shooting. Ma always said I was born restless. My pa wanted me to be a churchgoing dirt farmer like him, but my younger brother Thad was better suited to that life. I rode out one night after we'd had another fight on the subject and never looked back."

Rayanne looked shocked. "You never wanted to see your family again?"

"It was the other way around. I rode through there a couple of years later. By then, I already had a reputation as a troublemaker with a talent for guns. When I stopped at the farm, I made a point of sharing some of my adventures with Thad. Pa cornered me with his rifle and yelled at me for filling the boy's head with sinful thoughts. Then he said I was straight on the road headed to hell, and that he'd give me just one chance to turn my back on Satan. If I left this time, not to bother coming back because he had no use for fornicators and drunkards."

Even after all these years, he could still hear the cold fury in his father's voice. He'd sounded like one of those old prophets in the Bible, preaching at him about hellfire and brimstone. Sometimes he wondered where he would've ended up if he'd made a different decision that night.

Rayanne sat up straight, her outrage obvious. "What kind of idiotic father would say something like that to his son?"

He loved that she would leap to his defense, but his father hadn't been wrong. "He was protecting Thad and my ma from the likes of me. He was right about me being nothing but trouble. After all, look where I ended up."

She would have none of it. "And maybe you wouldn't have if your family had reached out instead of turning their back on you. I'm the first to admit that my parents drive me crazy, but I've never doubted that they loved me."

Right now, Rayanne was upset because she thought he'd been mistreated. That was bound to change as the rest of his story unfurled, and he hated that. He needed to be up and moving, even though no matter how fast he walked or how far he went, he'd never figured out how to outdistance his past.

"Mind if we walk?"

He didn't wait for her to answer but immediately stepped off the porch and headed down the street. With the sun beating down, the day had grown uncomfortably warm. Not that he was complaining. If he could feel the heat, it meant he was still real. He stripped off his duster and tossed it on the railing outside of the mercantile. That still wasn't enough, so he rolled up his sleeves.

The sun wasn't the only source of heat right then. Rayanne stood close by staring at his arms with the same expression in her eyes that she'd had right before he'd taken her back there on the saloon floor. What had he done to fan that particular fire?

He retreated a step, not sure how to respond. "Rayanne?"

She slowly grinned. "Sorry, my mind went off track there for a minute. Just so you know, women love the look of strong forearms with rolled-up sleeves. At least this woman does."

He wasn't used to how outspoken modern women had become, but he liked it. "Anything else I should know about?"

Rayanne hooked her arm through his. "Well, that duster is pretty hot."

"I know. That's why I took it off."

Something about what he'd said set off a fit of the giggles. Then she apologized. "Sorry, I shouldn't have laughed, but we're talking about two different kinds of hot here. There's the sun," she said, pointing to the sky. "And then there's the kind of hot caused when a man rolls up his sleeves or wears a piece of clothing a woman thinks is sexy."

Well, all right, then. "And you think my old duster is sexy?"

"Don't look at me like I'm crazy. There's a reason so many men on the covers of romance stories set in the Old West are wearing coats just like yours."

"So if the books were meant to appeal to me, the woman on the cover would be wearing those shorts?"

Now she was blushing, probably remembering how easy it had been for him to get her out of them. "Maybe we should take that walk you mentioned."

That quickly, his good mood disappeared. He let her tug him along in the direction of the creek. It would be cooler in the shade of the trees, and for the first time in more than a hundred years, he was actually thirsty.

As they walked along, he kept watch for the others who'd intruded on Rayanne's dream. It occurred to him that he'd forgotten something. "I just realized this is the day I promised I'd take you to the meadow that your uncle liked. There's still time if you want to go."

She considered the suggestion. "Would you mind? How are you feeling?"

Did she think he was weak? "I'm fine, other than I'd like a drink of water. I'll tell you the rest of my story on the way back."

"We'll get some drinks at the cabin." She gave him a puzzled look. "So if you're feeling thirsty, are you hungry, too?"

It hadn't even occurred to him to wonder about it. "Come to think of it, I am."

How odd to be feeling so human again. "I don't know how long this is going to last, but I'd love an apple—and some of those cookies you keep hidden in the top shelf of the cabinet."

"It's a deal."

They were in and out of the cabin in a matter of minutes. She really wanted to honor Uncle Ray on his birthday, but it was tempting to put the whole thing off to take advantage of this time with Wyatt while he was solidly in this world. In fact, she'd like to take advantage of Wyatt period, especially with a repeat performance of the time they'd spent on the saloon floor. But as long as he was willing to share his story, she sensed it was important for her to hear it. He obviously worried what she'd think of him once she knew the truth, but she wouldn't judge him for mistakes he'd made decades before she'd even been born. She loved the man he was now.

She was following behind him on the narrow trail, enjoying the opportunity to watch him move with his usual powerful grace. Oh, yeah, when they got back, maybe she'd coax him into spending the night with her. Perhaps starting off in that big, claw-foot tub.

What did gunslingers think about taking a bubble bath by candlelight?

He happened to look back right then, looking as if he were about to speak. Something of what she was thinking must have been right there for him to see. Without a word, he tugged her close enough to press a kiss on her mouth, one filled with promise and just a hint of heat.

"We turn off this trail just ahead. From there on, I'll mark the way to make sure you can find your way back."

Why would he do that? "Won't you be with me?"

"Yes, but it's better to be safe. We don't know how all of this works, and I don't want to take a chance on you getting lost on the mountain because I'm not around to show you the way back."

"Good thinking."

His reasoning made sense; that didn't mean she

liked the possibility of him disappearing. If that was in the cards, she would've thought it would have happened after they made love, not when they were simply taking a long walk. She'd fed him an apple, a sizeable ham and cheese sandwich, and a handful of those cookies he'd mentioned. Maybe that would keep him fueled until they returned to the cabin.

"How much farther?"

He pointed ahead. "Just past that pair of rocks up ahead."

When they got past the trees, her breath caught in her chest. The vista in front of her was simply beautiful. A small stream cascaded down the side of the mountain, and the sun made sparkling rainbows in the mist coming off the water. A few late-blooming lavender-and-white columbine were scattered throughout the grass. In a word, it was perfect.

"I can see why Uncle Ray loved this spot."

Her eyes filled with tears, and the words came out in a whisper. Wyatt's strong arm supported her as they made their way to a rocky outcropping that overlooked the small waterfall.

His voice was a deep rumble, the vista clearly affecting him, too. "I think your uncle came here whenever he needed to find some peace. I would watch from the woods as he stood right here, gazing at the water tumbling down. The first few times I thought he was considering jumping, but then I realized he found the sound soothing. After a while, he'd walk away looking as if he'd left a burden behind."

Grief clogged Rayanne's throat. "The war changed

Uncle Ray. My mother said it was like the man she knew never really came home."

She let the silence settle over her, seeking the same comfort Uncle Ray had taken from the beauty of the mountain. In truth, though, her real comfort came from the solid presence of the man standing beside her.

It was time to say goodbye to Ray, and so she did.

On the way back to the cabin, Wyatt started talking. Maybe he wanted to distract her. Maybe he just needed to get his story told. Either way, she held his hand and listened.

"You know that Blessing grew up around the mine. Anytime there's gold or silver involved, there's going to be trouble. Every so often, a group of hard cases would ride into Blessing and start raising hell. Most of the time, they'd drink, gamble, and…um, visit with the two ladies who worked upstairs at the saloon."

He shot her a quick look before adding that last part. Did he really think that would shock her? She grinned at him. "Wyatt, I'm a history professor who specializes in the American West. I'm familiar with the kind of work those ladies did. I also know there weren't that many choices for a woman to make a living, especially in remote areas."

He squeezed her hand. "That's true. They had a hard time of it, but Molly and Tennessee Sue were nice women."

"I believe that."

"Right before I came to town, the mining office had been robbed a couple of times."

The trail narrowed down, forcing them to walk single file. Wyatt started talking again as soon as they could walk side by side once more. "I rode with one of those gangs. I did my share of drinking and carousing in the saloon, but I didn't go after the gold."

Wyatt glanced down at her. "Don't go thinking that it was because I was too honest to steal from the fine people of Blessing. I probably would've been in the thick of it if I hadn't fallen down and broken my leg the night before the last robbery. One of the men got mad over losing at poker and was about to take his temper out on Molly. I charged up the stairs to stop him, but lost my footing and we both fell. The bastard was so drunk, he walked away without a scratch."

She noticed that Wyatt was rubbing his thigh as if it still ached. "Molly made them carry me down to your great-great-grandmother's place on a plank. A couple of those old miners sat on me while Amanda set my leg."

"So that's how you got to know her."

"Yes. Amanda was a decent woman, with all that meant back then. Her first husband died in the mine, leaving her a widow with a young son to raise on her own. She earned her living teaching the children in town how to read and write, but it was summer so school was out. She also occasionally took in boarders, so she agreed to let me stay until my leg healed."

He drifted off into a few seconds of silence. "I was pretty much confined to bed for a couple of weeks before I was strong enough to get around on crutches. Her boy Billy kept me company playing checkers. I was also teaching him how to play chess. He was a quick learner. Good-natured, too. He didn't complain overly much about having to wait on me when he could have been out playing with his friends."

Wyatt smiled. "He tried to talk me into teaching him how to play poker. His ma threatened to tan both our hides if we even thought about sneaking a deck of cards into her house."

Rayanne was relieved to see that not all of Wyatt's memories of Blessing were bad ones. How weird was it, though, to be feeling jealous of her own ancestor? It was obvious that Wyatt had liked Amanda. Had they been more than friends? After all, Amanda had been a widow with a handsome man living under her roof.

"When my leg healed, I found myself reluctant to leave town. I owed Amanda and the others for taking care of me. If they hadn't, I could've ended up dead or crippled. I figured I could pay Amanda and her son back by doing odd jobs around the house. Chopping wood, mending the roof, weeding her garden and the like. I even did some hunting. People get right friendly when you bring back a deer and are willing to share."

He stopped to stare up at the sun. "Funny, they were the same damn chores that I hated doing around my parents' farm, but it felt good being useful. I didn't drink or smoke from the night I broke my leg right up until that last day."

They were almost back to the cabin, but he seemed reluctant to resume their walk.

"Three months went by. My leg was pretty much back to normal, but I wasn't in any hurry to leave. For the first time since I'd ridden away from the family farm, I was content to stay in one place. People started treating me like I belonged here, like I was one of them. Then one of the men I'd been riding with came back through town. He spotted me and stopped to talk."

Did Wyatt even realize that his hands had strayed down to grip his pistols?

"Seems Earl had been sent ahead to do some scouting for the gang, to see if the mine had been producing. They'd already run through the gold they'd stolen last time. He was surprised to see me, but figured I was there for the same reason he was."

Wyatt looked pale, the memories obviously taking their toll. Maybe she shouldn't have insisted on hearing his story, but until she knew what had happened that day, she had no way of knowing how to help him.

"Why don't we go inside? I can fix us some dinner and then you can finish telling me."

"I'd rather just get this over with."

She hated seeing him looking so stressed. Some of it might stem from the fact he wasn't used to thinking about eating and drinking.

"I don't know about you, but I'm tired from all this hiking and everything. Would you mind sitting on the porch? I'll get us some cold drinks and maybe some snacks."

"That sounds good."

He followed her onto the porch, settling in the same chair he usually took. He sank into a dark silence. Not wanting to leave him alone for long, she grabbed some bottled water and crackers and cheese and hurried back outside.

He resumed talking as soon as she sat down beside him, his words coming in a rush. "I played along with him to find out as much as I could about their plans. Finally, I ran him out of town at gunpoint with orders to tell my former associates that they'd have to face me if they came back to Blessing."

"Did that work?"

"You know damn well it didn't. I should've known that I couldn't do anything right. I was better with a gun than any of them, but they had me beat in sheer numbers."

"And none of the other residents of Blessing would stand with you?"

"I wouldn't have let them if they'd offered. They were miners and storekeepers, not gunfighters." He took a long drink of water. "I think I wanted them to look at me like some kind of hero, especially Amanda and her son."

"And did she?"

For the first time in hours, Wyatt's mood lightened. "No, she railed at me for hours. Said I was a fool for thinking I could stop them. That there'd always be more gold and more men to steal it. What good would I be to anybody if I was dead?"

Then his smile faded. "Turned out she was right, but I was willing to die to protect her and the boy."

He was up and pacing now. "As long as no one ever stood up to those bastards, the attacks would never end."

"You were courageous for even trying, Wyatt."

"Don't go trying to make me out to be a hero, Rayanne. People died that day."

He stopped to stare out toward the woods. She followed his line of sight, already knowing what she'd see out there. Or rather, who. A ragged line of people, all wearing clothes right out of a history book, stood at the edge of the meadow, staring back at Wyatt. Right in the front of the bunch stood a young boy. When he raised his hand to wave, Wyatt turned his back, his face contorted in a mask of grief and shame.

"And it was the wrong people who died."

Then in a flash of light, he was gone.

Chapter 16

The sun was coming up when Rayanne sank back down in her chair on the porch. The night had not been one bit restful, her bed lonely, and her dreams empty and so damn sad. Her heart hurt for Wyatt, plain and simple. She now understood the burden of guilt that he'd carried around on his broad shoulders all these years. He'd died on the dusty streets of Blessing, gunned down by men he'd once ridden with, but he'd willingly taken that risk.

The problem was that somehow Amanda's son had died, too.

She scanned the surrounding woods. Where had Wyatt gone? How long would he stay away this time? Always questions and no answers. If he didn't show up soon, she'd head into town to see if he was back in Blessing. Even if she couldn't see him, she'd give anything to simply feel his presence, to know that he was all right.

It hadn't hit her until she'd been in bed that the last few minutes before Wyatt had disappeared, he'd been wearing his duster again, even though he'd left it hanging on the railing back in Blessing. Obviously, at some point he'd returned to his ghostly state, and she hadn't even noticed.

That was because no matter what form he took, Wyatt was real to her. A man, not merely the memory of one. And she loved him. What would he do if she told him? Would it help heal his wounds or only make them worse?

There was one way to find out. With so many other ghosts drifting through the woods, she hadn't wanted to risk running into them in the dark. Once the sun was up high enough to chase away the worst of the shadows, she'd head straight for Blessing and hunt for Wyatt.

She finished the last of her coffee and took the cup back inside, trading it for her backpack. Once she found Wyatt, she'd make it damn clear to him that she wanted to be with him regardless of the events of the past.

Maybe she was being overly optimistic, but she'd made sure to wear another pair of her drawstring shorts—just in case. Her bed might be more comfortable, but she'd happily settle for saloon-floor sex, too. She smiled at the memory of the conversation they'd had over what was hot and what was really hot.

As she stepped off the porch, she realized there was a noise in the distance, one she hadn't heard since the day Shawn had driven off in a huff. Damn it, just what she needed. Someone was coming. Her first temptation was to take off for the woods, but there'd be no hiding her trail through the dew-dampened grass. Besides, with her car parked by the cabin, they'd know she was around somewhere.

No one would drive this far without good reason. Maybe it was Phil dropping by for a visit, but she couldn't be that lucky. She sat down on the porch step and waited.

Sure enough, a few minutes later she caught sight of her mother's car. Maybe she should have run for Blessing and stayed there until her mom gave up and went home. God knew what kind of tales Shawn had told her.

The car hit a rut just as it came to a stop, causing it to lurch sideways. Her mom gunned the engine, sending up a spray of gravel. Rayanne winced, knowing how much her mom babied her car. If it got scratched, she'd never hear the end of it.

Her mom parked right in front of the cabin and climbed out of the car. She hobbled her way around to the steps, her shoes totally inappropriate for walking on rough ground.

"Mother, as usual a call would've been nice. Another five minutes, and you would've had to sit on the porch all day until I got back or give up and head back down the road."

Where she belonged. Lana had never been one for

roughing it. The cabin had all of the usual amenities like running water and electricity. However, it failed to meet her mother's definition of civilization because it was more than five miles from the nearest mall.

Her mother glared at her. "If I'd have called, you would have told me not to come."

No use in arguing that one. It was true.

"So if you knew I wanted to be left alone, and you hate this place so much, why are you here?"

Lana gave her a thoroughly disgusted look. "Can't this discussion wait until we're inside? I need a cold drink and a bathroom."

"Fine. I'll let you in. Help yourself to anything you want to eat or drink. The bathroom is upstairs."

Her mother pushed a button on her key ring, which released the trunk lid. "Get my luggage out of the car for me."

Rayanne's first instinct was to refuse. If the suit-case stayed right where it was, there was always the chance her mother would head back down the road again today. Once the luggage was inside, she'd be staying for sure.

Rather than immediately fetching it, she unlocked the door and followed her mother inside. "Why are you here, Mom?"

"I was already worried about you, but then Shawn stopped by after you ran him off. I still can't believe you did that after he drove all the way up here to see you. Seriously, I don't know why he hadn't given up on you long before this."

Rayanne pulled a bottle of water out of the fridge

and handed to her. "Need I remind you that Shawn also showed up uninvited? Not to mention he wanted me to blow off my work and go hang out with him, instead."

Lana picked up the water in a white-knuckled grip. "Which is exactly what you should have done. I don't have to tell you how much you hurt his feelings. Luckily, I reminded him that you'd just lost your uncle. If you make nice the next time you see him, I'm sure he'll forgive your rude behavior."

Enough was enough.

"First of all, Shawn and I have agreed that there is no future for us except as friends. Secondly, I'm a historian, Mother, and Shawn knows that. I only have so long to do my research and start writing before the summer is over. It's already getting to be late August. If I decide to return to my job, I still have a lot of work to finish before school starts."

Her mother only heard one thing. Her voice went up two octaves. "*If?* What do you mean *if* you decide to return to your job? Of course you're returning to the college. That's where your life is."

Right now Rayanne had more important things on her mind than picking up the pieces of her life down below. Things she couldn't share with her mother. Yes, eventually she'd have to return to reality, but not until some things up here on the mountain were settled.

Rather than point that out, she drew a long, deep breath and changed tactics. "Mom, you must be tired from the drive up here. Why don't you eat something and then lie down? I'll set your bag on the porch on my way out."

Lana planted herself between Rayanne and the door. "Where are you going?"

"Into town."

Her mother brightened and immediately pulled out her keys. "Great. I'll drive. We can get a hotel room and a spa treatment. My treat."

"Not that town, Mom. I'm going to spend the day working in Blessing."

Her mom didn't budge. Instead, she dug in her heels and crossed her arms over her chest. "I don't want you rambling around in that death trap by yourself. Shawn told me that you almost got killed falling through the floor of one of those old buildings."

Darn the man. "He exaggerated the danger. Now please step out of the way, Mom. I'll be back before dark."

"Fine. Do what you want. You always do." Her mother stood her ground a few seconds longer. "But understand that you're forcing my hand, Rayanne. Living up here allowed my brother to avoid dealing with his problems, and he ended up spending his whole life alone. He could've gotten help, and maybe, just maybe, he could have lived a normal life again."

She finally gave ground, but her voice cracked. "I lost my brother to this mountain. I don't want the same thing to happen to you, too. One way or another, I want you back home. Then we'll see about putting this place up for sale. It's been a burden to our family long enough."

Rayanne understood her mother's concerns, but her own connection to this mountain wasn't ever going to change. "I'm sorry you feel that way, Mom. Uncle Ray left this place to me and enough money to live on for years. It was his gift to me, and it will not be going up for sale, ever. If you can't accept that, I would prefer that you were gone when I get back."

She walked out, pausing by her mother's car long enough to slam the trunk lid shut, leaving the luggage locked inside. Not exactly a subtle hint, but right now she didn't have time for subtleties. Not with Wyatt gone missing and time growing short.

The first thing she noticed was the silence in the woods. No flutter of bird wings, no scurrying feet in the undergrowth. What were they sensing that had them all hiding? She took a cautious look around. Just as she suspected, there was movement in the trees, but the ghostly forms made no sound as they passed.

If they were aware of her, they gave no sign of it. This time it was a group of three men, miners by the look of them. One carried a pickax resting on his shoulder; the other two had shovels. When they reached a patch of sunlight, they flickered out of existence again.

She kept moving, preferring the open space of town to the close confines of the woods. So far, outside of her dream with Wyatt, none of the spirits had paid the least bit of attention to her. She hoped it stayed that way.

About halfway down the trail, another ghost appeared, this one much shorter. His shock of red hair marked him as the same boy who had waved at Wyatt. Billy, her long-dead great-uncle. She slowed down, hoping he'd disappear before their paths crossed, but no such luck.

Instead, he stopped to look directly at her. "You were with Mr. Wyatt by the creek."

Maybe she could have ignored one of the adults if they'd spoken to her, but this was a child, and family at that. He shifted from foot to foot, too full of energy to stand still. His overalls had been neatly patched, his shoes scuffed and worn. It was uncanny how much he looked so much like Uncle Ray as a young boy.

"Yes, I do know Wyatt. He's a friend of mine. You must be Billy. I hear you play a mean game of checkers."

The boy grinned at her. "Chess, too. I'm hoping Wyatt will teach me to play poker, but he can't while Ma is around to see."

She laughed. "He told me that, too."

Billy looked back over his shoulder as if watching for someone. "Are you going to town?"

"Yes, I thought I'd go check on Wyatt." If he was there.

She was sure she hadn't said that last part out loud, but Billy answered, anyway.

"He's there, all right. I saw him go in the saloon earlier. I'd take you there, but my ma would tan my hide if she caught me near the saloon. She won't be happy if she finds out Mr. Wyatt is in there, either. She done told him as long as he rented our spare room, he couldn't come home stinking like whiskey and those ladies who work there.

"I don't know why she said that last part." He scrunched his nose up in confusion. "Miss Molly smells real nice. I sniffed her when she came into the store one day."

Rayanne fought to keep a straight face. Definitely time to change subjects. "I should get going. Want to walk with me?"

He shook his head. "No, I'd better not. Nice to meet you, Miss—" His eyes widened. "You never said your name."

"It's Rayanne, Billy."

"Nice to meet you, Miss Rayanne."

Then with a wave, he ran off. A few steps away he blinked out of sight. Goose bumps danced over her skin. Despite all the time she'd spent with Wyatt, she wasn't sure she'd ever get used to seeing people pop in and out of existence.

At least the unnatural silence had ended as the usual rustlings in the woods returned to normal. A few minutes later, she left the trees behind and the town came into sight. It looked the same—deserted and falling apart. With everything that had happened and the number of ghosts she'd seen over the past two days, she'd been afraid the missing buildings would've reappeared.

What a relief. After the confrontation with her mother and then meeting Billy in the woods, she could use a bit of normal. Well, if hunting down her ghostly lover could be considered any kind of normal.

She stopped at the end of the street and looked around. Other than a breeze stirring up some of the dust, the place was still. Empty.

Billy said Wyatt had gone into the saloon, so she'd look there first. Of course, there was no way to know if Billy meant he'd seen him today or back in the past.

She stepped onto the porch, wishing the town had come with some kind of instruction manual. It would sure be nice to know what she was doing when people's lives, or rather, their deaths were at stake. Her gut feeling was that she was here for a purpose other than cataloging the history of the town. That somehow, she was meant to play a role in ending the tragedy once and for all.

Even if it meant never seeing Wyatt again, never sharing another kiss, never making love with him again. She hated the whole idea, but the man deserved some peace. Then maybe she could get back to the life her mother had been talking about, one free of nightmares from her own past.

After setting her pack down, she stepped through the doors into the saloon and breathed a sigh of relief. He was there. Not visible, but she could feel his energy. She'd take him anyway she could get him.

"Wyatt, are you all right?"

There was a shimmer of energy over in the corner near the pictures she had tacked up on the wall. She stepped closer, hoping he would solidify, at least enough so that she could see him, maybe even hear him.

The struggle went on for several seconds with

bright flickers of light fading in and out. A loud pop startled her, but then Wyatt was there. Tears of relief stung her eyes.

"You're back."

He nodded, looking reassuringly solid. She started toward him, but he held up his hand in warning. When she stopped, he swung his hand at the table. It passed straight through without a sound. The stacks of papers rippled a bit, but that was all.

"Can you talk?"

He tried, but no sound came out, at least none she could hear. His clear frustration had him fading again.

"Don't worry about it, Wyatt. I'm just glad that you're here and all right. I was worried."

That didn't seem to please him, either. Somehow she doubted he'd be any happier to find out that she'd met his friend Billy in the woods. Rather than push the issue right now, she'd finish sketching the last building she'd measured out. Even if she was only going through the motions, it might help him deal with the powerful emotions yesterday had triggered.

She pulled a chair up to the closest table and started sketching. This time she added a few people strolling in front of the store now that she'd seen what they looked like. An hour or more passed before Wyatt moved closer, looking more solid. She'd finished the first picture and started a second, this one a portrait. Drawing Billy was a risk, but it felt right.

"You've caught his likeness. You've only seen him twice, both times at a distance."

She kept her focus on the sketch as Wyatt stood

behind her, watching her intently. "I met up with Billy on my way here this morning. We had a nice talk."

"He spoke to you?"

Wyatt's hand came down on her shoulder, his touch feather light. She brushed her fingers across his as she turned to look up at him. "Yes. I told him you and I were friends and asked if he'd seen you. He told me you were here in the saloon, which would make his ma mad. Something about her not wanting you to show up smelling like whiskey and Miss Molly."

He smiled a little, looking far happier than he had when he first appeared.

"He couldn't understand that last part because evidently Miss Molly smelled nice. He knew that because he sniffed her once when she came into the store."

This time she couldn't hold back a grin. The relief at finding Wyatt again coupled with the image of that little boy checking out Molly's perfume sent her off into peals of laughter.

Wyatt chuckled. "His ma would've tanned his hide if she'd found out about that."

He gave her shoulder another squeeze and stepped back. Cocking his head to the side, he studied her. "So who drove up the mountain this morning?"

She should have known he'd sense the intruder. "My mother. She wants me to leave with her. She's worried that I'm going to turn into my uncle and end up living up here all alone."

"She's right. It might have been better if you'd gone with her."

She ignored the stab of pain his words caused and focused on the one positive. "She left?"

He nodded. "A few minutes ago. Is she the type to give up easily?"

"No. She hates this place for the effect it had on my uncle and then again on me. You know, after seeing…what I saw back then."

Wyatt frowned. "You never mentioned having problems."

She hated the memory of that time. "I had nightmares for months. My parents and the idiot doctor they took me to kept insisting I had just imagined it all. That I'd gotten scared because I couldn't find Uncle Ray and blew it all out of proportion."

She'd hated the endless hours of rehashing the same things over and over again. "I didn't believe them, but they thought it was all in my imagination. But I knew deep down inside that it was all real—all those people, the gunshots."

Then she stood up and turned to face Wyatt. "Especially you. Even if somehow my mind made up all the rest, I always knew you were real."

He wrapped his arms around her, pulling her in close and wrapping her in a cocoon of leather and his strength. "I never forgot that day, either. It was the only time something changed."

Okay, maybe now was the time to talk about that.

"Why do you think that is, Wyatt? There had to be times when Amanda or Hattie or even Uncle Ray were here when everything played out again."

His voice was a quiet rumble. "I don't know. I always meant to do something different. Maybe if I could tie Billy to a tree or warn Amanda that he'd sneak out. Something. Anything to keep him from dying."

"Do you know which of the gang shoots him?"

Wyatt immediately released her, almost shoving her back out of his reach. "None of them."

"Then who did, Wyatt? I need answers if I'm going to find some way to end this nightmare for both of us."

He stared at her, his blue eyes looking faded and dull with pain. "Who the hell do you think it was, Rayanne? The answer is obvious. I pulled the trigger. No one else. Just me. The last thing I saw before I died myself was Billy crumpling to the ground, a gaping hole in his chest, and Amanda screaming his name."

Chapter 17

Wyatt braced himself for her revulsion and rejection, not that he'd blame Rayanne one bit for feeling that way. After all, he'd hated himself for over a hundred years. He'd done some pretty questionable things in his life, but nothing—NOTHING—could be worse than killing that little boy. Even if Rayanne could forgive him for not telling her before they'd crossed the line to becoming lovers, she'd never forgive him for killing her great-uncle.

He wouldn't be surprised if she stormed out of the saloon, never to speak to him again. Hell, if she wanted to borrow one of his guns and shoot him with it, he'd stand still and let her take aim. Maybe this would all end if she torched the place and let Blessing burn to the ground.

But none of that happened. Instead, this one incredibly strong woman looked up at him with such compassion in her beautiful green eyes.

"Oh, God, Wyatt. I'd figured out that Billy died that day, but I'd never for a second thought that it was you who'd pulled the trigger."

She reached up to cradle his face with her soft hands. "I'm so sorry. How awful for you."

Wait a minute. He backed up a step as he tried to make sense of what she'd just said. Rayanne felt bad for him? His chest hurt from the force it took to spit the words out.

"Awful for me? Are you deaf, woman? I killed that boy right there in front of his mother. They were nothing but good to me, and my stupidity cost them everything. They trusted me. I promised to make the town safe for them. Instead, Billy bled to death in the street with my bullet in his chest."

He turned his back to those eyes that saw too much. Tears burned his eyes, the images in his head not just memories, but something he had lived through over and over again. Each time was fresh and horrible as when it originally happened. He closed his eyes and remembered the heat of that day, the gritty dust that had clung to his damp skin, the burn of whiskey in his throat from the one shot he'd drunk for courage only moments before stepping out into the street.

The fine citizens of Blessing had all scurried for cover, knowing death was about to stalk the streets of their small town. He drew no comfort from knowing that he'd killed enough of his former associates to keep them from coming back again. Looking back, he'd rather the bastards steal every speck of gold dust that mine ever produced if it meant that Billy could have lived a long and happy life.

He realized Rayanne was trying to get his attention, planting herself right smack in front of him again. He blinked hard, trying to focus on her, the one bright spot in his existence.

"Wyatt McCain, I heard what you said, and I understand what you did. Yes, it was a horrible tragedy, but it was a mistake, an accident. Nothing more. Even Amanda knew that. Did you know that she blamed herself for Billy's death?"

Now that made no sense. "She didn't pull that trigger. I did."

"Yes, that's true. However, she knew Billy was curious about what was going to happen, but she left him alone, anyway. If she'd stayed home like you told her to, he wouldn't have died, not like that. But who knows, maybe in the great scheme of things it was just his time."

Knowing he wasn't the only one who'd suffered because of Billy's death didn't help at all. Rayanne was still talking.

"So back to what I was saying, Wyatt. I have to think there's a reason I can see you, hear you, feel you when no one else can. Aunt Hattie said all it took was someone believing to make it all real. You and I changed things fifteen years ago. If we believe we can do it again, maybe the two of us can change things for good this time."

He wanted that more than anything. Well, almost anything. Right now he wanted Rayanne something fierce.

"Change it how?"

"I don't know, but we've got two days to figure it out."

She snuggled close again, holding on to him with such fierce strength. "You don't have to face this alone anymore, big guy. And if we don't figure it out this time, then we'll try again next year."

"No, we won't." He pressed a kiss to the top of her head. "The last thing I want is you wasting your life on me, Rayanne. You need to find a man from your own time, someone who makes you happy, and build a life with him. Not that jackass who was here, but a good man who deserves you. Promise me that if I let you watch this play out this one last time, you'll walk away no matter how it turns out."

She didn't want to do it. It was clear in the way her eyes shifted away from his face to stare at some point past his shoulder. It had to be the belfry on the old church, the one place she'd been avoiding since right after she'd shown up on the mountain.

He wanted to shake some sense into her. Instead, he gently tilted her face up toward his. "I mean it, Rayanne. I can't bear the thought of you caught up in this nightmare year after year."

"But—"

Rather than listen to all of her foolish reasons for wanting to tangle her life up with the tragedy, he hushed her the only way he could. He kissed her. He'd never been a man of many words, preferring action to get his point across. No one misunderstood the solid impact of a fist or what it meant to stare down the barrel of a gun.

If only he dared tell this beautiful woman what she'd come to mean to him. He poured everything he had into the kiss, hoping she'd understand. She sighed and settled into his arms, allowing him to deepen the kiss, to savor the sweet spice that was uniquely Rayanne's.

When he lifted her up onto the table and moved to stand between her knees, he felt her smile. He pulled back, trying to decide if he should be insulted. "You find this amusing?"

Her eyes sparked with good humor and a lot of heat. "No, I find it arousing. But I have to wonder if we'll ever actually get around to doing this in the comfort of a bed."

Leave it to her to make him laugh when only minutes ago he'd been hurting so damn bad. He stepped back and tugged her back to her feet.

To let her know he was only banking the fire, not putting it out altogether, he kissed the palm of her hand before saying, "How about we finish what you need to do here today and then go back to your cabin for the night?"

Her eyes glittered with hunger. "Sounds perfect. Even better, if we get a move on, I promise to knock off work early."

"Then by all means, let's get down to it."

She trailed her fingers down his chest and kept going. "Exactly which *it* are you talking about?"

He caught her hand in his. "Keep that up and we won't get anything else done."

She gave an exaggerated sigh and gathered up her sketch pad and walked away. He laughed and followed her out of the saloon.

Rayanne was glad that she'd managed to improve Wyatt's mood because she was about to rip all those old wounds open again. She hated to hurt him that way, but she remained convinced that the only way they'd break the awful pattern that he'd been caught up in for more than a century was to figure out how to change what happened.

Outside, she stood in the bright sunshine and stared up at the intensely blue sky above. Wyatt stood beside her, ignoring the beautiful day to watch her, instead.

"Spit whatever you have stuck in your craw, Rayanne. If I'm not going to like it, anyway, just say it."

"Fine." She did a slow turn, looking from one end of the street to the other. "I want you to walk me through that day again. Tell me everything, good and bad. All the things you did right and all those that went wrong."

He glared down at her, his hands clenched in fists. "Why the hell do you want me to do that? You already know all the important stuff. You saw most of it play out right in front of you. I walked out of that saloon to face down the men I used to ride with. When the gunfire ended, most of them were wounded or dead."

He waved his hand toward the other end of town. "They rode in from that direction, but they sent one guy around from the other end to hide out in the belfry. He's the one you warned me about. That was the only year when I shot him instead of the other way around."

But then he stopped to stare up at the belfry, his eyebrows riding low over his eyes. "Why do you think that happened? And if it happened once, why not again?"

He strode off down the road. "People were hiding in all of the buildings. Someone had to have seen him up there, but no one said a word. Never tried to warn me."

"Maybe for fear of drawing attention to themselves?" Although as far as she was concerned, that was cowardice of the worst kind. They could have banded together to face down their attackers, not let a single man take on the whole bunch by himself.

"That and I told them to stay out of sight. I didn't want to shoot one of them by mistake." His mouth twisted up in a bitter smile. "See how well that worked out."

"Start at the beginning and go from there, Wyatt."

She flipped open her pad and prepared to take notes because she'd never get him to go through this a second time and wouldn't want to. She quickly sketched out a rough map of the town and began marking down the details as he described them.

Speaking in a soul-weary monotone, he might as well have been reciting the alphabet for all the emotion he conveyed with his words.

It took them nearly an hour to go through it all before she was satisfied that she had all the details down. Start to finish, the whole gunfight had probably lasted a handful of minutes, but the memories of it seemed to play out in slow motion in Wyatt's mind. As he talked, he'd flickered in and out of existence, most of the time in that halfway state where she could see him, but he had no real substance.

He looked like hell right now. She hoped a change of scenery would let him come back to her, solid and real.

"All right, that's enough for today. Let's head back to the cabin where we can relax."

He'd just shown her where Billy had died in front of the mercantile. Wyatt knelt down, touching the faded and cracked wood as if he could still see the pool of blood and the boy's sightless eyes staring up at him from where he lay sprawled on the ground. In reality, Wyatt hadn't actually seen Billy bleed out. He'd been too busy dying himself.

She tried again. "Let's go, Wyatt. I don't know about you, but I could use a cold drink and something to eat. I'll go get my things from the saloon. I'll meet you at the edge of town."

That is, if he even noticed she'd deserted him. She wasn't sure what she'd do next. In his current state, she couldn't touch him, much less physically drag him away from Blessing to her cabin.

Inside the saloon, she gathered up her things and stuffed them all back in her pack. Outside, Wyatt stood at the edge of the porch, waiting for her. They fell into step together and made their way toward the tree line.

"That wasn't the most pleasant experience I've ever had," he said, his voice tight with emotion. "However, I have to admit that it was a relief to talk about it, especially with you."

Wyatt wrapped his arm around her shoulders, once again solid, as if she somehow grounded him in the world. "None of the others who show up every year seem to remember what happened. They think they're real with no knowledge that a hundred or more years have passed. Then on the twenty-third, all of a sudden, the town is back to exactly the way it was. Everyone says and does the same things. Even me."

Inside the cool shade of the trees, he pointed toward some vague shapes in the distance. "They get more real, hang around longer as we get closer to the anniversary. Then it all explodes again, gunshots coming from every direction. I know what is going to happen. I even know how many times I'm going to get shot before I die. It's as if I'm caught in a flooded river, getting swept along with the current and drowning in my own blood."

He stumbled to a halt. "But you're different. At least in the beginning, your uncle thought maybe he was imagining me, like I was one of those memories he brought back from the war with him. Before him, Hattie wasn't sure for a long time. I can only think of a handful of times when she tried to speak to me. But from the first, you've always treated me as if I'm more than a fragment of some nightmare."

She hurt for him. The other ghosts might not be sentient, but he was. "You are real to me and always will be."

For the first time since they'd kissed in the saloon, there was less pain in his gaze and a note of excitement in his voice. "You've seen the others, and you spoke to Billy like he was real, too."

Where was he going with this? "Actually, he spoke to me first. But for those few minutes, he existed in this place and time, just like you do."

"So like the last time, maybe you can make yourself heard on the day of the gunfight."

His excitement had a dark edge to it as he spun her around to face him. "But this time, when you make yourself heard, it won't be me you'll try to save. It will be Billy."

His words stabbed right through to the heart of her. "But, Wyatt, I can't let you die. Not if I can stop it. I love you too much to let that happen."

Okay, she hadn't meant to let that slip out, but she wouldn't deny the truth of her words, either. He stared down at her for the longest time.

He drew a long, slow breath. "I love you, too, Rayanne. More than you'll ever know. I'd give anything for the two of us to have a future together, but I belong in the past. If you really do love me, promise me you'll do what you can to save Billy. It's the only way I'll ever know any peace. All I'm asking is that you try this one time. No matter how it turns out, it's time for you to get on with your life down below."

Wasn't that what she wanted for him, too? A chance to stop this travesty? But if Billy didn't die in the past, how would that change everything that had happened ever since? Would none of this have happened? What if that meant she'd never met Wyatt at all? None of it made sense.

The woods closed in on her, leaving her feeling trapped and choking on the pain. She was the one to turn away this time. "This hurts so much, Wyatt."

He moved up behind her and wrapped his arms around her shoulders, holding her with such care.

"Do you want me to go back to Blessing?"

She actually considered it, but then shook her head. "No, I want you with me. We're down to less than two days, and I don't want to waste a single minute of that time."

"If you're sure." He rested his head next to hers. "I don't want to cause you any more pain than I already have."

"It only hurts because you've made my time up here so special, Wyatt. I love the way you make me feel."

Several more former residents of Blessing appeared a short distance away. Wyatt's hold on her tightened. "Let's go to the cabin and forget about all of this until tomorrow morning."

She shivered at the sheer number of ghosts she could see at the moment. It was as if they'd stolen all of the heat from the summer day.

"Good idea. We'll lock the door, pull the blinds and pretend the rest of the world doesn't exist. There's just me, you, a claw-foot tub and that bed I mentioned earlier."

He pressed a soft kiss to her temple. "Lady, I do like the way you think."

Then they ran down the narrow trail all the way to the cabin, laughing when she closed the door and threw the lock.

"Food first."

Rayanne had been trying to drag Wyatt up the stairs, but he dug in his heels. She'd looked ashen back there in the woods when the fine citizens of Blessing had strayed too close to them. Although he didn't seem to need much of anything in the way of food and water, that wasn't true for her.

"But taking a bath first would feel so good."

The heat in her eyes made it clear just how good it would feel. It was damned tempting to take her up on the offer, but she hadn't been able to hide the slight trembling in her hands when she tried once again to coax him to follow her.

Two could play at that game. "Eat something first. You're going to need all your strength for our—" he studied her with all the heat he could muster "—bath."

She stopped right where she was, her mouth slowly curving up in a smile. "Well, then, there is that. I'll fix a quick sandwich. Do you want one?"

"No, thanks. Right now I don't appear to need anything."

Rayanne had been about to open the white cabinet that held cold air. "Are you all right?"

He suspected what she really wanted to know was if he were solid and was reluctant to find out for herself. He quickly stripped off his coat and hat, tossing them on a nearby chair. Then he picked up a book off the counter and thumbed through it, answering her without words.

She shot him a relieved grin and returned to fixing herself a quick meal. At the moment, he was alive or at least solid and able to impact his surroundings. That could change at any moment, but he hoped it wouldn't. He was really looking forward to that bath.

Rayanne slapped two pieces of bread together with a piece of cheese between them and then devoured it all in very little time. When she swallowed the last bite, she grabbed his hand and dragged him toward the steps again. He outweighed her by a lot, but he let himself get towed along.

"That's not much of a meal."

"It was enough for now."

At the top of the stairs she ducked into the bathroom and turned on the water and added some pink liquid that bubbled up when the water hit it. The scent of roses filled the damp air. Holding her hand under the stream of water, she adjusted the two knobs until she was happy. "That feels about right. Gotta love hot and cold running water."

Her hands immediately grabbed the hem of her shirt, leaving wet prints on the cloth as she tugged it up and over her head. When he didn't immediately follow suit, she tapped her foot impatiently. "Get started, mister. I need you to wash my back."

He'd taken his share of baths over the years, but he'd never once shared a tub with anyone. The possibilities left him fumble-fingered as he started working on his own buttons.

It didn't help watching his lover fling her clothes aside and slide into the steaming water without him. He slowed down, determined to savor the moments. Rayanne had settled back in the bathtub, watching his every move with hungry eyes. That was only fair. He'd been needing this moment with her ever since she'd stormed into the saloon, looking for him earlier that morning.

He wanted nothing between them except the sweet slide of her skin against his. Sex would be great, but right now he needed more than that. Her touch soothed him in ways he couldn't find the words to describe. He'd been alone for so damned long, and being with her kept those lonely shadows at bay.

Rather than rush things, he took his time folding his shirt and laying it neatly on the floor. Next he toed off his boots and set them side by side next to his shirt. Socks followed next. When he reached for the first button on his trousers, Rayanne shifted positions, leaning forward with her arms crossed on the side of the tub, her chin resting on her hands.

Clearly, she was enjoying the show. He dropped the trousers and kicked them off, giving up all pretense of being in control. She immediately moved to the end where the faucets were, giving him the end where he could lie back against the side of the tub. He made room for her between his legs, settling her against his chest, her head leaning on his shoulder. The mounds of bubbles played peek-a-boo with all of his favorite parts of her body. Her bottom sat snugged up against his shaft, offering undeniable evidence that he was enjoying himself.

In fact, if all they did was cuddle in warm water and bubbles, he could die a happy man.

But then she reached for the washcloth and soap and showed him just how much happier he could be.

Chapter 18

Rayanne lathered up the soft cloth and handed it over her shoulder to Wyatt. "If you'll wash my back, I'll return the favor."

Then she leaned forward to give him room to move. She sighed with sheer pleasure as he dragged the cloth across her skin in slow, thorough circles. He didn't limit his ministrations to the elegant length of her back. Her shoulders received their fair amount of attention, as did each of her arms.

Then he dropped the cloth into the water and gathered up a handful of the bubbles and used them to massage her aching breasts until she could no longer sit still. He tightened his hold on her with one hand and used the other to explore the slick folds at the apex of her legs.

One thick finger tested her readiness, pressing deep inside her as he nibbled along the side of her neck, moving on to trace the shell of her ear with the tip of his tongue. She tried to break free, intending to turn around and straddle his lap. He would have none of it.

"Wyatt! Please!"

"We'll get there, sweetheart, but right now I'm enjoying myself."

He showed no mercy, continuing to torment her in such wonderful ways. Finally, he loosened his hold long enough for her to turn around. She settled her knees on each side of his hips.

"My turn for some fun."

"I'm all yours."

She rose up and carefully guided his erection right to the entrance of her body and then slowly impaled herself on its rigid length. They both moaned as she settled him deep inside. Then she rocked forward and back, sending ripples of water lapping at the top edge of the tub.

This was about to get messy, and she didn't care. There'd be plenty of time later to mop up spilled water. Right now, all she cared about was stoking this hunger between them. As she came down hard, Wyatt slid farther down in the water and grabbed onto both sides of the tub with his hands. If she wasn't mistaken, his eyes had just about rolled up in his head.

She did it again, unsure which of them she was tormenting the most. When she repeated the maneuver, her lover lost all control. In a slick move, he had her pinned beneath him, but making sure her head was well above the water line as he started pumping his hips, surging in and out of her. She raised her ankles high up on the edge of the tub, taking all of him.

Wyatt's climax was building. It was there in the way he held her so tightly in his arms, in the way his breath came in short bursts as his body shuddered deep inside of hers. Her ability to make him lose control was intoxicating and drove her flying over the edge right along with him.

As he poured out his passion deep within her, she chanted the only thing that really mattered.

"I love you, I love you, I love you."

And when Wyatt finally collapsed, sinking heavily against her, he added words of his own.

"For now and for always, Rayanne, I will love you."

Life might offer very few perfect moments, but in her heart, she knew this was one of them.

She wrapped her arms around him and just breathed in the scent of sex and roses. Both of them were content to savor the moment. Eventually, the water grew too cold to be comfortable. It took all of her energy to move at all.

"Hey, big guy, want to try out the bed next?"

He lifted his head and grinned at her. "That's a bit conventional for us, don't you think?"

"I'll bet we won't find it boring, especially if we…" Then she whispered a few ideas in his ear to prove her point.

He blinked twice. "Well, I'm willing to give it my best effort."

It took him a couple of tries to start moving. Finally, he managed to climb out of the tub and grab a pair of thick towels. They helped each other dry off. When she reached for the robe she kept on the back of the bathroom door, Wyatt stopped her.

"You're not going to need that. You have me to keep you warm."

With that happy thought, she hung the robe back up on the door and led the charge down the hall to her room. She turned back the covers and scooted all the way to the far side of the bed to make room for Wyatt. After a bit of shifting this way and that, they found a comfortable position and drifted off to sleep.

Morning came way too early. Today would be their last day together. With luck, they'd come up with a plan to break the cycle, and Wyatt would finally rest easy in his grave on the hillside outside of Blessing. If not, then he'd continue to die year after year, a man trapped in his own special hell. The only difference would be that he'd have the memory of these days and nights with Rayanne to keep him company.

He'd reminded her during the night that he fully expected her to make a life for herself without him no matter which way things turned out. She'd argued with him, but he'd held firm. When she'd cried, he'd held her close. And when they'd made love, he'd given her his best.

She'd made him feel alive, and maybe for her he

was. If so, was it possible that he could have gotten her with child? Was it selfish of him to hope he had?

He stared up at the ceiling and let his thoughts drift, imagining what their child would look like, how it would feel to share this amazing love with a third person, one they created together. It was foolish and sweet and most likely an impossibility. Besides, how was he supposed to fit into this modern world? There was so much Rayanne took for granted that was new and scary to him.

Cars were bad enough, but he'd seen those machines flying high in the sky, too. Even that bath they'd shared the previous night had been the first time he'd experienced hot water he hadn't had to heat on the stove and carry to the tub. This dream world they shared here on the mountain wouldn't exist for him down below. Blessing was his world, the one place he belonged.

Rayanne rose up to look at him. "What's wrong?"

"Nothing at all."

"Liar." She rolled on top of him. With her hands on his chest, she pushed herself up to stare down at him. "You were relaxed and cuddly. Now you're all tensed up."

Maybe he could distract her. He cupped her backside with both hands and squeezed. "I was thinking about how we should start the day."

"Nice try, but I'd hope that thinking about some hot sex in the morning wouldn't have put that particular look on your face."

She leaned down to brush her lips across his.

"Don't try to protect me, Wyatt. We both know these next two days are going to get ugly."

He brushed her hair back from her face. "I was thinking if somehow I managed to survive tomorrow—really survived, not just caught up in the same old vicious circle, that I'd never fit into your world."

Damn, he hadn't meant to put even more sadness in her eyes.

"Look, forget I said anything, Rayanne. But it's true I'm not like the men in your time."

She smiled, but it was clearly a struggle. "True enough, but then I've always had a thing for gunslingers."

"Really. What kind of thing would that be?"

Before she could answer, the telephone rang. Rayanne stared at it as if it were a rattlesnake about to bite. Finally, she sighed and slid off the bed to answer it.

"Yes, Mom, I'm still here. Where else would I be?"

He couldn't hear the other half of the conversation, but it was clear that Rayanne was not enjoying anything her mother had to say.

"We've talked about this. And yes, I do know what tomorrow is."

Her lips were white with tension as she listened. "Please, Mom, don't drive a wedge between us that won't be easily mended."

Wyatt sat up on the edge of the bed and debated what to do. Whatever her mother was saying was tearing Rayanne apart. He wished she'd simply hang up. When she didn't do it herself, he gently pried it from her fingers and wrapped his arm around her, holding her close. Would her mother be able to hear him if he tried speaking to her?

"Mrs. Allen, you need to stop this now. You're hurting your daughter with these unkind words."

Success. She sputtered to a halt. "Who is this?"

How was he supposed to answer that? *I'm the ghost who haunts Blessing? I'm your daughter's lover, except I died when your grandmother was a young woman? I'm the man who is going to break your daughter's heart? I'm the man who loves her?*

There were no good options. He settled for, "I'm a friend of Rayanne's, and I can't stand seeing her hurting like this."

Then he hung up.

No doubt there would be consequences for his actions, but right now he was more worried about the woman whose tears burned against his skin. He stroked Rayanne's back, hoping it would soothe her pain. As he did so, he noticed their image reflected in the mirror over the old bureau.

They were a picture of contrasts. He was tall, his body lean and rough-hewn from years of hard riding and even harder living. His skin was dark from hours outside without his shirt on as he'd chopped wood and hauled water to Amanda's garden. His hair was longer than he liked. He'd been due for a trim and a shave when everything had gone to hell.

Rayanne, on the other hand, was everything he wasn't. Soft. Gentle. A strange mix of strong and fragile all at the same time. And so damned lovely that it hurt.

She looked up, meeting his gaze in the mirror. It wasn't their lack of clothing that left him feeling raw, exposed. No, it was their love for each other reflected there in the silvered glass. Despite the shimmer of tears in her eyes, Rayanne smiled at the man in the mirror.

"I could sit and stare at you like this all day."

Then that small bit of joy faded. "I'm sorry about that phone call. My parents can't seem to get it through their heads that I'm fine up here."

No, she wasn't. Not really. "I hope I didn't cause you more problems by talking to your mother."

The smile was back. "I'd love to have seen the look on her face when she realized I'd had an overnight guest. She's been saying I need a man in my life."

He bet he wasn't what her mother had in mind. "In my day, your father would come after me with a shotgun."

Rayanne's smile was all temptation. "Because you had your wicked, wicked way with me repeatedly and hopefully plan to again? Like right now."

It wasn't in him to refuse her, not with the clock ticking and their time running out so damned fast. They both needed something to distract them, even for a few minutes. He picked her up in his arms, lifting her legs high around his waist as he tumbled them both back down on the bed.

The real world was right outside, ready to tear them apart. But for now, for these few minutes, they could find comfort in each other's arms.

* * *

Two hours later, they finally stepped outside. As soon as the sun hit his skin, he felt a familiar tingle. Not now! It was too soon—and already too late.

"Rayanne!"

She'd been locking the door of the cabin, but looked up when he called her name. A look of horror crossed her face as she took two steps in his direction. When she reached out to him, her hands passed right through his.

They both stared at the shimmer working its way up his arms. "I'm sorry. It's time."

"Wyatt, I'll meet you in town."

He wanted her with him, but caution had him shaking his head. "Not until tomorrow. Stay here. Stay safe."

She looked distraught. "I can't hear you!"

He tried to touch her one last time and mouthed his final words to her, hoping to make himself understood. "No matter what happens, I love you, Rayanne. Never forget that."

Rayanne stood there looking fierce and determined. "I won't forget. And I love you, too, Wyatt McCain. I'll do my best to end this for you."

He nodded, knowing she would. The tingling had worsened to a burn. He could no longer feel the warmth of the sun or the ground beneath his feet. Rayanne seemed to be standing at the far end of a tunnel, growing smaller and more distant until he couldn't see her at all.

His heart broke as the darkness washed over him.

* * *

The next time Wyatt grew aware of his surroundings, aware of himself, it was late in the day, getting on toward dinnertime. He was walking down the street in Blessing on his way to the mercantile to pick up a length of fabric that Amanda had ordered to make new shirts for both him and Billy.

Before he got that far, he spotted that sneaky bastard Earl ducking into the saloon. What was he doing back in town? He veered off his intended path and followed Earl inside.

The old clock on the wall said it was after five. In less than twenty-four hours from right now, he'd be dead and buried up on the hillside. Regrets wouldn't change a thing so he ordered a beer and walked over to sit down with Earl. Even though he already knew the answers, he'd buy a few rounds to loosen up Earl's tongue and start asking questions.

Come sundown, he'd run the bastard out of town with a special message for the rest of the gang. They wouldn't listen, not when they thought the town was easy pickings. Fine. At least he'd warned them.

If this played out the way he expected it to, tomorrow they would die. Soon, the dust in the streets of Blessing would soak up their blood and their dying screams.

Chapter 19

Rayanne used to think Uncle Ray's cabin was cozy and comfortable. She'd been rattling around inside for hours now, alone and lonely. She missed Wyatt. Plain and simple. If he hadn't asked her to stay away until tomorrow, she would've headed straight for Blessing hours ago.

She considered the wisdom of digging out her uncle's old sleeping bag and camping out on the hillside overlooking the town. Anything to keep from missing a single minute of the drama about to unfold. But no, she'd promised to stay away today. For Wyatt's sake, she'd stay right where she was.

There had to be something to do. She considered stripping her bed and washing the sheets, but they carried Wyatt's scent. She wasn't ready to lose even that much of him.

That left Uncle Ray's room. She'd put off cleaning it out long enough. Bracing herself, she opened the door and took a determined step across the threshold. Listening to the silence, she realized the room now felt empty, abandoned. The memories were still there, but they were comfortable and familiar, their pain no longer fresh.

She started by emptying the closet, sorting out the clothes that were usable from those that should have been tossed in the trash years ago. When that was done, she started on the chest of drawers. One glance in the top drawer had her grinning. How many pairs of socks did one man need?

An hour later, everything was bagged up, labeled and sitting out on the deck. Eventually, she'd haul it all to town. After a quick break for lunch, she turned the mattress and made up the bed with fresh linens and another of the old quilts from the linen closet.

Already the room seemed brighter, welcoming. Maybe it was time for her to leave her childhood room behind and move into this one. She'd think more about that later. Right now, she needed to go through the bedside table and the bookshelves, which didn't take long. She set aside a few photographs that her mother might want along with some of Ray's favorite books. By the time she was finished, the sun was setting.

She'd worked herself into a pleasant exhaustion. Maybe she'd be able to sleep, after all. Food held little appeal, but as Wyatt had told her yesterday, she'd need all her strength to get through the next day—and all those days afterward.

Thinking of Wyatt made her chest ache. She stared at the grainy photograph she'd kept pinned to the wall. He looked so grim in the picture, as if he'd forgotten how to smile. She knew better.

She'd made it through twenty-four hours without him. The prospect of an entire future of such days weighed her down until it was hard to keep moving. After putting soup on to heat, she walked out onto the porch to watch the sun set. The spectacular display did nothing to lighten her mood.

Where was Wyatt right now? By this time, that guy he used to ride with should have arrived in town. What was the man's name? It started with a vowel. Irving? Ed? No and no. Earl. That was it. The two of them would share a few drinks, Wyatt buying them both shots of whiskey to lull Earl into revealing what he and the others were up to.

Was Wyatt thinking of her at all? Could he even remember who she was now that he was caught up in his own life again? Was it selfish of her to not want to be the only one who hurt this much? Probably.

With that cheery thought, she went back inside. She curled up on the couch, looking around for some kind of distraction. Nothing in Ray's movie collection held any appeal, and she couldn't focus well enough to follow the plot in the mystery she'd been reading.

Finally, she reached for Ray's journal. Maybe now would be the right time to finish reading it. Her heart hurt over the loss of her uncle, but she suspected that pain would pale in comparison to how she'd feel losing Wyatt, as well.

At first her tears blurred the words on the page, but she blinked hard until Ray's writing came back into focus.

My time on the mountain is growing short. The doc says my heart is worn out, and I can't say that I'm surprised. He tried to get me to move closer to town, but I've found it peaceful up here on the mountain and see no reason to change things this late in the game. I could probably live down below now, but maybe not. I know my sister has never understood my love for this place, but that's all right. She never once felt the power of the mountain and the people that it claims as its own.

I only catch the occasional glimpse of them passing through the woods, mostly in the summer as the time grows near for tragedy to play out again. I've gone years without watching it all happen, but I did climb to the belfry one final time last summer. I felt I owed Wyatt McCain that much for keeping me company for all these years. Granted, I didn't talk to him much, but that was just me.

Despite or maybe because of how the gunfight turned out, I've always felt a certain kinship for the man who put his own life on the line to protect the others in Blessing. I know all too well the cost of being a warrior in this world. Eventually, my heart will simply stop, and I will finally rejoin my unit.

Rayanne, if you're reading this, know that I loved

you, and I'm so damned proud of the woman you've become. It's my greatest hope that you'll find a way to lay Blessing's past to rest once and for all. That last summer you visited, you not only saw Wyatt Mc-Cain, but he heard and saw you. Your warning didn't change the final outcome, but it did change a few things.

I tried for years afterward to do the same, but with no luck. I have to think that somehow you managed to forge a special connection between you and Wyatt. Not sure how or why. Maybe because you still had the innocence of a child.

One thing I do know is that a man's soul can't find peace until he forgives himself for the things that he's done in his life. Once I managed to do that, the ghosts of my past finally faded away.

But enough of this. Embrace the mountain, Ray-anne, because it has chosen to share its secrets with you.

Uncle Ray

She reread the last few paragraphs, their truth resonating with what she believed. Wyatt needed to forgive himself because no one else who mattered held him responsible for Billy's death. Amanda certainly hadn't blamed him, and Rayanne knew the price he'd paid for his mistake. A hundred-plus years of Wyatt reliving his own personal hell was punishment enough. She could only hope that her love and her promise to try to save Billy would finally help Wyatt let go of his pain.

An hour later she crawled into bed, breathing

deeply of his scent on her pillow. It eased her heart almost as if he'd been there to hold her close all night long.

But only almost.

By the time she awoke the next morning, the sun had already cleared the horizon. Realizing how late it was, she lurched out of bed and grabbed some random clothes and ran for the bathroom.

How could she have slept so late on such an important occasion? She'd meant to be in town before sunrise, hoping to watch it all unfold. What if she'd already missed her chance to affect the outcome of the day's events?

She ran a brush through her hair and charged down the steps to the kitchen. Pausing only long enough to grab a couple of bottles of water and a box of granola bars to shove in her pack, she headed out the door.

To her horror, she wasn't alone. This time it wasn't the ghostly remnants of Blessing standing in the meadow outside of the cabin. No, the three people climbing out of the car were far scarier. Her parents were bad enough, but it was the third member of the group that left her mouth as dry as cotton.

She walked down the steps, her heart in her throat. Rather than try to talk when she wasn't even sure she could swallow, she stopped to take a swig of water first. It didn't help much. "Mom, Dad, Dr. Long, what an unpleasant surprise. I'm assuming you'll be leaving soon."

Judging from the looks and nods they exchanged,

that wasn't the smartest approach she could've taken. Her father stepped forward, clearly planning on being the spokesperson for their group.

"Rayanne, I'm sorry we came unannounced, but we all know you would have told us to stay away. Your mother has been very worried about you."

Oh, brother. Her own worry for Wyatt lit her already short fuse.

"Why? Because I inherited Uncle Ray's estate instead of her? Or because I didn't leap at the chance to sleep with Shawn when she sent him up here, hoping I'd do just that? Hell, the only thing that he was missing was a big red bow with an 'Open me next' tag on his shirt."

Her mother gasped in outrage. "Rayanne! I did no such thing."

"Then how did he find his way up here, Mom? I sure didn't tell him where to find me. That alone should have told you that there was nothing serious between the two of us." At least not on her part.

Her father shot his ex-wife a dark look. "Is that true, Lana? Did you send him up here without asking Rayanne how she felt about him first?"

"Well, she never even gave the man a decent chance. While she spends all of her time caught up in research, life is passing her by."

Then her mother did an end run around her father to get right in Rayanne's face. "Shawn is perfect for you. I thought if the two of you spent some time together away from the college and away from this place," she snarled, pointing at the cabin, "that maybe, just maybe, you'd come to your senses. Obviously, that didn't work."

Rayanne rolled her eyes. "No, it didn't. Three points for the melodramatics, though. Now, if you'll excuse me, I have work to do."

When she started past them, her father blocked her path. "I'm sorry, sweetheart, but even if your mother made a mistake with this Shawn guy, that doesn't mean she isn't right about the fixation you've developed for this place. It's not healthy for you. Just ask Dr. Long."

For the first time, the psychiatrist spoke up. "Rayanne, it is my opinion that the death of your uncle may have caused you to have a relapse. With prompt treatment, we should be able to keep this episode from becoming as severe as the one fifteen years ago. I've already blocked out two appointments a week for the next month for you."

She could only laugh. "Nice that you can make a diagnosis without ever speaking to the patient, Doc. Well, sorry, but you can take those appointments and pills and…"

Rayanne paused to rethink what she was about say. Calm was far better than hostile. "And cancel them. Please."

Her mom started in again. "Rayanne, I will not watch you go through that hell again. I'll have you forced into care if that's what it takes."

Her words cut like shards of glass, sending Rayanne staggering back several steps. "Mother!"

The shock on her father's face was too genuine to be faked. "Lana! Now you've gone too far."

It was all too much. Maybe they'd be able to mend fences later, but right now there were more important matters that needed Rayanne's immediate attention.

Before she walked away, though, she laid it out plain and simple for all of them. It took every bit of willpower she could muster, but she kept her voice even, her manner nonthreatening, when what she really wanted to do was shake some sense into the lot of them.

"Dad, I'm very sorry you made the trip up here because of Mom's hysteria. I understand that Uncle Ray's death hit her hard, and that has intensified her worry about me being up here. But truly, I've been working hard to complete my research on the town before the end of the summer. Go home. I'll call you when I get a chance."

What could she say to her mother that wouldn't permanently damage their relationship?

"Mother, this is my home, and you are no longer welcome here. Don't come and don't call. If necessary, I will get a restraining order. I'd rather not involve my attorneys, but I will if you force my hand. I know you have issues with this place, but that's not my problem. It's yours, plain and simple. Don't push me on this. You won't like what happens."

Her mother flinched as if Rayanne had actually struck her. It was tempting to relent, but right now it was more important that the three intruders leave.

Finally, she turned to the final member of this little

party. "Dr. Long, thank you for your concern, but let me make something clear. I'm a historian, and studying a place like Blessing is what I do for a living."

She glanced back at her mother before once again meeting Dr. Long's gaze head-on. "If you're planning on billing somebody for this little trip up the mountain, it better not be me. After all, I have not been your patient for fifteen years.

"Now, if you all will excuse me, I'm going to return to my research. I will be eternally grateful if you are gone by the time I get back."

Then she turned her back and walked away.

That calm lasted less than half the distance to Blessing. As she walked, she scrubbed at her face with the hem of her shirt to wipe away her acid-hot tears. If only she could do the same with her memories. Right now, she needed all of her wits about her just to get through the rest of the day.

She'd just reached the edge of the slope leading down to the town when the sound of running footsteps brought her to an abrupt halt. They coasted to a stop a short distance behind her. She forced herself to turn around.

"Dad—"

He held up his hands to cut her off. "I just wanted to make sure you're all right. You know, after that debacle back there. Your mom knows you don't want to see her right now, but she wanted me to tell you that she's sorry. Hell, even Dr. Long seemed impressed about how well you handled the situation."

His mouth quirked up in a half smile. "He also said to tell you that he wouldn't dream of billing anyone for a nice drive in the mountains."

Okay, that helped.

"Thanks, Dad. Tell Mom…" She paused while she tried to find the right words. She settled for, "Tell her I'll call when I'm back in town."

"Do that, honey. I know you like to putter around in places like Blessing, but it's hard not to worry about you being up here all alone in those derelict buildings."

Then he frowned as he stared past her toward the town. "That's odd. I know it's been years since I've been up here, but I don't remember there being that many buildings still standing."

Oh, God. Rayanne had been too caught up in her pain to even notice. The last thing she needed right now was for her father to get curious. All her efforts to convince him and the others that she was fine would go to hell in a handcart if she pointed out that her ghost town was currently full of ghosts— real ones.

"I think maybe Uncle Ray had done some restoration work since you were last up here."

That wasn't even a lie. He'd replaced those steps in the church. That counted.

Her father smiled at her. "Maybe sometime you'll take me through the town. I'd like to see it through your eyes."

As peace offerings went, it was a good one.

"I'd love that, Dad. Now you'd better get back to Mom."

He gave her a quick hug and hustled back the way he'd come. She waited impatiently until he disappeared behind a bend in the trail to take off running for Blessing, praying she wasn't too late.

Bert, the saloon owner, poured Wyatt a shot of whiskey from a bottle he normally kept under lock and key. He thanked the man and savored the burn on its way down his throat. He didn't often get to enjoy the good stuff. When Wyatt tossed a couple of coins on the counter, Bert shoved it right back toward him.

"Your money's no good here today, Wyatt." He picked up the bottle. "Want another one?"

It was tempting, but Amanda was already mad at him for smelling like cheap liquor when he went back to her cabin last night. He didn't figure on surviving the day. But on the chance he was wrong about that, he didn't want to provoke her temper unnecessarily.

She'd already torn a strip off his hide with that sharp tongue of hers for what he was about to do. The woman had strong opinions on many subjects, one of the reasons he liked her, and evidently him facing off against his old gang was one of them. He'd tried to explain that the thieving bastards would keep coming and coming if someone didn't put a stop to it. She didn't understand why Wyatt had to be that someone.

In truth, he didn't want to be, but he was the only one in town with any chance of reasoning with Earl and the rest. If words failed to convince them to leave, he was also the only one with the ability to state his case with bullets.

Outside, he could hear the townspeople talking, a rising note of panic in their voices. He nodded to the bartender and headed for the door where Tennessee Sue blocked his way.

"What?"

"Be careful out there." Then she kissed him full on the mouth.

He brushed a lock of her hair back behind her ear. "I'll try."

Before stepping out onto the sidewalk, he paused when a shiver of fear waltzed up and down his spine. Not for him, although that was there, too.

No, he was worried about Billy. He'd made Amanda promise to stay home and to keep the boy with her. No matter how this all turned out, he'd needed to know they were safe. That was all that mattered to him. They'd find out soon enough if he lived through this.

If he didn't, well, neither she nor Billy needed to see that. He'd do his best for the town, but he had a bad feeling about how things were going to turn out. He could almost see it in his head, as if it were a play and they were all following the script.

For some reason, the first place he looked was across the street at the church. Why was that? Despite Amanda's urging, he'd never set foot in the place. It was a little late for a man like him to find religion. Even so, there was something about the belfry that drew his eye. A memory danced just out of reach, something he couldn't make sense of. Then the image of a woman's face flashed through his mind. Who was she? She looked a bit like Amanda, but different enough to know that it wasn't her.

Whoever she was, simply thinking about her calmed his mind. The cards were already on the table. Only time would tell if he'd been dealt a winning hand.

He took one more step forward, hoping he looked a hell of a lot more calm than he actually was. He took a deep draw off his cigarette and blew out a cloud of smoke. Something else Amanda wouldn't like, but a man deserved a few vices in life. Despite his brief relapse into drinking and smoking, he hoped Amanda knew he'd been a better man because of her.

Someone from down at the mercantile shouted, "They're coming!"

The remaining few people on the street scattered like quail. Doors slammed. Windows closed. The only sounds now were the pounding of hooves in counterpoint to his heartbeat. He tossed the cigarette down and ground it out with his boot heel.

He shifted his rifle to his right hand and shoved the front edges of his duster back so he'd have easy access to his pistols.

Earl and the others were in sight now, riding hard toward Blessing. At the edge of town, they slowed to a walk. He noted that the riders checked all the doorways and windows they passed for any sign that he had backup in place. He smiled. If they were that nervous, maybe they'd make a mistake.

They slowed to a stop at the far edge of shooting distance. He stood his ground, preferring they come to him.

Evidently, Earl wasn't only their scout but also their spokesman. "Wyatt, and here I thought we was friends, especially after all those drinks you kindly bought me last night. Hell, all these boys were jealous when I told them how generous you were."

"That was last night. This is today." Wyatt made sure his smile couldn't be mistaken for friendly. "Earl, I have to admit I'm disappointed that you've ignored my advice to avoid Blessing. Things are about to get dangerous. I'd hate to see you get shot."

"I ain't too worried, Wyatt." Earl leaned forward, resting his shotgun across the front of his saddle. "See, there's just one of you and a whole bunch of us."

"Well, that's true enough. To be honest, I'd just as soon buy another round of whiskey for you boys if you'd promise to ride on out of town without causing any trouble."

Earl exchanged a knowing grin with his friends. "We'll take you up on that offer as soon as you turn over the gold from the mining office. Stealing is thirsty work and a few drinks will taste mighty good."

They were already laughing. He didn't give a damn. He'd known all along it would come to this.

"Well, Earl, that's not going to happen, and we both know it. And you're right about there being more of you. I'm better with guns than any of you, but I'm not good enough to take out all of you before someone gets off a lucky shot. But there's one thing you can count on, Earl."

"Yeah, what's that?"

"That you'll be the first I shoot."

Then Wyatt pulled the trigger and the dying began.

Chapter 20

Past experience had made it clear that shouting a warning wouldn't save Wyatt. Despite it being mid-morning, a time when the town would normally be at its busiest, there was nothing but a heavy silence hanging over the town.

It was as if the entire world held its breath, waiting for a storm of blood and pain to be unleashed on the people of Blessing. Rayanne couldn't stop events that had unfolded over a century before. But maybe, just maybe, she could save one person. One innocent. Billy. That's all Wyatt had asked of her.

Neither of them knew if she could pull it off, but she would try. The selfish part of her argued that if she could rescue only one of the players in this tragedy, it should be Wyatt. Surely he'd earned a reprieve after all these decades of suffering through this alone. But in her heart, she knew the man she loved would never forgive her if she didn't try to save the boy.

So rather than heading toward the belfry as she did the last time she'd lived through this horror, Rayanne ran to the spot where Amanda's cabin used to stand. What would she do if the woman and her son weren't even there?

She approached the cabin cautiously, not sure what would happen if she entered a building that didn't really exist in her own time. The door was certainly solid enough when she rapped her knuckles on it.

"Amanda! Billy! Are you in there?"

No answer.

She pushed the door open and looked around. The interior looked much as she'd imagined it would. In fact, if she wasn't mistaken, that exact same vase now sat on the mantel over the fireplace in her mother's living room. The small connection with the great-great-grandmother she'd never had a chance to meet had Rayanne smiling. If only she could tell her mother about it.

Yeah, like that would ever happen.

She checked the second room and the loft, each as empty and silent as the next. Back outside, she ran around the house to see if there was a cellar they could be hiding in. No such luck. She passed the rick of wood that Wyatt had chopped for them. For a man who thought so little of himself, he'd done some awfully nice things for people, including sacrificing himself to keep them safe.

But right now, her fear for Amanda and her son had ramped up to new levels. She'd never forgive herself if she failed to find them in time. As long as Billy kept dying, then Wyatt would, as well.

She pelted back down the way she'd come, skittering to a halt when she reached the back of the church. Time for some caution on her part. Fifteen years ago, Wyatt's bullet had been real enough to kill that man in the belfry. More than one of the townspeople had been hit by stray shots that day. She didn't want to add herself to their number.

The silence was broken by panicky voices. The riders were on their way into town, the gunfight only seconds from starting now. She wouldn't accomplish anything cowering here behind the building. Entering the church from the back door, she made her way through to the front. She dropped to all fours and scrambled across to the small window by the front door.

Rising up, she saw a scene right out of her past and a whole lot of nightmares after that. Wyatt walked out of the saloon. If memory served her right, he'd pause there to finish his cigarette. Next, he'd step out in the street and die.

She'd never seen that part, but that didn't matter. Except for the one year when she'd interfered, he'd taken a shot in the shoulder from the guy on the belfry and seven more before it was over.

Even then, Wyatt had lived long enough to realize that he'd killed Billy. Maybe if he hadn't been so stubborn about dying, he would never have realized what he'd done. Would he have found peace then?

A movement at the opposite end of town caught her attention. It was Billy making his way along one of the buildings that had reappeared overnight. He was moving slowly, no doubt doing his best to sneak close enough to watch without being caught. At the moment, the boy couldn't be seen by Wyatt or any of the riders who rode right past the boy as they headed toward the center of town. She had to get to Billy before that changed.

Rayanne bolted out the back of the church at a dead run, knowing she had only a minute, maybe two before the firing started. She rounded the corner and charged toward where Billy was inching forward again. By now he was holding on to the side of the building, his feet dragging as he walked.

When she yelled his name, he froze and glanced back in her direction. At the same time, Rayanne spotted his mother across the street, looking horrified that her son had disobeyed her orders to remain at the cabin.

"Miss Rayanne, I need my ma," Billy called as he reached out toward her, his words a harsh whisper.

Before she could answer, the bullets started flying. She charged forward and tackled Billy, dragging both of them down to the ground.

A bullet hit the wall right over their heads, showering them both with splinters. She raised her head long enough to see what was going on. Wyatt looked straight at her, recognition dawning in those pale blue eyes.

"Rayanne! Stay down!"

She didn't need to be told twice. Maybe it was cowardly of her, but she couldn't bring herself to watch the man she loved die. Eventually, the shots died away; the only thing left was the fog of blue smoke drifting on the summer breeze. A riderless horse wandered by, its reins dragging in the dust.

"Miss Rayanne, help me."

Had Billy been hit, anyway? She sat up, checking him for any sign of blood. Nothing.

"What's wrong, Billy? Are you hurt?"

"I was playing by the woodpile. Got snake bit twice."

He held out his arm to show her twin sets of punctures. The fear in his eyes broke her heart. Without prompt treatment, the venom would likely prove fatal. The thought made her sick.

By then, Amanda had reached them.

"Who are you?"

Now wasn't the time for introductions. Rayanne pointed toward the wound. "Your son's been bitten by a snake."

Amanda blanched. "Billy! I told you to stay inside!"

The boy was in obvious pain, his eyes glassy and feverish. His voice was so weak as he whispered, "I'm sorry, Ma. I'll listen next time."

Amanda met Rayanne's gaze, her dawning horror painfully clear. Without a word, she stepped past

Rayanne to scoop Billy up off the ground and ran toward the mercantile where so many of the townspeople had taken refuge.

There was nothing Rayanne could do for the boy, and her presence would only be a distraction. Leaving Amanda to see to her son, Rayanne whispered a prayer for them all as she ran to where Wyatt lay sprawled in the street, the surrounding dust splattered with his blood.

Oh, God, the reality was so much worse than anything she could have imagined. His breath rattled in his chest, and blood bubbled and pulsed out of too many holes to count. He blinked up at her, looking confused at first, but then clarity returned. She lifted his head onto her lap, trying not to hurt him any further even knowing nothing she did would save him.

"Billy?" Even that one word was a struggle for him.

"He's with Amanda."

That much was true, but there was no way to know if he'd survive. Maybe as she'd told Wyatt before, it was simply the boy's time.

The tension in Wyatt's face eased, and his smile was so sweet. "Thank you for that."

Tears poured down her cheeks. "I wanted to save you, instead. God, Wyatt, I love you so much."

"Love you, too…with you always."

He said those last words with strength, conviction and his last breath. He shuddered slightly, then he was gone.

Literally.

A powerful wave of energy washed through Blessing and caught Rayanne up in its maelstrom. She was buffeted with dust and gravel, and even the sun overhead blinked out of sight, trapping her in total darkness. She screamed for Wyatt, and she screamed for help.

The wave was gone as quickly as it had come, but it left Rayanne dizzy and sick. Rather than fight it, she let the darkness sweep away her pain and grief and simply slept.

When consciousness returned, Rayanne had no idea how long she'd been passed out in front of the saloon, but the sun was already low in the western sky. She sat up slowly, fighting dizziness and nausea. Realizing that this was the exact spot where Wyatt had died sent her scrambling up to her feet. She took a cautious look around.

Everything was back to normal; the only buildings surrounding her were the ones that had survived the past century. The others had faded back out of existence again. The past was back where it belonged, the only question being if it would stay there this time.

She needed to get back to the cabin before nightfall, inside thick walls. Once inside, she'd take a long, hot bath and try not to think about how it had been to share that tub with Wyatt. She'd curl up in Uncle Ray's old robe with a cup of tea laced with brandy and then cry herself sick.

In the morning, she'd...what? At this point she didn't know. Tomorrow would have to take care of itself. For now, she had a plan of action that would get her through the next few hours. Anything to keep her moving forward.

Her bones ached as if she'd aged forty years. Who knew that grief carried so much weight? It was all she could do to stand upright. One step at a time, she made her way through the trees to the meadow that surrounded the cabin.

It was full night by the time she let herself in the cabin and locked the door. Safe at last from ghosts and family alike. What a shame she couldn't leave her memories out on the porch to deal with later when she found the strength. With that happy thought, she headed upstairs to that bath. She sank down in the hot water up to her chin, gave up all pretense of control and let the tears come.

Chapter 21

"You look like hell, young lady. Haven't you been taking care of yourself?"

Phil glowered at her from the other side of the counter. He added a third scoop of ice cream to the banana split he'd insisted on making for her. She watched as he smothered it with chocolate sauce, whipped cream and chopped nuts. He plopped a spoon down in front of her.

"I asked for a single scoop of chocolate, Phil. That's more ice cream than I normally eat in a month."

He just huffed at her. "There's nothing normal about this week of August up here on the mountain, and you know it."

Okay, what did he know about what went on in Blessing? How much had Uncle Ray told him over the years? Rather than respond immediately, she took a big bite of chocolaty goodness to buy herself some time.

Her friend crossed his arms over his chest and leaned back against the cooler behind him. Clearly, he didn't plan on going anywhere until he got some answers. When he arched a single eyebrow, he might as well have shouted, "I'm waiting."

"Yesterday was the twenty-third." She set the spoon down and waited to see how he'd respond.

His shoulders slumped down, but whether it was because he was relieved or worried was impossible to tell. "Damn it, Rayanne, did you watch from the belfry again?"

Evidently, he knew quite a bit.

"No. I didn't see the actual gunfight. I was down the street between two of the buildings."

"And those scratches on your back and shoulders?"

She took another small bite before answering. "A bullet tore into the wood right above us."

This time both eyebrows slammed down over his eyes. "Us? Who was up there with you? Tell me it wasn't that ditzy mother of yours. Wasn't that her car I saw go by early yesterday morning?"

She had to laugh. "It was, but I sent her and my dad packing before I headed into Blessing."

Her smile faded as she went on. "I tried to save the boy who got hit with a stray shot. His name was Billy, and he was my great-uncle. Or would've been if he hadn't died that day."

"Did it work? Saving Billy, that is."

She shrugged as she stared down at her ice cream. "I don't know. Fifteen years ago, I changed one link in the chain of events when I yelled out a warning about the shooter in the church belfry. It didn't change the ultimate outcome of the gunfight. Wyatt McCain still died that day, and so did Billy."

She looked up at Phil. "So I don't know if anything is different. Billy didn't get shot this time, but he was in town looking for his mother because he'd been bitten by a snake. If he survived, wouldn't my family already know? I mean, if he lived past that day, it would've been in my great-great-grandmother's journal. By the way, that's what was in the box you gave me from Uncle Ray."

Phil tossed her a couple of napkins as if she'd spilled something, but then she realized they were for her tears. "I'm sorry. I can't seem to stop crying. It's all so awful."

"So Ray was right."

Phil dragged another stool over to the counter and sat down beside her, his heavy hand on her shoulder. "Your uncle knew what was going on in Blessing every year. Some old-timers around here always claim they've heard the gunshots or maybe caught a glimpse of someone in the woods. Hell, one year Ray and I were out hiking together and we saw some riders heading in that direction."

He smiled. "Scared the hell out of me when they rode by in absolute silence and then disappeared a second later. That's when Ray told me the whole story."

It was good to know that she wasn't alone in this. "What do you think he was right about?"

"That the gift for seeing the truth of Blessing was growing stronger from generation to generation. Ray knew what went on in town on the twenty-third, but most years he only got glimpses of the action. Sometimes he'd see people and at other times he'd only hear sounds."

Phil let his hand drop back down to his knee. "But that year you were up on the mountain, you saw everything. He felt real bad about that."

She'd never blamed him for anything. "Uncle Ray had no way of knowing what would happen."

"Feeling guilty and being guilty don't always walk hand in hand, Rayanne."

Phil gave her ice cream a pointed look. She picked up the spoon and started eating again.

"He thought maybe you were the one who could fix what was broken up there. End it for everybody and let those folks rest in peace."

"I hope it worked. I can't go through that again."

"You're stronger than you think, Rayanne. Most folks would have come screaming down the mountain at the first sight of a ghost. You hung in there right up to the last."

She swallowed her ice cream and wished she could swallow her pain as easily. "It's not that. I promised Wyatt McCain I wouldn't spend my life up there on the mountain trying to change things for him."

"You spoke with him?"

She blushed furiously. They'd done a whole lot

more than talk, but she wasn't about to share that bit of news with her elderly friend.

"We spent a lot of time together. He helped me map out the whole town the way it used to be."

"What was he like, this McCain fellow?"

What could she say that wouldn't give too much away? Even if Phil did believe that there were ghosts on the mountain, that didn't mean he wouldn't think she was crazy for falling in love with one. She settled on the simplest truth.

"He was a good man, Phil. A real good man who sacrificed himself for that town. He knew full well he was outmanned and outgunned, but he did his best to protect the people of Blessing. He died for them."

She smiled, letting herself remember some of their special moments, starting with his blue eyes staring down into hers as he made love to her. How funny he'd been when she told him modern women would think he was hot with his sleeves rolled up or if they saw him in his duster. How he'd made her feel complete, special and loved.

"I'm not going to ask what's going through your mind right now, but I'm guessing you have some strong feelings for McCain. Call me an old softy, honey, but I think you being up there wasn't some accident. It was meant to be."

Another customer came in. Phil stood up and patted her on the shoulder again. "Finish your ice cream. Something tells me you're going to need all your strength."

She almost choked when his words echoed what

Wyatt had said to her the night he'd made her finish her sandwich before he'd let her take him upstairs to make love. Right now the memories were too raw to dwell on for long, but it was nice to know she could still smile.

Back up on the mountain, she sat on the front porch and stared up at the sky while the sun came up. Another day had passed with no sign of Wyatt. She still needed to go back into Blessing to retrieve the last of her papers and to finish the last of her sketches and measurements. The only building left was the old church.

She'd put it off until last, although she didn't know why, exactly. Maybe because that was where all of this had started for her fifteen years ago. It seemed fitting that the church be the last place she added to her portfolio.

Now that it was light enough to see where she was going, she set her coffee cup aside and rose to her feet. She hadn't yet decided whether to return to the college or if she'd winter over here in the cabin. Right now, she was taking each day one at a time.

The birds were busy in the trees, their chittering a welcome sign that she was alone. She paused at the edge of the trees to stare at Blessing. The morning sun was kind to the faded wood, reminding her how different the place had looked when the buildings were all new.

She took that first step on her return to Blessing and found that it wasn't as hard as she'd feared.

Wyatt had told her that once the gunfight was over, sometimes it was late fall before it all started again. She wanted to finish her work now while there was no chance of running into him.

She couldn't stand the thought of Wyatt getting caught up in the same old pain again. In town, she gathered up all of her work in the saloon and packed it away. With that finished, she drew a slow breath and headed across the street to the church.

Inside, she stopped to look around. Of all the buildings in town, this one had withstood the passage of time the best. Maybe the people who had built it had done so with more care. Although she didn't attend church herself, she savored the profound sense of peace that seemed to have soaked into the walls of the building.

For a few seconds, she bowed her head and offered up a silent prayer that the man she loved and that boy he cared so much about had finally found peace on the mountain. Hoping somebody up there had been listening, she set her stuff down and got busy. It didn't take her long to measure everything. Then she took a few minutes to sketch in the few details she remembered from the short time she'd been inside the building as it had been in its prime.

Finally, she reluctantly headed up the stairs to the belfry. This time, the memories from fifteen years ago stayed firmly in her past. Instead, she concentrated on the present as she stepped through the door onto the platform outside. The sun warmed her skin as she walked over to the railing to look down. The view from the roof gave her a new perspective of the town. She opened her pad to a new page and started drawing as fast as her pencil would move.

Slowly, the town took shape. When the buildings were all in place, she added the people—miners, storekeepers, ladies running their errands, children kicking a rock down the street. She could see it all so clearly in her mind.

And one lone man wearing a dark red shirt with his hat pulled down low over his face stood down on the sidewalk, staring across at the saloon. She closed her eyes and then looked again. He was still there.

The point on her pencil snapped, and her pad slipped out of her fingers.

"Wyatt?" she whispered.

From this angle, she couldn't see his face. That shirt was different, and he wasn't wearing a duster. Even so, there was something about him that looked so familiar.

Spots danced in her eyes and there was a loud roaring in her head. She tried to hold on to the railing, but her fingers wouldn't cooperate. When her knees refused to support her, she sat down before she fell down.

What had she just seen? She braced herself for the worst and peered through the railing toward the street below. Just as she feared, it was empty. Perhaps by drawing the town as she wanted to remember it, her imagination had filled in the few details she'd most wanted to see. Maybe it had been too soon to come back.

She was done for the day. Maybe for good. She started to gather up her sketches. Where had she left her pack? She spotted it a few feet away, but before she could make a move in that direction, she heard the familiar creak of the door to the belfry opening.

Okay, the last time someone had shown up on the belfry when she was there, it hadn't turned out all that great for her or Wyatt. Rather than face a potential threat sitting down, she rose to her feet and grabbed her pack to use as a weapon if it became necessary.

The man she'd seen down on the street stepped out onto the roof. His hat now tipped back off his face, and the sun gleamed off his blacker-than-night hair. A pair of sky-blue eyes stared right at her.

The boards beneath his feet creaked in protest as he took a cautious step toward her. She stared at his feet in amazement. He had weight. Substance.

This time she shouted his name. "Wyatt!"

His answering smile was everything she could have hoped for. "I should've known I'd find you up here."

He held out his arms and she ran straight into them. "Wyatt, what are you doing here? You said you'd disappear until fall. I didn't break my promise to stay away."

The rush of words came out in a single breath. Instead of answering her, Wyatt picked her up in his arms and swung her around and around.

"I'm back, but not like before. I'm real again, Rayanne. For good this time. I don't know how I know that, but I do."

When he set her back down on her feet, she was breathless. "Really real? How can that be?"

"I don't know." Then he looked down at the street below, his expression haunted. "Why isn't Billy here with me?"

She had to tell him the truth. It wasn't going to be easy. "I'm sorry, but Billy didn't sneak into town to watch the gunfight, Wyatt. He stayed home like he was supposed to, but he was bitten by a snake near the woodpile. He was in town looking for Amanda, not you."

"Damn it, so he died that day, anyway, didn't he?" Wyatt tightened his hold on her.

"I have to think so. Amanda's journal said she lost Billy that day, but not how he died. I'm so sorry, Wyatt."

"Me, too, but maybe you were right, and it was just his time. Nothing we did changed a thing."

She hugged him back. "But it did. Now you know that it wasn't your fault that Billy came to town, no matter how he died. I told you Amanda never blamed you for her son's death. You shouldn't, either."

She caressed his face with her fingertips. "My uncle, a surprisingly wise man, said that a man had to forgive himself for the things in his past before his soul can find peace. Now that you know Billy's death wasn't all your fault, maybe you can make peace with what happened."

Wyatt closed his eyes and took a deep breath and then another one. When he finally opened them, she saw nothing but a calm acceptance in their depths.

"Maybe your prayers were answered, and I am getting a second chance to live my life right. But it's going to take a powerful lot of adjustment to this new world, and I'm going to need some help with that."

Wyatt tightened his hold on her. "Know anybody who would be willing to take on the job? It would take a special woman to love an ex-gunslinger."

The last vestige of pain in her chest melted away. "That all depends. Think that ex-gunslinger could put up with a woman who likes to spend her time wandering in ghost towns and reading dusty, old books?"

Wyatt stared down at her with a world of love in his smile. "She sounds perfect, the kind of woman worth waiting more than a century for. The kind a man would be right proud to call his wife."

Rayanne retreated a step. "Is that a proposal?"

He took his hat off and crumpled the brim in a tight grip. "I reckon it is."

"Then I accept."

For the second time, Wyatt grabbed her up and swung her around and around and then kissed her to seal the deal. For the first time, she didn't worry that it was too much, that he'd blink out of existence if she demanded more than he had to give. It was amazing, a gift she'd never take for granted.

When he set her back down, his expression turned solemn. "It won't be easy, Rayanne, explaining me to your folks and friends. And I'm not sure what I can do to earn a living, either. Things have changed so much since I died."

She understood why he was worried, but at least he was looking forward, no longer trapped in his past.

"Not to worry. I have a friend who owns a small store near here who could use some help. I suspect he'd be thrilled to meet you. Besides, Uncle Ray left me both this land and the cabin free and clear along with enough money to ensure neither of us has to work. But even if he hadn't, we can handle anything as long as we're together."

Then she tugged Wyatt toward the door back down to the church. "But we'll worry about all of that later. Right now, let's head back to the cabin. I think we both could use a long soak in the tub."

Wyatt's blue eyes sparkled with heated intent. "Lady, I like the way you think."

After he stepped through the door, she realized she'd left her sketch pad and pack behind. "I forgot something, but I'll catch up in a second."

With her artwork tucked under her arm, she paused to take in the view below. Everything looked the same and yet there was a different feeling in the air. Something calm and soothing. And then she knew. For the first time in over a century, the streets of Blessing were at peace.

* * * * *

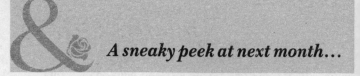

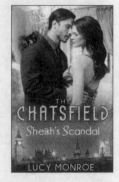

When five o'clock hits, what happens after hours...?

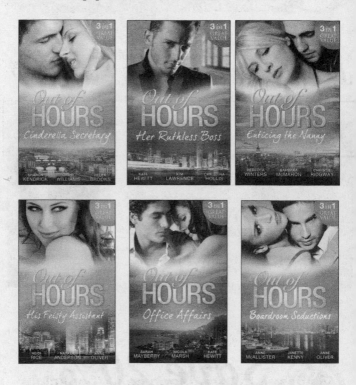

Feel the sizzle and anticipation of falling in love across the boardroom table with these seductive workplace romances!

**Now available at
www.millsandboon.co.uk**

Join the Mills & Boon Book Club

Want to read more **Nocturne**™ books?
We're offering you **1** more absolutely **FREE!**

We'll also treat you to these fabulous extras:

- 🌹 **Exclusive offers and much more!**

- 🌹 **FREE home delivery**

- 🌹 **FREE books and gifts with our special rewards scheme**

Get your free books now!

visit www.millsandboon.co.uk/bookclub
or call Customer Relations on 020 8288 2888

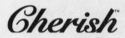

Discover more romance at

www.millsandboon.co.uk

- ❤ WIN great prizes in our exclusive competitions
- ❤ BUY new titles before they hit the shops
- ❤ BROWSE new books and REVIEW your favourites
- ❤ SAVE on new books with the Mills & Boon® Bookclub™
- ❤ DISCOVER new authors

PLUS, to chat about your favourite reads, get the latest news and find special offers:

- 🅕 Find us on facebook.com/millsandboon
- 🐦 Follow us on twitter.com/millsandboonuk
- ❤ Sign up to our newsletter at millsandboon.co.uk